Praise for DEATH STAL
the first Dave Cubiak

"Can a big-city cop solve a series of murders whose only witnesses may be the hemlocks? An atmospheric debut." *Kirkus Reviews*

"Murder seems unseemly in Door County, a peninsula covered in forests, lined by beaches, and filled with summer cabins and tourist resorts. That's the hook for murder-thriller *Death Stalks Door County*." *Milwaukee Shepherd Express*

"Skalka's descriptions of the atmosphere of the villages and spectacular scenery will resonate with readers who have spent time on the Door Peninsula. . . . [She] plans to continue disturbing the peace in Door County for quite a while, which should be a good thing for readers." *Chicago Book Review*

"The characters are well drawn, the dialogue realistic, and the puzzle is a difficult one to solve, with suspicion continually shifting as more evidence is uncovered." *Mystery Scene Magazine*

Praise for DEATH AT GILLS ROCK,
the second Dave Cubiak Door County Mystery

"In her atmospheric, tightly written sequel, Skalka vividly captures the beauty of a remote Wisconsin peninsula that will attract readers of regional mysteries. Also recommended for fans of William Kent Krueger, Nevada Barr, and Mary Logue." *Library Journal* (**Starred Review**)

"Will give mystery lovers food for thought along with the pleasure of reading a well-crafted book." *Chicago Book Review,* **2015 Best Books of the Year**

"Skalka writes with unusually rich detail about her story's setting and with unflinching empathy for her characters." *Publishers Weekly*

"A new hero to enjoy. . . . Skalka has a hit with both this story and her featured character, Sheriff Dave Cubiak." *Mystery Suspense Reviews*

Praise for DEATH IN COLD WATER,
the third Dave Cubiak Door County Mystery

"Starring a tenacious cop who earns every ounce of respect he receives." *Booklist*

"A fast-paced story highlighted by the differences in temperament and style between the local law enforcement officer and the federal agents, [with] a final, satisfying conclusion." *Mystery Scene*

"A haunting depiction of heartbreaking crime. Skalka does a wonderful job of showing how people can both torment and help each other."
Sara Paretsky, author of *Fallout*

"Patricia Skalka has pulled off the near impossible—a tale of grisly murder filled with moments of breathtaking beauty. Sheriff Dave Cubiak is the kind of decent protagonist too seldom seen in modern mystery novels, a hero well worth rooting for. And the icing on the cake is the stunning backdrop of Door County, Wisconsin. Another fine novel in a series that is sure to satisfy even the most demanding reader." **William Kent Krueger, author of *Desolation Mountain***

Praise for DEATH RIDES THE FERRY,
the fourth Dave Cubiak Door County Mystery

"A smooth yet page-turning read. . . . [Skalka] brings the region alive for readers with a you-are-there verisimilitude." *New York Journal of Books*

"Another deftly crafted gem of a mystery novel by Patricia Skalka. . . . A simply riveting read from cover to cover." *Midwest Book Review*

"An intricate, intriguing plot in which Door County Sheriff Dave Cubiak can stop a ruthless killer only by finding the link between a spate of murders and a forty-year-old mystery." **Michael Stanley, author of the *Detective Kubu* series**

"Skalka is equally skilled at evoking the beloved Door County landscape and revealing the complexities of the human heart, as Sheriff Cubiak's latest case evokes personal demons. This thought-provoking mystery, set in a beautiful but treacherous environment, is sure to please."
Kathleen Ernst, author of *The Light Keeper's Legacy*

DEATH BY THE BAY

A DAVE CUBIAK DOOR COUNTY MYSTERY

PATRICIA SKALKA

THE UNIVERSITY OF WISCONSIN PRESS

The University of Wisconsin Press
728 State Street, Suite 443
Madison, Wisconsin 53706
uwpress.wisc.edu

Gray's Inn House, 127 Clerkenwell Road
London EC1R 5DB, United Kingdom
eurospanbookstore.com

Printed in the United States of America

This book may be available in a digital edition.

Library of Congress Cataloging-in-Publication Data

Names: Skalka, Patricia, author. | Skalka, Patricia. Dave Cubiak Door County mystery.
Title: Death by the bay / Patricia Skalka.
Description: Madison, Wisconsin: The University of Wisconsin Press, [2019]
| Series: A Dave Cubiak Door County mystery
Identifiers: LCCN 2018049609 | ISBN 9780299323103 (cloth: alk. paper)
Subjects: LCSH: Door County (Wis.)—Fiction. | LCGFT: Detective and mystery fiction.
Classification: LCC PS3619.K34 D38 2019 | DDC 813/.6—dc23
LC record available at https://lccn.loc.gov/2018049609

ISBN 9780299323141 (pbk.: alk. paper)

Map by Julia Padvoiskis

Door County is real. While I used the peninsula as the framework for the book, I also altered some details and added others to fit the story. The spirit of this majestic place remains unchanged.

For
Aunt Rose,
who was denied so much in life

The greater the power,
the more dangerous the abuse.
Edmund Burke

DEATH BY THE BAY

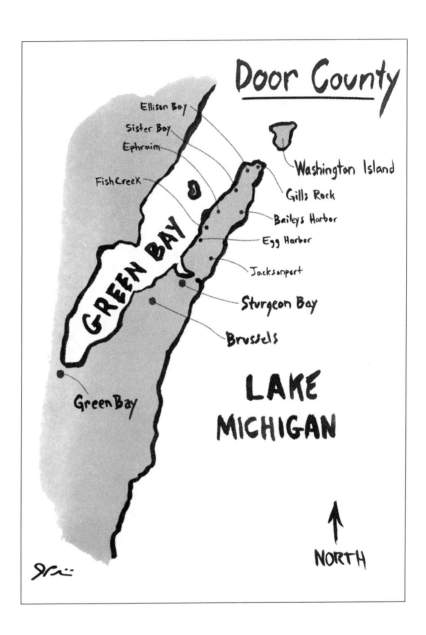

A DISRUPTED LUNCH

The doctor was late. In the ten or so years that Door County Sheriff Dave Cubiak and Evelyn Bathard had met for their weekly lunch, the retired coroner had been unerringly punctual. They had a one o'clock reservation at the Green Arbor Lodge, and it was already half past. Cubiak was concerned. Not worried yet. But concerned. Trying to ignore the slow sweep of the second hand on his watch, he studied the whitecaps that were forming on the gray surface of Green Bay. He had requested a window table for Bathard's benefit. Although his elderly friend had sailed only once during the previous season, he remained a mariner at heart, and Cubiak knew he would enjoy the cliff-side view from the restaurant. So where was he?

It was possible that Bathard had forgotten the date. Or the time. But Cubiak didn't think either was likely. He wondered if his watch was wrong, but that seemed doubtful as well. The timepiece was a high-school graduation gift from his parents, the only thing of value they had ever given him, and despite being treated with great abandon through the years, it had always proved accurate. To be sure, he checked it against the clock on the wall. It was one forty-five.

The sheriff picked up his phone and started to call Bathard, but then he stopped. He needed to give his friend a little more time. Cubiak had assumed that on a Monday in late May the dining room wouldn't be busy, but he had been wrong. There were more people in the restaurant than he had expected—more men in suits and women in dresses, more wing tips and heels than he had seen in a long time.

"What's going on?" he asked the waitress.

"A medical meeting in the conference center. Bunch of docs all over the place," she said.

Cubiak relaxed. That explained things. Bathard was probably circling the lot, looking for a parking space.

"More water?" the waitress said and held up a lemon-laced pitcher for him to consider.

"Sure, thanks." What he really wanted was a beer, but he didn't drink on duty. He had been down that road before, when he was a Chicago cop, and he had no intention of making a return trip.

Cubiak looked down at the water again. The bay buffeted the western shore of the Door County peninsula, which, like Lake Michigan to the east, had remained stubbornly cold through the spring. Six weeks earlier, the sheriff had seen small ice floes riding the crests of the waves outside his house. The ice disappeared overnight with little fanfare but with great relief to the tourist board. It was time for the first summer visitors to arrive. In the distance, a gray freighter slipped effortlessly through the water, following the shipping lane that kept it a safe distance from the rocky shore of the peninsula. The boat rode low in the water, probably carrying a load of steel or electronics to one of the shipyards in Sturgeon Bay.

Another fifteen minutes passed, and the sheriff started to worry. For more than a decade, he and Bathard had met weekly at Pechta's in Fish Creek. The old-style bar and grill was convenient, the food was good, and they both enjoyed the brash banter with Amelia Pechta, the witty and sharp-tongued proprietor. But she had retired in the fall, and the new owners had transformed the restaurant from a comfortable old shoe of an eatery, with distressed wooden booths and dim lighting, into a pinched-toe stiletto. High-tech tractor seats replaced the worn but comfortable chairs, and fishing nets were draped on the walls in an unseemly combination of surf-and-turf décor. For the two friends, the changes were a bad fit. There were plenty of restaurants in Door County, and as each week rolled around, they tried a different one. This was their first lunch at the one-hundred-year-old Green Arbor Lodge.

Cubiak checked the time. Two twenty. Phone in hand, he turned toward the lobby. From his seat, he had a clear view to the mullioned windows behind the registration desk and to the landscaped entrance outside. Between two rows of clipped hedges, an elderly gentleman made his way up the path to the lodge door. The man was stooped, as if weighted down by the heavy overcoat he wore despite the relatively warm weather. With each uncertain step, he propelled a wooden cane forward along the stone surface. If you live long enough, old age catches up, Cubiak thought. Suddenly he realized that the man on the walkway was Bathard. The image tugged at the sheriff's heart. They were all on a steadfast journey through life, but when had his friend grown old? When had he started using a cane? Cubiak pocketed his phone and pushed away from the table.

On his way to the door, he passed his waitress.

"Back in a sec," he said.

Cubiak elbowed through the crowded lobby. He reached the heavy wooden door just in time to push it open for Bathard.

"Sorry I'm late," the coroner said as the sheriff clasped his shoulder.

"Is everything okay?"

"Yes, certainly. Oh, this?" Bathard brandished the cane. "I sprained my ankle. Nothing to fuss over. I meant to call but—"

A woman screamed, interrupting him.

In the refined setting of the old lodge, the disruption was unseemly. Startled, Bathard lurched into Cubiak. Around them, conversations stalled. Then everyone started talking at once.

"Quiet!" the sheriff shouted over the bedlam, as he steadied his friend.

"I'm fine. Go," Bathard said.

When the inn started, it boasted a dozen simple guest rooms, a small private dining room, and a patch of lawn groomed for bocce and croquet. Over time the residential wing was enlarged and a second added. Eventually the dining room was opened to the public, and the lawn was torn up to make room for a recreation wing with an indoor pool, separate saunas for men and women, and a fully equipped workout room. The latest addition was the wing that housed a state-of-the art conference center.

The cry had come from one of the four wings.

On instinct, Cubiak started toward the nearest guest rooms. A shout from the opposite direction made him spin around and head toward the conference center corridor.

The passage was packed with people from the conference who had been drawn by the scream. Some milled about and glanced one way and then the other, holding their phones high as they snapped photos, trying to capture anything of interest. Others pushed forward, as if eager to help.

"Sheriff's department. Let me through. Get back," Cubiak said as he pushed through the human logjam. The well-dressed crowd looked at him askance. Who was this man with the shaggy hair, plaid shirt, and blue jeans to give them orders? Most of them stayed their ground, but a few grudgingly gave way.

Six meeting rooms opened off the hallway. There were three on each side, and they had picturesque names like Pinestead and Tree Top. Each room had planked maple floors and was painted a calming, soft green and furnished with upholstered chairs of dark wood. Through the open doorways, Cubiak glimpsed signs of hasty exit—overturned chairs, papers and binders scattered on the floor, briefcases left standing alongside empty seats. In one room he saw an open purse and tablet on a chair and a red scarf hanging over the back of another.

The commotion had come from the room at the end of the hall where a rotund, middle-aged woman blocked the entrance. Her salt-and-pepper hair was pulled back into a bun, and with a manner as severe as her hairstyle, she stood with arms akimbo under a sign that read Woodlawn Theater.

"No one comes in," she said sternly when Cubiak tried to get past.

He flashed his badge. "Sheriff's department."

"Oh," she said. Flummoxed, she glanced into the room as if hoping for further instructions. Cubiak had one foot in the door when she meekly stepped aside.

Eight people were in the theater, an inflated name for what was essentially a large presentation room that sloped gently toward the raised platform that filled the front like a low stage.

Pale and rigid with alarm, the three women at the rear gave Cubiak a fleeting glance as he entered. Then they turned their attention back to the five people on the dais.

Three of them were lined up behind a long conference table: a young man with a pale mustache, an even younger woman with half of her brown hair dyed neon blue, and an elegant, mature woman in a fitted gray suit. Two men in suits were on the other side of a podium, which stood near the table. One knelt on the floor; the other lay on the floor and was not moving.

As Cubiak approached, he studied the tableau at the front of the room. Out of habit, he committed the details to memory, as he would if he were viewing a crime scene.

The woman in the gray suit leaned against the wall of windows. Her short silver hair hugged her head like a helmet. Her eyes were shut, and both hands were pressed to her mouth. The young couple stood shoulder to shoulder. He had his arm around her in a partial, awkward embrace. They were a mismatched pair: he unusually tall and dressed formally in suit and tie, she petite and outfitted in a short red dress, denim jacket, black leggings, and heavy combat boots. The man looked at her with great concern, but she stared past him toward the podium, clasping her laptop to her chest and seemingly oblivious to his presence.

The man on the floor still had not moved. He had white hair and the frail physique of the very old. He wore a charcoal suit and new shoes whose soles gleamed in the light. His arms and legs were flung casually to the side, as if he were relaxing at the end of a yoga session. But his striped green tie was loosened and tossed to the side, and his shirt was opened to the waist, exposing his sunken chest.

The kneeling man looked up momentarily. His face glistened with sweat. His arms were taut, and his hands were pressed against the bare chest of the figure on the floor.

When he reached the platform, the sheriff paused. As he did, the woman in gray opened her eyes. The woman in red elbowed the gangly man. He flushed with embarrassment and stepped away as she set her computer on the table and laid her jacket on top of it.

On the other side of the lectern, the kneeling man fell back on his heels. "I'm afraid he's gone. Looks like a heart attack," he said.

Close up, Cubiak saw that the man on the floor had a narrow, chiseled face. His complexion was ashen. His eyes stared at the ceiling, their blueness faded and the luster dimmed.

The sheriff identified himself but got no response from the other man. When Cubiak reached for the victim's wrist, the kneeling man suddenly righted himself and pushed at the sheriff's arm.

"Who are you? What are you doing?" he said. He had a strong voice, and, despite thick hair that was more salt than pepper, he was probably at least thirty years younger than the man he had been trying to resuscitate.

Cubiak glanced into a pair of murky brown eyes and repeated himself. "I'm the sheriff." Then he added, "I'm checking for a pulse."

"I'm a physician, and I've done that already. This gentleman is dead."

Cubiak nodded and gently released his hold. The man's wrist was limp, and its warmth, the only sign of life remaining in the body, would fade soon.

"Did anyone call nine-one-one?"

"There's no need for that," said the man with the dark eyes.

Cubiak ignored him and turned to the trio on the other side of the podium.

They stared at him, looking to the kneeling man and then back to the sheriff. Finally, the tall man reached into his pocket just as the woman who had rebuffed him dug into her purse. She dropped a large ring filled with keys on the table and then extracted her phone as well.

"One call is enough," Cubiak said. He was on the line with his deputy Mike Rowe.

"Get to the Green Arbor. Now," he said.

The kneeling man joined the group.

"We don't need outside help." His voice was as hard as his stare was cold.

"And you are?"

"Doctor Harlan Sage, the director of the institute. The Institute for Progressive Medicine. We're here for our annual conference."

Cubiak indicated the deceased. "And he is?"

Sage turned toward the fallen man, but before he could respond a voice from the back of the room rang out. "His name is Leonard Melk."

Cubiak turned to find Bathard leaning on his cane inside the doorway. His look was somber, and beneath his neutral tone, the sheriff detected an undercurrent of disapproval.

"Yes, the deceased is the renowned Doctor Leonard Melk," Sage said, addressing the coroner.

The director started back toward the podium but Cubiak caught his elbow. "I'd rather that no one touch Doctor Melk again until Doctor Bathard has had a look."

Sage yanked his arm free. "Why him? He's not part of the institute or the conference. This is an internal affair and he"—Sage pointed a finger at Bathard—"isn't one of us. He doesn't belong here."

The director's arrogance riled the sheriff. "You're wrong on two counts," he said. "Doctor Melk's death occurred in a public venue, so it comes under my jurisdiction as sheriff, and I have the full authority to solicit the opinion of anyone I wish on the matter. Doctor Bathard is the former county coroner, and as such, he may, as you say, belong here more than anyone else in this room, conference or no conference."

Sage crossed his arms and glowered. "This is bureaucratic nonsense. Doctor Melk died of a heart attack."

"I'm inclined to agree, but we don't know for certain, do we?"

Cubiak held Sage's gaze. The sheriff had an uncanny ability to read people. He wasn't always correct. In fact, when he had met Cate, the woman who was now his wife, he had misunderstood almost everything about her. But most of his initial impressions were on target. He had immediately pegged Bathard as a man of depth and integrity. The sheriff was sure that Sage was hiding something, probably his relief that Melk would no longer overshadow him and his delight at being freed from his influence.

All business, Cubiak went on. "I'll need the names and contact information of everyone who was here when the doctor collapsed. When my deputy arrives, he'll get statements from the three at the back of the room and the woman at the door. I'll talk to the rest of you now."

"Statements?" Sage said. He sounded ready to launch a new protest, but one glance at the sheriff and he swallowed his objections. "Very well, if we must. No one here has anything to hide. Let's just get this over with." He looked at the woman in gray. "There's nothing we can do about this afternoon, but perhaps we can salvage the rest of the conference."

As he talked, Sage pulled a cream-colored card from his breast pocket and shoved it at Cubiak. The MD that trailed the director's name led into an impressive alphabetic litany of credentials. The IPM logo was embossed on the upper right and the institute's motto printed in a large font along the bottom: For the Greater Good.

The woman in gray stepped up next. Her card was flimsier than the director's, but it carried the IPM logo, as well as her name, Noreen Klyasheff; her title, executive assistant; and her contact information.

The card belonging to Adam McGill, the earnest young man in a drab brown suit, bore only his name and email address. The two were a good match, modest and subdued.

"You're not with the institute?" Cubiak said.

"I'm Doctor Melk's personal assistant." Then blushing, McGill corrected himself: "*Was* the doctor's assistant." A shadow passed over his face. Had he just realized that the physician's death meant he was now unemployed? Cubiak wondered.

The woman with the two-toned hair was the last to step forward. She was even more pale than before, but Cubiak sensed an underlying steeliness that belied her fragile appearance.

"Linda Kiel, our own personal scribe," Sage said with a mixture of amusement and derision.

"I'm a journalist," she countered.

"Writer of Words" read her card. Was the title meant to be pretentious or self-mocking? the sheriff wondered. Did the pronouncement describe what she did or who she was? In either case, it was meant to elicit a response, and he deliberately did not react. The rest of the card was blank except for a phone number, an email address, and the name Cody Longe.

"My pen name," she said before Cubiak could ask.

Another pretension? The sheriff wasn't sure; he had never known anyone with a pen name, but beyond talking with a few local reporters he had limited experience with journalists. "Sounds impressive," he said and was certain he heard the woman in gray snigger.

He took in the trio. "The three of you can wait over there," he said, indicating the chairs on the side of the dais away from the body. "I'll start with Doctor Sage."

The writer stayed her ground. "How long is this going to take? I have an appointment."

"You'll need to reschedule."

The young woman's manner bothered Cubiak. There was a duplicity to her that he couldn't pinpoint. In the face of the day's unfortunate events, she seemed flippant. Perhaps she was in shock, he thought, deciding to give her the benefit of the doubt for now.

"I'll try and be quick," he said by way of consolation.

He was about to suggest they send for coffee when Rowe came through the door. The sheriff gave the deputy a quick rundown on events and pointed him toward the women at the back of the room.

"Get everything you can from them, what they saw, who was where when the doctor collapsed. You know the drill."

As he conferred with Rowe, Cubiak watched the others. Sage talked on his phone. Klyasheff rummaged in her purse and finally pulled out a lipstick, which she uncapped and dabbed at her mouth. McGill trailed Linda Kiel to the table and reached around her for her jacket. She snatched it from him and said something sharp under her breath, leaving McGill red with embarrassment again. Then she grabbed her laptop and stomped off to a seat in the middle of the first row, pointing him to a spot at the end. Her meanness annoyed the sheriff. McGill only meant to be helpful, Cubiak thought. Kiel had no reason to humiliate him.

"That's it?" Rowe said.

"What? Yes. I don't expect anything to come of this. Things seem pretty cut and dried."

"SNOW"

2

Cubiak walked Sage toward the window near where Doctor Melk had collapsed. He wanted the body in full view while he questioned the institute director. The sheriff pondered which role he should play: should he be bad cop or good cop? He didn't suspect any untoward activity in Melk's death, but he was put off by Sage's arrogance and was tempted to come down hard on him. He knew that, TV cop shows notwithstanding, the tough guy approach was counterproductive in most situations and reserved it mainly for dealing with recalcitrant witnesses and in cases that involved an abusive spouse or parent. In those situations, he figured the offenders should consider themselves lucky that was the worst they got from him. No, most situations did better when the good cop showed up on the scene. The average Joe was more at ease talking to Officer Friendly. He felt a bond with the kind of lawman who, under other circumstances, would sit down and buy him a beer and nod sympathetically as he complained about the raw deal he had gotten from life.

Sage was better educated and more polished than the average citizen, but he wasn't immune to a touch of human kindness.

On the other side of the glass, a patch of yellow jonquils bloomed in wild profusion. The flowers' cheerful demeanor contrasted sharply with the mood in the room. Cubiak looked from them to Sage and started with condolences.

"I'm sorry about the loss you've suffered today. Doctor Melk's death must be a blow to the institute and to you as well. I gather that you've been associates for many years."

Some of the stiffness went out of Sage's shoulders. "Doctor Melk and I worked together for more than four decades."

"He was your mentor?"

"Yes, in many ways. He brought me into the institute."

"Ah, that's tough." Cubiak switched gears slightly. "I hope you'll understand that my questions are merely routine. Personally, I'd rather forgo the formal process under these kinds of circumstances but . . ." He let the thought trail off.

"Whatever you need," Sage said.

From his tone, the sheriff knew that the director felt in control of the conversation. That was his first mistake.

"Tell me what happened," Cubiak said.

"I don't know. I wasn't here. I'm giving a lecture later this afternoon, or I was until now, I guess. At any rate, I was down the hall preparing for my session when I heard the scream and came running."

Sage exhaled and ran a hand through his hair.

"Adam had already reached Doctor Melk. He'd loosened his tie and unbuttoned his shirt and was about to start CPR. I'm sure he's been trained, but he's not a physician. Instinctively, I pushed him aside and took over just before you showed up."

"Doctor Melk was scheduled to give his presentation at three o'clock?"

"That's correct."

"What time did he arrive?"

"He was here all day. In fact, he was here all day yesterday as well. He had a room at the lodge. Today, I saw him at breakfast, probably around eight."

"Did he attend any of the sessions?"

"That I can't say for sure. He liked to keep his hand in things, so he may have sat in on one or two presentations. At some point he probably went out for a short walk. He liked to spend time outside. He said it helped him clear his mind."

"When you saw him, what was his manner?"

"What do you mean?"

"Was he anxious? Did he seem unduly concerned about anything?"

Sage shook his head. "Doctor Melk is—was—one of the most sanguine men I've ever known. He was completely himself when we spoke." He hesitated. "If anything, he may have been a bit melancholy about stepping aside from the institute after all these years."

Time for a touch of bad cop. "It was about time, wouldn't you say?"

Sage stiffened. "I'm not at all sure what you mean."

You're not? Cubiak thought.

"Melk started the institute and ran it from the beginning. If he was true to human nature, that could mean he'd be resistant to change. After all those years, maybe it was time for new leadership, new ideas." The sheriff almost said new blood, but caught himself. "Surely by now you were ready to take the reins."

Sage's mouth tightened, but he, too, stopped before he said what he really meant. "For all intents and purposes, I'd done so years back."

"Right." But always under the watchful eye of your mentor, another thought Cubiak kept to himself. He paused a moment and shifted tactics again.

"Tell me about the institute."

Sage took his time answering, but what he finally offered sounded like the standard overview found on the opening page of an annual report. "The Institute for Progressive Medicine embodies a forward-thinking approach to health care. We incorporate the latest advances in traditional Western medicine with alternative methodologies that have proven effective in other regions of the world in an ongoing quest to cure disease and alleviate patient suffering."

"You hold an annual conference?"

"This is our fifth. The conference is open to our member doctors as well as those in the profession who are interested in widening their horizons, medically speaking. Unlike most conventional medical conferences, we also offer sessions designed for the lay audience."

"Do you mean patients?"

"Some patients come, as do their families, but the sessions are open to anyone interested in learning more about new or alternative approaches to the diagnosis and treatment of disease and disability. These are often of special interest to people in the media. Writers, bloggers, and such."

"And Doctor Melk always participated?"

"Of course."

"He appears to have been quite elderly."

Sage smiled. "Doctor Melk was just shy of ninety-three, but his age was largely irrelevant. Physiologically he was at least a decade younger than he was chronologically. In other words, Doctor Melk had the body of a healthy eighty-three-year-old. He liked to say that based on genetics he had at least another decade to go. His father lived to ninety-eight, and his mother died quietly in her sleep at one hundred and three after she'd spent an afternoon in her kitchen canning pears."

"He had no health issues?"

"Nothing out of the ordinary. A touch of arthritis in the spine. Elevated cholesterol that was controlled with medication. He has an ICD, an implantable cardioverter-defibrillator, but that's not unusual either."

"Was there any chance the device malfunctioned?"

Sage gave Cubiak an exasperated look. Another ignorant layman. "That's a fairly common misconception among the general public. Of course, when they were first introduced, in the 1980s, there were issues, but every generation represents an improvement over the previous one. I won't say the devices are foolproof, but they are getting there. Besides, they're monitored on an ongoing basis."

"There's virtually no chance of a malfunction."

"None. Or at least very little."

"But a device like that can't keep the patient alive forever."

"Correct. At some point even the healthiest heart runs its course." He sighed. "There are none of us immortal, Sheriff."

McGill, the personal assistant, had nothing more to add. He had been sitting at the table checking emails on his phone when Melk collapsed.

"You didn't see anything?"

"When I got here, Doctor Melk was sitting over there talking to Noreen." He pointed to the other side of the podium. "I didn't want to disturb them, so I sat at the table and waited, knowing he'd call me if he needed anything. Like I said, I was busy catching up on email. The next time I looked up, Doctor Melk was at the podium. I went back to what I was doing and didn't pay attention until . . . ," he faltered, "until it was too late."

"How much time elapsed between the time you got here and Doctor Melk collapsed?"

"Five, ten minutes. Fifteen at the most." McGill blanched. "I heard a thump and then a scream. When I looked up, I didn't see Doctor Melk, but I didn't realize what had happened until I saw Linda staring at the podium. Then I knew something was wrong, so I got up and ran over."

"Where was Ms. Kiel standing?"

"Over there, by the window."

"Behind the podium?"

"Yes, and a bit off to the right."

"Who screamed?"

"It must have been Noreen, Ms. Klyasheff. She was kneeling by Doctor Melk when I got there."

"What about Linda Kiel? Did she come over to the doctor?"

McGill shook his head. "Like I said, she was plastered up against the window, white as a ghost. I thought she might faint."

"Did Melk say anything?"

"Not to me. By the time I reached him, I think he was already dead."

Cubiak pulled two chairs to the window and offered a seat to Noreen Klyasheff. She smoothed her skirt with manicured hands and pulled her feet back toward the chair. She took her time getting settled and he didn't rush her.

"You're the executive assistant to Doctor Sage?" he said when he sensed that she was ready.

"Now, yes. Before that I worked for Doctor Melk."

"How long?"

"Eighteen years."

"You must have known him well."

She smiled weakly. "I think so, yes."

"I'm sorry; this must be hard for you."

She closed her eyes and nodded.

Cubiak waited a moment before going on. "You saw the doctor collapse?"

"Yes."

"Where were you when it happened?"

"There." She stood halfway and pointed to a front-row chair on the other side of the podium. "I was looking right at him."

"Tell me what happened."

Klyasheff settled back and folded her hands in her lap. "I wanted to have a good seat for the talk so I got here early. A few other people were doing the same; I could hear them behind me. Several minutes after I sat down, I saw Doctor Sage leave. I presume he wanted to check on the presentations that were scheduled for the end of the day, to make sure everyone was prepared with what they needed. You know how annoying it is when someone stands up to give a talk and something goes wrong with the mic or the PowerPoint. Anyway, a few minutes later, Doctor Melk came in. He sat down next to me for a bit, probably just to be polite—he was that kind of man. Then he went up to the podium. There was still plenty of time before his speech, but he liked to get in early and make sure things were right. I saw him check the mic—he always checked the mic—and arrange some papers on the podium, probably notes for his speech."

"Did he seem nervous?"

"Doctor Melk?" She laughed. For a moment, she seemed to retreat into happier memories. "Doctor Melk wasn't the nervous type. Public speaking came easily to him, and he relished the opportunity to talk about the institute and his work there. He may have been a little sad about leaving, but nervous? No, never."

"He was alone at the podium?"

"Until she came up and started talking to him." Not attempting to hide her scorn, Klyasheff motioned toward Linda Kiel.

Cubiak hid his surprise. What did the journalist have to say that was so important that she would bother Melk before his speech?

"How did Doctor Melk react?"

"Well, as I said before, he was ever the gentleman. He smiled and pretended to be interested in what she was showing him."

"Could you see what it was?"

"No, her back was to me."

"Did you hear what they said?"

"I couldn't. A woman in back started coughing, plus Linda was practically on top of him."

"I thought Ms. Kiel was in front of the podium."

Klyasheff shook her head. "At first, yes, but then she moved to the side and stepped right up to him. That's when she held up a sheet of paper, practically shoved it in his face, if you ask me. I don't know what it was but his expression was . . . well, I don't know how to describe it except to say that he seemed stunned. He looked very stern and said something to her."

"How did she respond?"

"She laughed and then she gave him a hug."

"Did he hug her back?"

"Not really. He seemed startled. He said something else and she walked away. Afterward, he stood there with this odd look on his face. Then he grabbed the podium with both hands, like this"—she demonstrated for him—"and fell over. I could hardly believe it, even though it was happening right before my very eyes, but then I heard a loud thud and saw him lying on the floor. That's when I screamed."

"Where was Ms. Kiel?"

"I'm not sure. I think she was at the window. I jumped out of my chair and ran to the podium to help Doctor Melk, but she just stood and stared."

"You got to him before anyone else?"

"Yes."

"And Doctor Melk was still alive."

She pressed her fingers to her eyes. "Yes."

"Did he say anything?"

"He tried to talk but his voice was so faint I couldn't understand."

"If you had to guess what you heard, what would it be?"

Klyasheff narrowed her eyes and stared into the middle distance. "It sounded like he was saying the word *snow*." She looked at Cubiak. "It didn't make any sense."

"Then what?"

"Then he died."

Cubiak left Noreen Klyasheff sitting along the side wall and motioned Linda Kiel to the other side of the room. As she approached, he was struck by her apparent nonchalance.

Again he pulled out two chairs and waited for the young woman to sit first.

"You're not a doctor?" he said.

"Me? Heavens, no. I thought of going to med school at one point but never got through organic chemistry." She laughed as if she were sharing an inside joke with the sheriff, and he smiled in the way he knew she expected him to.

"Sage called you a scribe."

She laughed again. She was trying to be casual, but he sensed an undercurrent of excitement in her manner, as if she was pleased to be part of the day's drama.

"That's so like him to use such a very old-fashioned term, but he is sort of an old-fashioned guy, so it fits. And it is what I do."

Cubiak glanced at the walnut wainscoting and oversized ferns on the ends of the dais. "This hardly seems like the kind of event that warrants media coverage."

"It's not. But that's not why I'm here. I'm writing a book about the institute, and with Doctor Melk giving his farewell address, it was something I couldn't miss."

"What kind of book?"

She rolled her eyes. "The kind they want, of course. History, highlights, happy endings."

"Sweeping the negative stuff under the rug."

"More like keeping the spotlight focused on the positives. I've been imbedded with the institute for ten months." She stressed the word *imbedded* as if it heightened her status. "Interviewing doctors and patients and figuring out what's important and how to organize the material so it's not one of those boring beginning-to-end chronologies."

"You get to decide on the content?"

"It's a work for hire, but to some extent they depend on my discretion."

Cubiak took that to mean no.

"Ultimately the institute calls the shots?"

She shrugged.

A yes, he thought.

"And Melk was the final judge."

"One of them."

"You liked Melk?"

"I liked everyone at the institute."

It was Cubiak's turn to laugh. "Do you like doing this kind of work?"

Kiel twisted the silver ring on her right hand. "More or less." She hesitated. "Okay, less than more. *Like* isn't really the word for how I feel about the assignment. *Need* is a better fit. The honest truth, Sheriff, is that it's almost impossible to make a living doing straight reporting anymore. Instead, you write for established websites, which pay nothing or close to it, or you blog and starve waiting for readers to discover and follow you. Or, you swallow your pride and write happy news for those willing and able to pay for your time and expertise. It's akin to selling off pieces of your soul to the highest bidders."

"When will the book be published?"

"In about three months. But the first sample cover design was ready, and I brought a copy to show Doctor Melk."

"Is that why you went up to him at the podium?"

Kiel looked across the room at Ms. Klyasheff and glowered. "Apparently the all-seeing eye of the institute has already run through things for you."

Cubiak ignored the obvious dig at the senior staffer. "Is it?"

"He had to give his approval."

"You couldn't wait?"

"He'd told me earlier that as soon as it was ready, he wanted to see it. I don't understand what the big deal was. It's not as if I was cutting into his prep time. He had nearly an hour before he was to give his talk, so it wasn't like I was unduly pressuring him or anything."

"Did he like it?"

"Absolutely." The response came a little too quickly. "He asked me to email him a copy so he could give it his considered opinion—a favorite phrase of his—once the conference was over. But he was humming a bit when he saw it, and with him that was always a good sign." She looked at Cubiak. "Here, do you want to see it?"

"Isn't it proprietary?"

She shrugged as if to say words had to be protected but art was fair game.

The drawing was done in an art deco style and portrayed the traditional medical symbol of the winged staff entwined by two serpents. The caduceus was imprinted with the letters IPM and surrounded by rays of light that beamed out as if coming through the gates of heaven.

"Doesn't Sage have to approve it as well?"

"Of course, him and God only knows who else. They tend to make decisions by committee at the institute. But Doctor Melk's okay was still the most important."

"How well did you know the doctor?"

"Personally, not at all. He was very tight lipped about his nonmedical life. I know that his parents were from Brooklyn but that by the time he was born, they'd moved to Wisconsin."

"When was that?"

"Sometime around the 1920s."

"Why did his parents leave New York?"

She looked past Cubiak toward the window. "He never said. I'm not sure he knew."

"What can you tell me about him?"

Kiel rattled on. "In a nutshell, Doctor Melk started medical school just as the Depression was winding down. He married late and was widowed young. He and his wife had no children. He enjoyed studying biographies of famous men but also felt that any time he spent reading for pleasure was time away from his work. He was totally dedicated to his profession, but modest too. There were some things, like the institute, that he was happy to talk about and others that he minimalized."

"Such as?"

"His early days as a physician. It's all ancient history, he liked to say. We were like the blind stumbling around in the dark. The real advances are being made now. And we need to keep looking forward, not to the past."

"How much time did you spend with him?"

"Altogether, I have about ten hours of interviews with Doctor Melk. That was time I spent just with him but there's more in conversations that included Sage as well."

She hesitated. "You asked me before if I liked Doctor Melk. I think the most truthful answer is that I admired him. He was a fine person and a real gentleman. Mostly he was a good doctor, one of those who genuinely cared about his patients. His presentation today was supposed to be one of the highlights of the book. We—Sage and I—had any number of discussions about whether it should be used as the preface or an appendix." She dug around in her briefcase again and pulled out several sheets of paper. "His speech," she said.

"I'll need a copy of that."

Kiel hesitated. "I think you'll have to ask Sage for that. It's proprietary material."

"Was Melk in the room when you arrived?"

"Yes. He was sitting there." She pointed to the row of chairs on the other side of the podium. "He and Doctor Sage were discussing final arrangements for tonight's banquet." She made a noise and clasped her hands in a gesture of helplessness. "The banquet! It'll have to be canceled, won't it?"

"I would imagine so."

"All that planning. Anyway, I sat down at the end of the row and waited for them to finish. Doctor Melk saw me because he gave a little wave, and then when Sage got up and walked away he motioned me over."

"He wasn't at the podium when you showed him the book cover?"

"Oh, no. He was still seated over there, just as I told you. We talked about the cover, which he liked very much, and then he made a little joke about this being his swan song. 'I hope someone applauds when I'm done,' he said, and I assured him that he'd get a standing ovation."

As she talked, Cubiak tallied up the discrepancies between her version of events and what Noreen Klyasheff had told him. The differences probably didn't matter, unless there was a reason behind them.

"Where were you when Doctor Melk collapsed?" he asked.

Kiel pointed to the window near the podium.

"And just before that?"

"I was at the podium. Doctor Melk's tie was crooked. Doctor Melk was very particular about his image. He always said it wasn't about him; it was about IPM and he wanted the world to see the institute in the right light. I knew there'd be photos taken during the speech and felt he should look his best. So I went to straighten it for him."

"Ms. Klyasheff said you gave him a hug."

Kiel grimaced. "She would. I may have patted his arm or whatever after fixing his tie, but I assure you I did not hug Doctor Melk. No one did."

"Did anyone else approach him after you stepped away?"

"No, why do you ask?"

"No reason, but it makes you one of the last people to talk to him before he died."

Kiel's eyes flashed with triumph. The spark was unsettling, and she tried to cover it over with a flutter of her lashes and a diminutive "oh."

Cubiak wondered what else besides the book she intended to write.

"Can I leave now?"

Before Cubiak could respond, a second loud cry rang out. It sounded desperate and familiar, like a delayed echo of the first scream, which had brought him to the room where Melk had died.

DESAPARECIDO

3

For the second time that afternoon, Cubiak slalomed through the human obstacle course in the corridor. The crowd had thinned, but enough hangers-on remained to hamper his progress. They seemed confused by the ongoing turmoil. Some continued to look toward the room where Melk had collapsed, while others had turned in the direction of the second scream, as if they weren't sure which crisis deserved their attention. Sidestepping past the IPM signs that had been toppled and kicked aside, the sheriff sent another text to his deputy Mike Rowe: *Hurry.*

Before he left for work that morning, Cubiak had assured his wife that he would be home in time for an early dinner. He told Cate that he had a light morning at the office, lunch with Bathard, and several days' worth of paperwork to catch up on. It was supposed to have been an easy day, but instead he was moving from one hot spot to another. In one room, a well-regarded physician lay dead on the floor. He hoped that there wasn't another body waiting down the hall.

As Cubiak neared the end of the passage, he heard sobs coming from the Forest Room. The door was open and a bubble of people had formed around the entrance. He stepped through and closed the door.

Inside, a short, slim woman stood with her back toward him. She gripped the handle of a large wheeled cart that was piled with cleaning supplies and towels. Unlike the conference-goers in their smart attire, the woman wore the outfit of a lodge staff member: athletic shoes, black sweatpants, and a blue long-sleeved T-shirt with the words Green Arbor Lodge splashed across the back.

Cubiak stepped forward so he could see her. She was fairly young and Hispanic. Traces of tears glistened on her face.

"Are you okay? What's happened?" he asked.

She seemed not to have heard. Raising one hand, she pointed to a black-and-white photograph that was projected on the pale ivory wall behind the podium. The image showed a young boy in a white short-sleeved shirt and dark knee-length shorts. The photo was slightly out of focus and tightly cropped around the boy, cutting off the top half of the person standing behind him. All that showed of the unknown figure was the bottom part of a long white coat, the kind worn by a doctor or a lab technician, and the thick, gnarled fingers that gripped the boy's shoulders. The boy looked to be about six or seven, not much older than Cubiak's son, Joey.

As if she had just become aware of his presence, the woman's gaze shifted toward the sheriff and then moved back to the photo. When she finally spoke, her voice was fragile, as if it might break.

"*Mi hermano. Mi hermano gemelo.*"

To Cubiak, it sounded as if she were uttering a prayer. He tried to connect what she had said to the words and phrases he had heard living in Chicago, but he was never good with foreign languages. Time had blurred the memory of the little he had picked up from the taunts and slurs tossed around the neighborhoods, the intimate, hurried conversations exchanged on the L platforms as noisy trains pulled in to the station, the pleas whispered or shouted into cell phones in corridors of the police stations where he used to work.

Despite the bits of Spanish that came back to him, he didn't comprehend what the woman said. "*No comprendo.* I don't understand," he said.

Did anyone at the station speak Spanish? As he wondered whom he could call upon for help, the door opened and another woman slipped in behind them. She was Hispanic and older but of an indeterminate age. Although she wore her black hair stylishly short, the features of an ancient people were imprinted on her face. She had rounded shoulders, deep wrinkles, and soft, dark eyes that seemed steeped in sorrow. She too wore the uniform that identified her as a member of the lodge cleaning staff, but on her squat, padded frame the costume was taut.

The door clicked shut and the younger woman stiffened, but she did not turn around.

Instead, she slapped her fist to her chest. "*Mi hermano gemelo*," she said, as if she could convey her message through sheer force of willpower.

"The boy in the picture is her brother," the older woman said. She spoke quietly in the self-appointed role of translator. Despite her heavy accent, her words were clear.

Hermano. Brother. He should have known that.

Cubiak dipped his head to indicate his understanding. There was another word he had not recognized. "Is that his name, Gemelo?"

She smiled condescendingly. "*Gemelo* is not a boy's name. It is the word for *twin*."

As she talked, the older woman approached her colleague and wrapped an arm around her. Then wordlessly she guided her to one of the chairs along the back wall.

The younger woman sat without protest. She seemed lost in a daze. Her head drooped to her chest, and she sobbed for several seconds before her cries softened into whimpers. The older woman crouched at her feet and cradled her hands in her gnarled grasp.

The sheriff was struck by the tenderness between the two. Could they be mother and daughter? He dismissed the idea. If they were, then the boy in the photo would be the older woman's son and she would have identified him as such. It was possible the two women were related in a different way, or perhaps they were simply coworkers and friends. Or maybe the older woman was one of those rare souls who understood intuitively when kindness was needed.

Cubiak pulled up a chair and sat facing them, careful to remain several feet away. Both women wore ID tags, but he couldn't see them clearly enough to read their names.

He decided to talk directly to the younger woman. Even if she didn't comprehend what he was saying, he hoped that she would realize that he wanted to understand the reason for her distress.

Looking straight at her, he spoke. "What is your name?"

As he knew she would, her companion translated.

The younger woman raised her head and stared at Cubiak. For the first time she seemed fully aware of his presence. Her eyes brimmed with suspicion. She frowned and shook her head. Then she leaned toward her companion and unleashed a fury of words.

"She won't talk to you," the older woman said.

"Why not?"

"She thinks you're one of the doctors."

The response surprised him. Why would she be wary of doctors? And why would she think he was a physician? "Why does she think I am a doctor?"

The older woman waved a hand toward the door. "They are everywhere."

She kept her eyes pinned on him. "Are you?" she said, in an accusatory tone.

"*No es médico,*" Cubiak said. He spoke to the young woman again, uncertain if he had used the correct term for *doctor*. After a pause, he went on. "I am the sheriff." He spoke in English because he didn't know the Spanish words to use.

The young woman stiffened in alarm and pulled back as far as she could while still remaining seated.

She understood, he thought. But why was she so fearful of him? She had to be legal to be employed at the lodge. As he watched, her eyes narrowed and the muscles around her mouth twitched. She was battling with herself, deciding whether to talk to him. Whether to trust him.

He waited. Any sign of aggression would upset her further. To convey his good intentions, he sat back and let his hands fall over the arms of the chair in a nonthreatening pose.

When he spoke again, he kept his voice soft. "My name is Dave Cubiak," he said as he raised one hand to his chest.

The young woman scrutinized him. After a moment, her eyes softened and she relaxed. "My name is Francisca María Delgado," she said. Then she touched the other woman on the shoulder. "My friend is Lupita Esteban."

A truce of sorts had been reached.

"*Hola*, Señorita Delgado and Señora Esteban," the sheriff said.

"Francisca, please. And Lupita. At the lodge, we use first names only."

Motioning for Cubiak to pay attention, Francisca stood and pointed to the image of the little boy. "My *hermano se llama Miguel*. He is *desaparecido*," she said, using a mixture of English and Spanish.

"*Desaparecido*," Cubiak repeated. Another unfamiliar word. He looked to Lupita for help.

"She says her brother is missing."

"What do you mean 'missing'?" the sheriff said.

"*Desaparecido*," Francisca said again, her tone growing more insistent.

She bent to her companion and released another flurry of Spanish. Cubiak didn't catch a word. When the one-way conversation ended, Lupita slowly pushed up from the floor and turned toward the photo. She looked immeasurably sad and seemed uncertain as to where or how to begin telling him what she had just heard.

Francisca spoke sharply to her again.

"*Sí*," said the older woman. She bowed her head and moved her lips in silent prayer.

When she finished, she crossed herself and turned back toward Cubiak.

"It is a tragic story, Señor. Francisca's family lived in a small mountain village in Chiapas. One day, two men in white coats came to the village. One spoke only English, but one knew a little Spanish. They went to the priest and asked permission to examine the children. They had medicines with them that could help them breathe better; they would treat small injuries and check their eyes and ears and teeth for diseases. Of course, the priest said yes and even offered his small house for their use."

No doubt for a fee, Cubiak thought.

"The people in the village were excited and happily brought their children to the doctors. Francisca's parents did the same. They waited until it was late in the day and most of the others were already gone before they came with their family. When the gringos saw Miguel, they were very simpatico. But they seemed pleased as well. Francisca's parents were confused. Then the doctors told them it was a good thing they had the courage and good sense to bring the boy because they knew how to help him. At first, the mother was very suspicious. 'You can cure our son?' she said. And they said yes, in the U.S., they could. Can you can imagine how Francisca's parents felt?"

"Yes, sí," Cubiak said, trying to stem his growing concern.

Lupita went on as if he hadn't interrupted. "The doctors were an answer to their prayers. The village was very poor and Francisca's parents had no money to pay, but the men said they belonged to a big charity that provided medical care for children like their son. They said that all the costs would be paid. Miguel would have to leave with them and fly to Los Estados Unidos, but it was the only way he could be treated. If they agreed, all they had to do was sign a paper giving their permission. They said they had been in Mexico for six months and that this village was their last stop. The next evening, they were flying back to their clinic and so there was little time to deliberate."

The old woman said something to Francisca and then continued. "The men said they needed the parents' approval and gave them a paper to sign, but they did not know how to read English. And there was no one in the village who could."

"Not even the priest?"

Lupita repeated the question in Spanish for Francisca.

"He knew how to read but not English. The priest's only concern was that the boy did not have any papers, not even a birth certificate. How would he be allowed to go to El Norte and then come back into Mexico when he was well without them? The doctors said that children brought to the country for medical treatment did not need documents."

"What did Francisca's parents do?"

"They prayed to Our Lady of Guadalupe and lit candles at her altar in the church. They stayed up all night asking her and her Son to tell them what to do. By the time the doctors returned the next morning they had made their decision. They felt that they had no choice. How could they refuse the miracle they had begged El Señor to give them? They were convinced that the angels had guided the doctors to their village so they could help Miguel. So, yes, they signed the paper."

Lupita made an *X* with her finger to indicate how that was done. Then she sat down and again took Francisca's hands into her own.

By now the noise in the hall had faded. Cubiak got up slowly, as if burdened by the enormity of what he had just heard. He gave a slight bow to the women, and then he walked up to the image on the wall. The boy had dark eyes and hair like the sheriff's son, but unlike Joey he was heavier and not as tall. He had a short, broad nose and an epicanthic fold near the inside corner of each eye. Cubiak had never seen a Hispanic child with Down syndrome, but he was familiar with the classic symptoms and recognized them in the boy's features.

The two women waited patiently at the back of the room. Although the sheriff was sure that he already knew the answer, he turned and asked Francisca the critical question.

"Did the men cure your brother?" He couldn't bring himself to call them doctors.

Without waiting for a translation, Francisca whispered a response in Spanish.

"She doesn't know," the old woman said.

The answer surprised Cubiak. "Why not?"

"Because Miguel did not come back to the village. His family never saw him again."

The sheriff cursed under his breath.

The men kidnapped the boy, but why? To be sold into child labor? Or worse? There were a dozen possible explanations, and none of them good. And how did Miguel's photograph end up as part of a presentation at a medical conference in Wisconsin?

Cubiak's best estimate put Francisca in her midthirties. If he was right about the boy's age, the picture was probably taken nineteen or twenty years ago. He studied the image again. Besides the boy and the cropped portion of the person behind him, there was only a bit of brick at the boy's feet and a sliver of what appeared to be a white wall behind the two, not enough background to determine if the picture had been shot in Mexico or somewhere in the United States. The boy's clothing looked American, but that didn't help to pinpoint the locale.

The photo was coming from a laptop and was probably part of a PowerPoint. Either someone had just finished a presentation or was setting up for a lecture when Noreen Klyasheff screamed at the other end of the corridor and many of those at the conference rushed out to see what had happened. Cubiak searched the computer for the name of the owner, but there was nothing on it and he didn't feel confident pressing any buttons to see what else would pop up on the screen. He didn't dare risk erasing the entire program.

The podium was empty but the floor was littered with papers. Most contained hand-scribbled notes left behind by people at the sessions.

Finally, on a chair at the end of a row, Cubiak found a brochure for the four-day event. There were three lectures every hour. Only one mentioned Down syndrome, and the speaker was Harlan Sage, MD, PhD.

"I'll be damned," the sheriff said. Even more surprising was the other disease mentioned in the title: Alzheimer's.

Cubiak's phone buzzed with a text from Rowe: *Here. Trouble with Sage. Need your help.*

The two women hadn't moved from their seats.

"I'll be right back. Wait here. Don't go anywhere," the sheriff said as he headed toward the door.

THE BRUSH-OFF

Harlan Sage had replaced the woman blocking the entrance to the Woodlawn Theater. The disheveled director stood in the doorway, his arms out to the side, and scowled at the approaching sheriff. Rowe and Bathard were inside the room, their frustration visible on their faces, while the EMTs hovered in the hall, alongside the gurney they had pushed down the passage.

The conference-goers who had lingered seemed to be enjoying the show.

"Put your cameras away," Cubiak said as he moved past them. He approached the director. "What's going on here?"

Sage continued to glare but said nothing.

"The doctor won't let the paramedics come in," Rowe said.

"He insists the body be returned to the IPM facility and not the morgue," Bathard said.

Sage finally spoke up. "There's no need for them to be here, no need for an autopsy, as it's obvious that Doctor Melk died of natural causes, and no need for you to waste county resources on our behalf. I have people coming from the institute for the body. I assume full responsibility."

Cubiak kept his voice low. "This is not your call; it's mine. It is not your responsibility to assume; it's mine. And it is not within your authority to take charge of Doctor Melk's body; it's within mine."

Sage's jaw clamped shut again but he did not move.

"If you don't step aside and allow the EMTs to enter and remove the body, I will arrest you and charge you with interfering with a sheriff's investigation. Is that what you want?"

The muscles in Sage's cheeks quivered. He opened his mouth, then shut it again.

Cubiak softened. "I realize that you are under considerable strain. These are not the kinds of circumstances you normally deal with. I have to ask you to trust that I know what I am doing and allow me to do my job."

Sage's shoulders sagged. He let out a deep breath and scrutinized the sheriff. Then wordlessly, he turned and walked back into the room.

Cubiak let him be. While the paramedics readied the body and lifted it to the gurney he called the county medical examiner, Doctor Emma Pardy, told her about Melk, and asked her to meet the ambulance at the hospital.

"What's going on?"

"Sage may try to interfere again. If he does, it might be best if you're there to meet the ambulance and ward him off."

Cubiak waited until the body had been removed before he approached Sage.

"We'll keep you fully informed of all results," the sheriff said.

The director nodded.

"In the meantime, there's something else I need to ask about." A flicker of anger flashed in Sage's eyes. Cubiak waited for it to fade and then showed him the brochure from the Forest Room.

The physician read the title of the presentation out loud. "This is from the talk I gave earlier today. It's a promising new area of study," he said.

"How long have you been interested in this type of research?"

"Since I joined the institute. I took over from Doctor Melk."

"Can you explain the connection between Down syndrome and Alzheimer's?"

"It's complicated. I doubt you'd understand."

"Give it a try."

In a professorial tone, Sage proceeded to lecture the sheriff. "Down syndrome patients have an extra copy of a chromosome, chromosome twenty-one to be precise, that carries a gene that produces the amyloid precursor protein, or APP," he said and paused for Cubiak to catch up. "APP is a sticky substance, and too much of it produces plaque and tangles in the brain that strangle the neurons and interfere with normal transmission of—"

"What does this have to do with Alzheimer's?" Cubiak interrupted.

"In layman's terms: people who suffer from Alzheimer's also have excess APP in their brains, and thus they develop the same kind of tangles that interfere with normal brain function."

"Does this mean that if you cure Down syndrome you can cure Alzheimer's?"

Sage smiled. "Not exactly, but it does mean that if you understand Down syndrome, then you have a chance of dealing with excessive APP and finding a way to help patients with Alzheimer's."

"That sounds like a pretty big deal."

"It could be." Sage grew more defensive. "What's this all about anyway? Why are you asking?" He stood, signaling his readiness to terminate the conversation.

"You heard the second scream this afternoon?" Cubiak said.

"Of course. We all did."

"I found this in the Forest Room, where you gave your lecture. There was a photo of a young boy on the wall. What can you tell me about him?"

"Nothing. It's a stock photo. We've used it dozens of times. I have no idea where it came from."

Cubiak told him Francisca's story.

"Her twin brother? Her parents were promised a cure? That's impossible. Obviously the poor woman is mistaken. How old would you say the boy is?"

"About six or seven."

"And the woman?"

"Mid to late thirties. I'm not sure."

"Well, that goes a long way to explaining the confusion. This young woman sees a photograph of a child with Down syndrome who is about the same age as her brother when these men allegedly took him away." He shook his head. "I don't see how her allegation is credible. All this supposedly happened when she was a child herself. And the accusations she made—that the doctors said they would cure the boy. Do you honestly think she's remembering clearly what was said that long ago? There is no 'cure' for Down syndrome. Surely you know that, Sheriff. And no physicians would ever make such a claim. They surely wouldn't abscond with an innocent child. I don't know what happened to that unfortunate boy, but to imply that Doctor Melk or I or any reputable doctor is involved in his disappearance is, well, beyond the pale."

Cubiak expected Sage to start in about libel and lawsuits, but he merely shook his head again. "We live in a dangerous world, Sheriff. I have spent my life devoted to science. As a doctor, I hold firm with empirical evidence and tangible proofs, but as a man I am often tempted to believe in the existence of evil, not because I want to but because of the manifestations we witness. I don't doubt for a moment that something untoward befell that village boy, but who knows the true story? Isn't it possible that the parents willingly gave him up for their own reasons? These were not an enlightened people in a compassionate age. Think of the stigma the family bore because of the afflicted child. We see this in developing countries around the world; it hasn't been that long since we finally moved beyond it in our own nation. They may have had him institutionalized and made up the story about a possible cure to alleviate their guilt or to help their other children accept their brother's absence. This all took place so far away and so long ago that it would probably take a miracle to discover what actually transpired. At any rate, I assure you that the boy's disappearance has nothing to do with me and certainly nothing to do with the institute. Now, if you don't mind."

Cubiak watched Sage walk away. Everything he had said made sense. But there was an element of insolence in his response that bothered the sheriff. Was it professional hubris—the notion that the doctor is above reproach—or something else that prompted him to dismiss Francisca's story and bundle it into a neat little package of denials that could be tied up with a white ribbon of innocence?

Uncertain what he would say to Francisca, the sheriff made his way back to the Forest Room.

When he got there, the women were gone, as was the laptop and with it the photo of the boy.

THE HIPPOCRATIC OATH

5

As Cubiak headed down the peninsula, he called Cate and told her he would be home late. It was twilight, and to the west the remnants of an orange sunset stretched along the horizon. In the other direction the first star already glimmered in the charcoal sky above the lake. The sheriff liked the in-between feeling of the hour. It was an interlude that offered a place to rest between the demands of the day and the solitude of night.

He was on his way to see Bathard. Over the years, he had come to increasingly rely on his friend's memory and expertise, and after the day's events, there was plenty that he wanted to discuss with him. More often than not, the men met in the early evening, and more often than not a glass of sherry accompanied the conversation.

From the highway, the sheriff followed a familiar back road toward the shore and eventually turned onto the lane that led to Bathard's home. He left the jeep under a patch of trees near the old barn that the doctor had converted to a workshop when he retired. It was there that Cubiak had apprenticed himself to Bathard and the two men undertook the hard, tedious work of rebuilding the skeletal remains of a decrepit sailboat and turning it into a seaworthy vessel. The doctor kept the

Parlando moored in Egg Harbor, where it was available for Cubiak to use. These days Bathard rarely sailed or spent any time in the workshop.

A chorus of crickets greeted Cubiak, and the crunch of gravel underfoot was the only other sound that accompanied him across the yard to the rear porch. As usual, the back door to the house was unlocked.

Cubiak let himself in. The interior was quiet and dim and haunted by an emptiness that the sheriff doubted would ever be filled again. From the mudroom he made his way into the large kitchen, where the redolence of freshly baked bread roused memories. From there, he passed through the dining room and into the living room with the great expanse of window that opened onto the bay, which was dark now but for the intermittent flash of the lighthouse at Sherwood Point. He watched the beacon for a moment and then moved down the hall toward the library, where he hoped to find Bathard.

Widowed twice in the past twelve years, the old doctor spent increasing amounts of time in the cozy room sequestered with his books. "My good friends," he called them.

A table lamp was on, and from the doorway Cubiak glimpsed the elderly gentleman. Bathard was neatly dressed in khakis and a sport shirt, his once gray hair gone white and long enough to curl at his collar. His head was down and his eyes closed. The black cane leaned against the arm of the chair.

Not wanting to disturb him, the sheriff hesitated. At the very moment he paused, the coroner suddenly looked up. "Caught me napping, did you?" he said with his familiar, gentle laugh. He waved Cubiak in and indicated the empty glass on the side table. "I had a nip of sherry earlier this evening. If I had known that company was coming, I would have waited. But you go right ahead," he said, pointing to the crystal decanter on a low shelf.

Cubiak poured a drink. For most of his adult life, he had been a shot and a beer guy, tossing down the familiar combination of cheap whiskey and cheap beer that had been a mainstay in the working-class neighborhood of his youth. Only recently had he come to appreciate the lingering comfort of a fine wine sipped leisurely at the end of the day.

"You need to start locking your doors at night," he said.

Bathard waved a hand dismissively. "It is not yet night."

"The sun's down."

"That means that twilight is nigh. But thank you. I appreciate the concern."

Cubiak smiled. He had been raised by a father who defined his masculinity by how much vodka he could hold and how loud he could yell and sometimes by how mean he could be to his wife and son. The old man, as he liked to call himself, had never thanked anyone for anything his entire life and had never seemed capable of seeing the good in anything. When Cubiak had met Bathard, the sheriff viewed his gentle manner and generous spirit with cynicism. No one could be that decent all the time, he thought. For weeks and then months, he waited to be disappointed, but the day never came, and gradually Cubiak came to realize that Bathard was a genuinely good man and that he was honored to call the old doctor his friend.

Bathard waited until his visitor was settled in the matching armchair across from the unlit fireplace before he spoke.

"Do you know how to make God laugh?" he asked.

Cubiak raised an eyebrow in question.

"Plan your life." The coroner paused and then gave the sheriff a quizzical look. "It is supposed to be a joke."

"Not a very funny one."

"Not at all, but if it were true then between the two of us we would have had him—or her—in stiches." Bathard said. "Do not look at me that way. You know it is the honest truth."

Cubiak turned away from the coroner's gaze.

Like his friend, he had once had a different life. Born and raised in Chicago, he had lived in the city until that night fourteen years ago when he drove more than two hundred miles through a snowstorm and knocked on the door of the ranger station at Peninsula State Park. He was a broken man, a husband and father who had lost his wife and daughter to a drunk driver, a homicide detective at the country's third largest police force who had drunk himself out of a job and was barreling headlong down a path to self-destruction when his former partner interceded. Malcolm dragged him out of the muck of self-pity, badgered him to go back to school and to start a new career, and then pointed him north to Door County. Cubiak arrived fortified by the vodka he had learned to drink at his father's knee and the assurance that he had to stay for only one year, long enough to keep his promise to Malcolm. He came to escape all memory of death and found himself surrounded by it. Not the kind of death that comes quietly in the night but the random, terrifying species of death that comes at the end of an arrow or a bullet or worse, weapons wielded by a vengeful killer. Others tried but failed to halt the rampage, and Door County lived in fear until Cubiak solved the case. Why? Because he knew how to track and stop a killer and because he was compelled to act, because the pledge to serve and protect had never really left him. Now he was sheriff. Now he was a husband and father again. Now he had new dreams, but if truth be told, the old ones remained as well. They were the dreams that would never come true.

Bathard had his unfulfilled dreams as well. He had lost his beloved Cornelia to cancer and had been swept into a new life with Sonja. But cruel fate revisited the aging physician and stole that life too. Cubiak worried about him.

The coroner pulled the hassock into place and swung his foot onto it. "You didn't come to listen to my feeble attempts at waxing philosophical about life."

"Actually, I'm hoping you'll talk about Leonard Melk."

Bathard grimaced. "I had a feeling that was what brought you here under the cover of soup. My apologies for not offering you any."

The sheriff smiled again. "I've had my soup. Let's just say I detected a coolness in your manner earlier today at the lodge. Correct me if I am wrong, but I get the feeling you don't approve of Melk. Or Sage for that matter."

"Or the Institute for Progressive Medicine. You may as well toss that into the mix too," Bathard said.

"Why?"

The physician lifted his empty glass. "Just a drop," he said. When Cubiak finished pouring, he went on. "I find it distasteful to tell tales on one's colleagues."

"Melk is dead. And anything you tell me goes no farther than this room."

"For now."

Cubiak shrugged. "I have a job to do."

"Leonard Melk died of a heart attack."

"I'm not disputing that. I'm wondering why Sage was so annoyed by your presence and determined to keep me out of the picture. It was almost as if he was trying to hide something."

"I must say, his actions didn't surprise me. Melk and his institute have always been shrouded in secrecy. I imagine that Sage has been steeped in the same culture."

Cubiak settled back against the cushions and waited.

"You're familiar with the Hippocratic oath."

"More or less."

"Well, more or less it goes like this: 'Into whatsoever houses I enter, I will enter to help the sick, and I will abstain from all intentional wrong-doing and harm, especially from abusing the bodies of man or woman, bond or free.' There's more to it of course, but that is the kernel of it. Most doctors take the commitment seriously, but to some it is more like a hypocritical oath."

"And you put Leonard Melk into the latter category?"

"At this point, I am not in a position to go that far but I can tell you this: his institute—the Institute for Progressive Medicine—literally appeared out of nowhere. One day, a meadow of daisies grew on that field outside Green Bay. Then the flowers were plowed under and a multimillion-dollar treatment facility sprang up from the rich loam of the Midwest, and Melk opened the doors to a medical Lourdes, promising to heal every conceivable malady with what I would consider little more than magical water."

"Sage said they practiced traditional as well as nontraditional medicine."

"I am sure they do, but what is the mix and what exactly are these alternative methods? I had several patients to whom I had to give the unfortunate news of serious illness, the kind we all dread: cancer, incurable heart disease, ALS. I presented them with standard treatment options and gave them the sobering data about their chances, and then I never saw them again, only to learn later that they had gone to Melk. Granted that in some instances I had little to offer because conventional medicine had little to offer. But Melk? He had the kind of answers that appealed to desperate people. A modern-day version of snake oil, if you want my professional opinion. For years, the sick and the dying have flocked to the institute."

"Do you think the sheer volume of patients is enough to fund the operation?"

"That may be how it is sustained, but my larger question is: where did he get the funding with which to start? I admit that after I lost several of my patients to his promises, I looked into his background. His medical credentials were unassailable. And his personal story the classic American success story of poor boy makes good. Certainly, he came from very limited means; his father drove a delivery truck for a meatpacking firm in Green Bay, and his mother was a grocery store clerk."

"How did he afford medical school?"

"Scholarships and such, no doubt. There's no question that he was a very bright young man, the kind who deserved the opportunities he was given. But more to the point: where did he get the money to underwrite the institute? As a doctor, he would have earned a comfortable salary—nothing like the incomes enjoyed today by many physicians, particularly those who specialize—but enough to set himself up in a modest private practice."

"But not enough to underwrite the institute."

"I would not think so." Bathard paused. "Have you ever seen it?"

Cubiak shook his head.

"There had to have been major money involved."

"Investors?"

"Perhaps."

"What about research? Is there money in that?"

"What do you mean?"

Cubiak told him about the boy in the photo in the Forest Room and related what Sage had said about Alzheimer's and Down syndrome.

"He is correct that this is a promising field of study, although I have never heard of children being involved, and I cannot imagine that the institute is equipped to handle that kind of work. As for the money, it probably runs into the tens of millions, taking into account government research grants and what the big pharmaceuticals spend to develop new drugs. The payoff, of course, would be enormous."

"What do you think all this means?"

Bathard frowned. "To be honest, I cannot really say."

"That's unlike you."

Cubiak was pleased to hear the coroner chortle at the remark. The moment passed, and the doctor turned somber again.

"I mean that in all seriousness. Melk and the institute may be clean as the proverbial freshly fallen snow, but it is also possible that there is something untoward going on that we are missing. If you like, I can do a little digging—play detective, as it were. I still have a number of reliable contacts, and I certainly have plenty of time on my hands."

"If you don't mind."

"Mind?" Bathard smiled. "It would be good to feel useful again."

TRUE IDENTITY

6

On Tuesday morning, Joey finished his breakfast first. After he went out to play, Cubiak told Cate about the previous day's events at the Green Arbor Lodge, starting with the death of Doctor Melk.

"*The* Leonard Melk? I haven't heard that name in years," she said as she stirred milk into her coffee.

"You know him?"

"Not really, but I remember hearing Ruby and Dutch talk about him," she said, referring to the childhood summers she spent with her aunt and uncle in Door County.

"What did they say?"

"I didn't pay that much attention, but I had the feeling they didn't really care for him, or for the institute that he ran. Why do you ask?"

Cubiak frowned. He wasn't even sure himself. "Comes with the territory, I guess. I see a dead man and I want to know if anyone had it in for him."

Cate passed him a plate of buttered toast. "People die, Dave."

The sheriff nodded. "First mystery solved."

"There's another?"

"Maybe."

He told her about the second event and his encounter with the two cleaning women. As best he could, he described the image on the wall.

44

"Is there any way to authenticate a photo like that?" he asked. Cate was a professional photographer, and early in their relationship he learned to rely on her expertise.

"I'd have to see it."

"You will, once I find it again. Everything was gone when I got back to the room. But Sage said it was a stock photo, so either he or someone at the institute must have a copy."

Cate had an odd look on her face.

"Is something wrong?" Cubiak said.

"That story you just told me. There's something vaguely familiar about it. Almost as if I've heard it before." She pushed an uneaten bit of toast around her plate. "It's like déjà vu, only I don't know where it's coming from. Maybe it's just my mind playing tricks." She looked up at him. "Does that ever happen to you?"

"Not really." But it had and he didn't want to talk about it. A month ago at the grocery store, he had seen a tall, slim woman walking away from him down the dairy aisle. She wore jeans and a red patterned top that looked exactly like one that Lauren used to wear. Without realizing what he was doing and with no rational basis for doing so, he started to follow her, convinced that she was his first wife. It made no sense: Lauren had died in his arms. Then the woman stopped. When she turned around, the sight of her unfamiliar face slapped him back to reality. Stunned and embarrassed, he spun away and grabbed a jar of mayonnaise off the shelf. The incident had haunted him for days, not just because of the intensity of the feeling involved but because it wasn't the only one.

What was he doing still chasing ghosts? he wondered as he stood and pushed away from the table.

"I'm late," he said and bent to kiss Cate good-bye.

He was in the jeep when she ran out after him.

"I remember what I wanted to tell you," she said. Her long hair had fallen loose around her shoulders. As she pushed it out of her face, she leaned toward the open window.

"For a couple of the summers that I was up here with my aunt and uncle, I was friends with a girl who lived in Southern Door. She had horses, and we used to go riding on the back roads around her house. There was one farm that she would never go past because she said that something about it spooked the horses. I thought she was being silly but she insisted. She said that the people who owned the place years ago had had a disabled daughter who vanished. According to my friend, a doctor came to the farm promising to cure her, and the father sent her away with him. The parents never saw her again, and the despondent father committed suicide. Whether it was his ghost or his daughter's that my friend was afraid of, I don't know, but she wouldn't go near the place."

"What was wrong with the girl?"

"She wasn't sure."

"Do you remember the name of the family?"

"No, but I can try to find out." Cate pressed her hand against the jeep door. "Do you think it means anything?"

"Probably not. I wouldn't worry about it. Kids like to make up tales about haunted houses. The story about the girl may not be true." He started to drive away and then stopped. "But if you learn anything, let me know."

In Jacksonport, Cubiak pulled off the road and checked his messages. Pardy hadn't gotten back to him with the autopsy results on Melk, and there was nothing from his assistant, Lisa. He called Sage to ask for a copy of the photo, but the doctor didn't answer his phone. He tried the general number for the institute, but no one picked up.

The sheriff was too restless to spend the morning at his desk. Nearing Sturgeon Bay, he detoured off the highway and took the scenic route along the water into town. From the east side, he studied the new developments on the other side of the bay. The upscale condos sparkled bright white in the morning sun, but where he was the houses were old and stately and set back from the street, their owners' wealth and good fortune unobtrusive under the shelter of the tall shade trees.

When he got downtown, he skipped the new coffee shop that catered to tourists and summer residents. Cubiak liked the lattes they served, but that morning he opted for the old diner favored by the locals. As usual, the wooden tables and booths were full. Cubiak slid onto a stool at the counter and ordered a coffee.

The radio was tuned to state and national news that played softly in the background, but he was more interested in the local gossip that buzzed from one patron to another. The "Hey, did you hear about . . ." kind of chatter that kept him informed of local goings-on. Cate had suggested the routine to him. Cafés and diners in the morning, an occasional visit to one of the bars in the evening. "People like to talk. You'll be surprised what you hear."

She was right. The banter he picked up ran the gamut from neighborly good deeds to rumors of layoffs at the shipyards, to gossip about battered spouses and kids behind barns sniffing substances that would fry their brains. He didn't know how much of what he overheard was true. But later Cubiak would share what he had gleaned with his staff, because the more he and his deputies knew about what was happening, the better prepared they were to do their jobs.

That morning, four women at a nearby table conferred in hushed tones about the deceased Doctor Melk. A miracle worker, one called him. "He cured my husband's cancer when the other doctors said it was fatal." There was awe and reverence in her voice. "Always a kind word, and so good with children," said another. The two companions murmured with appreciation.

Did Melk's institute dispense snake oil, as Bathard implied, or work miracles, as the one woman believed? What really went on there? Cubiak was tempted to ask the women for dates and details, but he stopped for fear that questions from him might prove incendiary. He came to the restaurant to pick up gossip, not to spark it.

The sheriff needed to talk to Francisca again about her missing brother. Yesterday, she and her coworker Lupita left the Green Arbor, although he had asked them to wait for him. Why hadn't they stayed? Was there something they weren't telling him, or did Francisca fear that she had said too much? He checked the note the manager had given him with the women's addresses and phone numbers. They lived about five blocks away, around the corner from each other.

Their houses were not in the tourist part of town. No lace-curtained bed-and-breakfasts tucked behind picket fences, no old money or water views, no private docks—only the modest frame homes of people who worked with their hands, the kind of people Cubiak knew from his childhood. These were residents who not only took pride in neat lawns and freshly painted trim but did their own work to keep their properties up to standards.

He thought of trying to get the two women together again so Lupita could translate, but decided to start by talking to the older woman without Francisca. He wondered if there were details that Lupita had left out of the story the day before and wanted to hear her version. A phone call would be too impersonal. He needed to see her face when they talked. He would learn more that way.

Although the jeep was unmarked, Cubiak took the precaution of parking around the corner from Lupita's house. He didn't want to prematurely announce his presence or give the neighbors anything to gossip about. Better to arrive on foot.

Lupita lived in a white frame duplex. Her neighbor's door and shutters were red; hers were green, giving the building a cheerful Christmas look even in summer. No one answered his knock on the green door. He tried the red one, hoping someone was home and could tell him where to find Lupita, but no one answered.

Still moderately optimistic, he proceeded around the corner to the pale blue cottage where Francisca lived. Wooden trellises framed the small front yard. The structures were empty but probably would be covered with flowering vines or green beans later in the season. Cubiak knew that without Lupita to translate, he wouldn't be able to talk with Francisca, but he hoped that he would be able to convey his concern. It was the least he could do for her.

She wasn't home either.

Cubiak checked his phone for a message from Cate. But there was nothing.

A mound of paperwork greeted him at the office. When he left the previous evening, the surface had been clean. The mind-numbing stuff of bureaucracy, he thought. It's as if it falls from the sky. Instead of reading the reports, he fished out Doctor Sage's card again and dialed the number.

Noreen Klyasheff, the doctor's assistant, answered.

"Doctor Sage is not in. Is there anything with which I can help?"

"I wanted to find out about getting a copy of a photo that was part of his presentation at the conference."

"You'd have to ask Doctor Sage about that."

Cubiak explained that he had tried reaching the physician to no avail.

"Well, I can't answer to that." She hesitated. "I haven't heard from him either."

Despite her starchy self-righteousness, Cubiak sensed an underlying trickle of concern.

"Is anything wrong?"

"No," she said. But this was followed by "not really," which told him different.

"Is it unusual for him to be out of contact like this?"

"Depending on circumstances, no. He often travels on institute business."

As she spoke, he caught her regret. Had she been too personable and given away more than she should have? "I assume he's upset about what happened yesterday with Doctor Melk. Understandably, of course," she said with cool professionalism.

"Of course, but have him call me when he gets in. Better yet, give me his cell number and his landline if he has one. I'll call him myself."

She demurred; it was against policy to provide personal numbers without permission. Cubiak envisioned the woman at her desk, her posture as rigid as the rule she enforced. It took some wrangling and mention of the word *subpoena* before he finally got what he had asked for.

When he dialed Sage's mobile, the call went to voice mail, much as he expected it to. The same thing happened when he tried the landline.

Cubiak imagined the doctor sequestered behind closed doors with his immediate subordinates or the board of directors, conferring about Melk's death and its impact on the future of the institute as they moved forward. Or maybe they were discussing Francisca's claim about the boy in the photo. If the picture was a stock photo, questions remained:

Where had they gotten it, and had they secured permission for its use? Were there undue ramifications that could reflect negatively on IPM?

There were other possibilities. Perhaps Sage had lied, and he or another institute physician was the unidentified man in the picture with the boy. Perhaps they knew the identity of the child. If so, could they prove he wasn't Francisca's brother? How many tracks did the institute have to cover? As he had done at the restaurant, the sheriff stopped himself. He was moving way ahead of the situation and getting caught up in speculation. He had no proof of any untoward activity. He had found no indication of illegal or unethical behavior on the part of Sage or the institute. For all he knew, the picture had been plucked off the internet or purchased from a photo supply house thousands of miles from Door County.

There hadn't been a serious crime in the county in eight months. Not like at his old job in Chicago when it seemed that one came across the wire every hour, or sometimes every ten minutes. Cubiak opened the top desk drawer. Then he shut it. He forgot what he was looking for. Don't be a fool, he told himself. He lived in a paradise compared to most of the world. He was fifty-four and rolling toward retirement. He didn't need to go looking for trouble.

Cubiak picked up a report from the stack and started reading. He was on page 10 when he tossed the document back on his desk. Under ideal circumstances, he disliked paperwork. After yesterday's events, he found it impossible to concentrate on the mundane. Something about what had transpired at the lodge wasn't right. At first, Sage had seemed almost matter of fact about Melk's death, and then he was overly eager to keep the sheriff out of the matter. He had been blasé about his Alzheimer's research and dismissive about Francisca's claim that the boy in the photo was her brother. Kiel's edgy excitement was disquieting as well. Nor could he get past the fact that the two cleaning women had disregarded his simple request that they wait for him. Had someone scared them away?

The sheriff unwrapped the ham-and-swiss sandwich he had brought for lunch and opened an online search for information about Down syndrome and Alzheimer's. This shouldn't take long, he thought as he took a bite, expecting not to find much information on the internet. Stories on advances in Alzheimer's treatments periodically popped up in the mainstream news, but he had never heard a report that connected the disease to Down syndrome. He hadn't understood much of what Sage had told him at the conference center and assumed the doctor had been talking about theory or even wishful thinking.

What Cubiak found shocked him. The first headline he came across read like something from a tabloid newspaper. "Down Syndrome and Alzheimer's Disease Have a Lot in Common: Scientists are studying them together to find underlying causes." He checked the source and was even more stunned to find that the article had been published in *Scientific American.*

He remembered paging through copies of the magazine in high school. He had seen it on the shelves in the Sturgeon Bay library and on the small table in Bathard's study where the doctor kept his current reading material. This was not a publication to be ignored.

"I'll be damned," the sheriff said.

He skimmed the article. Although he didn't fully understand the content, he picked up enough to realize that what the author was saying was essentially the same as what Sage had explained to him the day before: plaque and tangled brain function were found in both patients with Down syndrome and those with Alzheimer's. The vital difference was that patients with Down syndrome were born with the condition, while those with dementia developed it later in life.

Similar articles were published by the National Institutes of Health, the Alzheimer's Association, and other equally prestigious sources. They all said the same thing: People with Down syndrome were predisposed to developing Alzheimer's. Finding a way to stop the progression of DS meant finding a possible cure for Alzheimer's, a disease that affected more than five million people in the United States and was the sixth leading cause of death in the country.

How does anyone figure all this out? Cubiak wondered. He clicked another button, and the link jumped to academic research studies. The titles of the articles were dizzying, far more complex than anything he could understand with his high school knowledge of biology and chemistry. The sheer volume of material was staggering. He scrolled back to the start of his search and began counting the articles about the topic. When he reached three hundred, he stopped, though there were many more.

"They're all in a race to the finish line," he said out loud.

Most of the research was relatively recent, but there were articles from as far back as the mid-1980s. The oldest material he found was from the early 1970s. One of the earliest reports was based on a study of only thirteen DS patients.

Cubiak did the math. If he was right, the research was already underway by the time Francisca claimed her brother had disappeared. The sheriff skimmed through the material again, but he didn't find Sage listed as the author on any of the pieces. That seemed odd, but maybe it didn't mean anything. The sheriff wasn't sure.

He pushed back from his desk and turned toward the window. In the pasture across the way, a line of Holsteins plodded toward the barn. It was nearly time for evening milking, and the large beasts walked with leisurely intent, their massive heads bobbing and their rumps swaying gently with each step. The hall outside his office was eerily quiet. He reached for his coffee and was about to take a drink when he realized it was cold.

"What the hell is going on?" he said as he set the cup down next to his wilted sandwich.

When Cubiak arrived home that evening, Joey was on the beach tossing a Frisbee to Kipper. Inside, Cate was perched on a tall wooden stool at the kitchen counter. She had the phone receiver tucked under her chin and was bent over a notepad with pen in hand. He opened the door, and she stopped scribbling long enough to give him a thumbs-up sign and then resumed writing.

The sheriff cracked a beer and went out to the deck to watch his son.

A few minutes passed before Cate appeared. She looked triumphant.

"Remember our conversation this morning?" she said as she slipped into the chair beside him.

"About the missing girl and the haunted house?"

Cate squeezed his hand. "You were right. The house isn't haunted. I talked to my old girlfriend, and she admitted that she'd just been trying to impress me when we were kids. But as far as she knows, the bit about the girl disappearing is true. Even better, the last she heard, someone from the family still lives there."

"Did you get a name?"

"Fadim. Florence Fadim. If it's the same woman, she must be ancient by now. She was old when I was kid." Cate handed him a piece of paper. "Here's the address."

"Was the girl her daughter?"

"Apparently not, but she might have been her sister. No one seems to know for sure."

"Did the girl have Down syndrome?"

Cate shook her head. "Uh-uh. Polio."

A CUP OF TEA

7

Cubiak spent a restless night. In his dreams he sprinted through a maze of narrow, antiseptic hallways chasing a small red ball. The child's toy rolled on endlessly, always out of his reach. The passages were painted a blinding white and lined with crooked doorways that opened to dim, windowless rooms that smelled of bleach and human waste. In each room, long rows of empty beds lined the walls. The center aisle was filled with lopsided tables that were covered with microscopes, moldy test tubes, and evil-looking syringes. The dreams were silent and unpopulated, except for wavering shadows that eluded him no matter how fast he raced through the deserted corridors.

When he woke, the glaring early morning sunlight etched the nightmarish images into memory. Exhausted, he slipped from bed and went out to the deck. He hoped the fresh air would clear his mind, but instead the opposite occurred. The rising sun that hovered above the lake was as red as the ball he had pursued through the night. Cubiak rarely recalled his dreams, but when he did he knew what prompted them. He was certain that this recent nightmare stemmed from the stories Francisca and Cate had told of mysterious doctors and missing children.

Determined to follow his normal routine, he pulled on a cap and started down the beach. Three days a week, he did a slow five-mile run on the road with Kipper, but on the two days in between, he and the dog hiked along the shore. From the house, the sand beach stretched for two miles in either direction before giving way to slabs of gray table rock that made walking impossible. No matter which way he went, it was a four-mile hike to the rocks and back. He followed no set routine but let the wind be his guide, always preferring to head into it and to return home with the breeze at his back. That morning, he started off toward the south. At first, he walked on a long stretch of beach that had been pounded hard by the waves, and the going was easy. Then the sand turned to mush. Each step demanded effort, and the comfortable stroll turned into a slog. By the time he had made it to the rocks and back, his leg muscles were tight. Kipper was already limping toward the house when Cubiak called him back. "Not yet," he said. Reluctantly, the dog obeyed and trailed behind as Cubiak plodded on. He was midway to the rocks at the north end of the beach when he finally gave up. Six miles was enough for both of them. He felt a soft ache in his right hip and apologized to the dog for the additional steps, but he had needed the extra distance to try to erase the images from his dream and to think through his plan for the day.

After breakfast with Cate and Joey, he left the house. It was a few minutes before nine. He checked in at the office and then he headed toward the Fadim farm. He could have asked one of his deputies to handle the visit and talk to the old lady about the alleged missing girl, but he had a light schedule, and he was curious. Chances were the excursion wouldn't amount to much. Had Mrs. Fadim even been alive when the girl disappeared? The sheriff wasn't sure what he expected to find. Probably nothing. Even if there was something to the story, he doubted there was much he could do. The trails would all be cold and forgotten.

Still, it wouldn't be a wasted trip, he thought. Mrs. Fadim lived in the quiet southern part of Door County where the farms far outnumbered the few visitors who lingered on their way to Sturgeon Bay and the touristy part of the peninsula. Cubiak didn't get out that way often and figured the visit would give him a chance to reacquaint himself with the area.

From the justice center it was sixteen miles to the exit for Brussels. In town, he passed the old mill and several bars, and then he turned away from the water and drove another two miles along a series of country roads where both the houses and patches of trees grew sparser and farther apart. Finally he stopped by a weather-beaten mailbox. The numbers painted on the side were flecked and too faded to read from the jeep, so he got out and took a closer look. This was it: the Fadim farm. The box was empty except for last week's newspaper. He pulled it out to take inside. Life had to be pretty lonely out here, he thought as he turned off the road and onto the narrow, rutted lane. A border of thistle and tall weeds flanked the entranceway, but beyond the tangle of brush several cultivated fields stretched out in either direction. The green fuzz that poked up through the black earth might be soybeans or hay. Cubiak was still too much a city boy to distinguish one crop from another. Maybe the shoots were newly sprouted stalks of corn. If it was knee high by the Fourth of July, farmers could count on a good crop. That was all he knew about corn.

Abruptly the road ended at what had once been a front yard. Instead of grass, a patch of parched, brown stubble covered the ground. A low wooden fence that was missing most of the pickets encased the patch, which was split down the middle by a jagged sidewalk. The path led to a stucco house with splotched brown walls and high, tiny windows on either side of the door. A rounded roof curved over the eaves and made the house look like a mushroom in need of rejuvenation, a fixer-upper for elves or pixies.

As he mounted the single step to the recessed doorway, he caught a flutter of curtains at the window near the corner of the house, but there was no answer to his knock and no doorbell to ring. On a hunch, he reached under the straw doormat and found a key. He slipped the key into the lock and realized he hadn't needed to bother. The door was not locked.

Whoever occupied the house was one of those trusting souls.

Too trusting, like Bathard, the sheriff thought, but he knew that this was still the norm for many of the residents. Probably half the people in the county either didn't bother to lock their doors or hid the keys in a spot that even an amateur thief would find in less than a minute.

Wary of alarming the old woman or whoever was in the house, or of being shot as an intruder, he toed the door open.

"Hello," he called out to announce his presence.

There was no response.

He slid one foot over the threshold and tried again.

"Hello. Mrs. Fadim? I'm Sheriff Dave Cubiak. I was in the area and wanted to stop by and say hello, make sure everything was okay with you." A white lie but the kind that came in handy at times like this.

The stuffy interior muffled the greeting.

The small entryway was boxed in on three sides and smelled of mold and dust. Through the doorway on his left he made out a long, narrow room where thin ribbons of sunlight rimmed the curtains in the three windows that looked out toward the road. The pale light illuminated a hunched figure in a tall, overstuffed chair but left the rest of the room in dim shadow.

"Hello. Mrs. Fadim?" he said again.

The bent figure turned toward the sound of his voice, and slowly the profile of an old woman came into focus. As she looked at him, her eyes narrowed, and she shrank farther into the chair, but when she spoke her voice was unexpectedly strong.

"Tommy, is that you? It's about time you got back. I've been waiting for you."

Who's Tommy? Cubiak wondered as he approached. He reached the chair in a dozen steps, but Mrs. Fadim had already pivoted back to the window. She was cocooned in a thick brown shawl. The faded blue housecoat beneath the wrap covered her knees and fell to her ankles. Layers of other clothes peeked out from the neckline and around her wrists. The sheriff wondered that she could move at all.

Leaning forward, she parted the curtains. "Did you find her?" she said.

"Mrs. Fadim, I'm—"

At that moment, the elderly woman latched a clawlike hand to his arm and with strength that surprised him jerked him forward.

57

"I know who you are! Don't you play games with me, Tommy. Where have you been all this time? I've been worried sick. Where's your sister? Did you find her?" The old woman sounded desperate and near tears.

Careful not to disturb the wooden cane that rested against the sill, Cubiak crouched down before the chair. This close to the old woman, he could almost see through the thin, parchment skin that stretched over her fragile, birdlike cheekbones. Wispy gray bangs hung over a deeply creviced forehead. Veins traversed her hands like rivers and creeks coursing through a sunburned landscape. Her thin hair was caught up haphazardly in a bun at the back of her neck.

She even smelled old, but her eyes were bright and a smear of soft pink glistened on her lower lip, a match for the uneven splotches of rouge that she had dabbed on her cheeks.

"Mrs. Fadim, I'm Dave Cubiak, the sheriff."

"Sheriff! Smeriff!" she said in a sharp bark that sent spittle flying from her mouth.

She slapped his hand and raised her voice. "If I've told you once, I've told you a thousand times, you have to push yourself away from the table and go look for her. You need to find her. Don't you understand? Don't you care?"

Anxious to ease the woman's agitation, Cubiak kept his voice calm. "Need to find who?"

With a screech, Mrs. Fadim bolted upright. "Your sister!" she said.

Rage nearly lifted the elderly woman from the chair but as quickly as the outburst erupted, it dissipated, and she released her hold on Cubiak's arm and crumpled into herself.

"She's been gone for so long," she said. Slumped in the chair, she stared at the slit in the curtains. Then she closed her eyes and dropped her head to her sunken chest. Almost immediately she began to snore.

Cubiak pushed back to his feet and flexed the stiffness from his knees. As he rubbed the spot where Mrs. Fadim's fierce grip still resonated, he stared at the old woman. The outburst seemed to substantiate Cate's story about a missing girl, but the woman's insistence that he was someone named Tommy indicated that she was crazy, sick, or sadly forgetful. If Tommy was her son and the girl was his sister, then she would be Mrs. Fadim's daughter. But Cate said she wasn't. If there was a missing girl, who was she? What had happened to her? Why had no one ever reported her to the sheriff's office? Was she real or a figment of Mrs. Fadim's imagination? How long had the poor woman kept her sad, futile vigil at the window? And who the hell was Tommy?

"Fuck," Cubiak said half out loud. Life could be so cruel.

He glanced back toward the open door. He hadn't told anyone, not even Cate, about his plan to visit the Fadim farm. He could turn around and walk out and forget the entire episode. Let someone else try to make sense of her wild ranting. But he knew he couldn't do that. At the very least, he could fix a cup of tea for Mrs. Fadim and exchange a kind word before he left.

By now his eyes had adjusted to the thin light. From the windows, he moved past a sagging brown velour couch and a matching chair whose arms had been rubbed to a sheen by years of use, past a small round table littered with photos, past a narrow bookcase crammed with leather-bound books whose titles had faded to illegibility, past a faux gilded mirror on one wall and painted landscapes on another, past a set of tall lamps with torn shades. Everything in the room was as worn as the woman in the chair.

The small kitchen had an old feeling to it as well. The dull oak table by the window, the wall clock in the shape of a black cat whose tail no longer switched back and forth to keep the time. The speckled, creviced linoleum floor that reminded Cubiak of the one he had known as a kid, the one his mother scrubbed on her hands and knees and never got completely clean.

He filled the kettle with water and rummaged through the rough-hewn cupboards for food. Next to four half-empty boxes of cereal he found a canister of tea bags and an unopened package of vanilla wafers. He brewed the tea and when it was ready, he arranged everything on a small tin tray and carried it back to the living room.

Mrs. Fadim was awake, transformed by sleep.

"Hello, young man. My goodness, I do get the handsome ones, don't I? Usually it's my grandson who comes to check on me or some old biddy who comes with a tuna casserole and box of biscuits," she said when he bent to set the tray in front of her.

She exclaimed over the simple repast as if it were a feast. "Who are you anyway?" she asked as she dunked a cookie into the hot tea.

Cubiak told her.

"Well, I didn't realize I was that important. The sheriff, my goodness."

"You thought I was someone named Tommy."

"Oh, did I?" she said.

"You asked if I had found my sister."

"Not your sister. Not Tommy's sister. *My* sister." Mrs. Fadim closed her eyes and took a deep raspy breath. "I ask everyone."

"Why?"

"Because we have to find her."

"Do you know where she went?"

She opened her eyes. "No."

"Do you have any idea where she might have gone?"

Mrs. Fadim bit her lower lip. "Somewhere north, I think." She hesitated. "Or was it south?"

"When did she leave?"

"I don't remember. Last month, maybe. Or last year." Tears welled in her eyes. "I get confused sometimes, but I know she should be back home by now. He said she wouldn't be gone for long. He promised."

"Who promised?"

"The man who came for her. He said he would bring her home as good as new. That she would be strong again and could run and play like the rest of us."

A dreamy whimsical look came over Mrs. Fadim. "She was so pretty. The prettiest of us all."

The old lady grabbed the sheriff's arm again. "She didn't want to go. She wept and begged us not to send her away. She didn't understand that it was for her own good. Father only wanted to help her."

Cubiak felt cold. Was it a reaction to the damp chill in the room or to the tale the woman was relating. "Who took her away? Can you tell me the man's name?"

She hung her head. "I knew it once but now I can't remember." Then suddenly she perked up. "He was a doctor. He was someone important. He said that he worked at a place where they helped children get well and that he drove all the way here just for Margaret."

Mrs. Fadim laughed. "He had a shiny black car, and we said, 'Margaret, don't you want to go for a ride in the fancy car?' He gave her a chocolate candy bar and called her Peggy. She didn't like that. She got very annoyed with him. 'My name is Margaret,' she said. So then he called her Margaret. And after that, she took the candy and she got in the car."

The old woman looked at Cubiak. "She didn't even give me a hug or kiss me good-bye. She just got in the car and left. I waved to her. I ran to the end of the driveway, waving. I like to think that she saw me and waved back, but I don't know. The car was going so fast it was hard to see anything through the dust."

Would she know the vehicle make or model? Probably not, Cubiak thought.

"Was it a new car?" he asked.

"Oh, no. It wasn't like one of those cars people drive today. It was an old-fashioned one. Like you see in the gangster movies."

"Do you have a picture of Margaret?"

"Just one. Over there." Mrs. Fadim nodded toward the table with the photographs. "Please," she said, motioning at the cane.

He offered his arm instead, but she pretended not to notice. With a look of stubborn concentration, she lunged for the walking stick. Holding it with both hands, she lifted herself up off the seat cushion, one vertebra at a time. When she was upright, she smoothed her skirt and gave a small, triumphant smile. Then she turned and began the long, slow shuffle across the threadbare floral carpet to the round table.

For several minutes, she surveyed the small cluster of photos as if she were reacquainting herself with long-lost friends and family. Finally she lifted her bony hand and pointed.

"That one," she said, aiming her finger at a small silver frame in the middle of the collection. The image in the frame was a color picture of a young girl who looked to be about five or six. From what Cate had said, the mysterious Margaret had disappeared decades earlier. If the missing girl had really existed and there was a photo of her, wouldn't it be in black and white? he wondered. And if the girl in the picture wasn't Margaret, then who was she?

"Can I take this?" he said, reaching for the photograph.

Mrs. Fadim slapped his hand. "No, it's the only one I have. And you always lose things."

She thought he was Tommy again.

"I won't lose it."

"Why do you need it?" She sounded querulous.

"So I can make a copy to show to people. Maybe someone in town has seen Margaret."

Mrs. Fadim brightened at the prospect. "Yes, maybe they have. But I must have it back. Promise you won't lose it."

"I promise."

He gave her his card. "If you need anything, call me," he said.

Before he left, Cubiak escorted Mrs. Fadim to the kitchen. While she watched, he opened a can of soup, poured it into a bowl, and set it in the microwave. A red arrow pointing to the On button had been taped to the door. "To heat the soup, just push this," he said.

She flapped a hand at him. "Silly boy. Don't you think I know how to take care of myself? You go now or you'll be late for school."

Feeling helpless and unsure what else to do, Cubiak buttered a slice of bread and left it wrapped in a piece of paper towel along with more cookies. "Something to go with your soup, and then a little dessert for later," he said.

Mrs. Fadim had lost interest and sat staring out the window at the backyard. "We used to have a chicken coop and a granary and a building for the pigs," she said. She frowned. "There was a corncrib, too, and a doghouse for Shep, our collie. But Shep died."

Cubiak followed her gaze and tried to imagine what she saw. In the space behind the house, an unused driveway circled around an old well. The only structure left was a weathered barn at the far end of the weed-infested yard.

"Did you have cows?" he asked.

"Cows? Oh, yes. Of course. You can't have a dairy farm without cows."

She grabbed Cubiak's hand. "Find Margaret. Find her before something bad happens to her."

Back at his desk, Cubiak went online and searched county records for information about Florence Fadim. According to the official documents, she was born in Brussels, Wisconsin, to Mary and Joseph Stutzman, one of seven children and the only girl. At eighteen she married Elgar Fadim, who was nearly half again as old, and moved down the road to his family's small dairy farm. Elgar died following a fall from a ladder, leaving Florence a widow with a young son, Thomas. She was twenty-four at the time and the boy five. Twenty years later, Thomas was killed in a car accident. He left a wife and three children: a daughter, Lorene, and two sons, Thomas Jr. and Jason. It was a life punctuated with loss and grief.

The official records and the brief obituaries for the Stutzmans did not mention a daughter other than Florence herself. So who's Margaret? Cubiak wondered.

When Joey was three, he had an imaginary friend named Baseball. Maybe Margaret was Mrs. Fadim's imaginary sister. It was pretty lonely where she had ended up, the sheriff thought. He pictured late summer when lush green fields of twelve-foot-high cornstalks surrounded the little island of house and yard, choking the inhabitants off from the rest of the world. Left on her own, how easy it would be for Mrs. Fadim to conjure up a young girl stepping out from between the rows of green and crossing her small patch of lawn to keep her company.

The scenario made a certain kind of sense.

But he didn't entirely believe his own version of things. If Margaret was a fantasy companion, wouldn't Mrs. Fadim want to hold on to her? Wouldn't she imagine Margaret sitting on the sofa and chatting with her, reliving the good times and recalling those that weren't? The last thing she would want was for her companion to disappear.

He pulled the small photo from his wallet. There wasn't a name on the back, no hint of the subject's identity. But there was no question that the photo was not old enough to be a picture of Mrs. Fadim's sibling. Was there enough similarity between the missing Margaret and the girl in the picture to convince the old lady that this was a portrait of the sister she claimed had disappeared?

More important, did Mrs. Fadim have a crippled sister, and if so, who was the doctor, or the man posing as one, who said he could cure her? Mrs. Fadim's story predated the one that Francisca had told him by many years, perhaps decades, but it was the same sad tale. What were the odds of two women of such different ages and from such different cultures fabricating similar stories? Equally puzzling to Cubiak was how such a tragic event could occur not once but twice. And if twice, then how many more times?

THE GIRL
WHO NEVER WAS

8

Cubiak slipped the photo back into his wallet and started an online search for Mrs. Fadim's grandsons. Within minutes he found two Jasons and one Thomas with the same surname. The first Jason lived in Anchorage, but he was seventy-five and ruled out by virtue of his age. The only other Jason had a Janesville address and was forty-two. Thomas Jr. lived even closer and was two years younger than Jason. The two could be brothers. Tom Fadim was a CPA in Sturgeon Bay. His office was on the west side, a five-minute drive from the justice center.

Shortly after noon, the sheriff headed out the door. During the height of the season, parking spots were hard to come by in the town's main downtown district on the east side of the bay. But across the steel bridge where the office of Thomas Fadim Jr. was located, parking was rarely a problem, especially early in the summer. The street outside the CPA office was empty except for a beat-up silver SUV at the curb. The vehicle idled in front of a blue, wood-frame house in need of paint. Weeds filled the patch of lawn and obscured half of the sign for Fadim's office. Either business was so good that he didn't have to keep up appearances or so bad that he didn't bother.

As the sheriff pulled up, a scrawny man hurried out the door. He wore jeans and a yellow-and-black plaid shirt. His baseball cap was pulled down low over his face, and he carried a tackle box in one hand and a fishing rod in the other.

Given Mrs. Fadim's comment about Tommy needing to push away from the table, the sheriff expected her grandson to be a large man. This had to be someone else.

"I'm looking for Tom Fadim. Would you happen to know if he's in?" Cubiak said.

The man stopped short and flinched, as if he were a schoolboy caught sneaking out before the recess bell. "That's me," he said. Regaining his composure, he lowered the sporting gear to the ground and extended a hand. "I was going fishing but . . ." The rest went unsaid; there was always time for a new client.

When Cubiak introduced himself, Fadim paled. "What's wrong? Has something happened?"

"Everything's fine."

Fadim's expression swung from a look of relief to one of puzzlement. "Then why—"

"I was hoping to ask you a few questions about your grandmother. I was out to see her earlier today."

"Why'd you do that?" The retort was sharp and laden with suspicion.

This was not a conversation the sheriff wanted to have on the sidewalk. "How about if we go inside. This will just take a minute," he said.

Fadim tossed his gear into the back of the SUV and turned off the engine.

"This way," he said, leading Cubiak toward the house.

The inside was as dreary and poorly kept as the exterior. The CPA's office was at the front of the building, in what had probably once been a living room. Except for a desk, a couple of chairs, and two sets of metal file cabinets, the office was empty. Fadim took the chair behind the desk and motioned the sheriff into the one that faced him.

"Now, what is this about? Has the old lady gotten herself into trouble with the law?" he said, in a feeble attempt to be funny.

Cubiak hesitated. He had taken an instant dislike to the man and was trying to neutralize his feeling.

"There's nothing wrong. My wife used to have a friend out that way. She told me about your grandmother living there alone, and since I was in the area, I thought I'd stop in and see how she was doing. The department recently instituted a policy of wellness checks on elderly residents and I figured I'd do my part." It was Cubiak's second white lie that day but the CPA didn't question it.

Instead, he drew himself up in an attempt to make himself tall in his chair. "It's not like we ignore her. My ex-wife and I take turns. Even my daughter goes out to see her, now that she's back in Door County."

Cubiak ignored the whiny protest. "She called me Tommy. Do you think she confused me with you?"

Fadim laughed. "She calls every man she sees Tommy. I'm Thomas to her, always have been. Sometimes she knows who I am, but mostly she thinks I'm my dad. He's the one people called Tommy."

"It's sad when that happens," Cubiak said.

"Yeah, it is, but nothing we can do about it, is there?"

"She mentioned someone named Margaret. Do you know who she was talking about?"

The accountant tossed up his hands and sighed. "My ex-wife would tell you that Margaret doesn't exist and never did, that she's a figment of Florence's imagination, a tool the old lady uses to get attention."

"Do you agree with that assessment?"

Fadim shrugged. "My grandmother always was a pretty colorful person. She has one of those flamboyant natures, used to drive my ex-wife crazy with all her theories. But I'm pretty certain that Margaret was real, although I can't really say where she fit in the family. My best guess is that she was my great-aunt."

"Your grandmother's sister?"

"Yes." Fadim rolled back from the desk. For a moment the squeak of the wheels on his chair was the only sound in the room. Then he went on talking. "After my father died, my mother went back to work, and during the summer my brother and I stayed out on the farm with the old lady. She had us pick wild blackberries for jam, and every week she made us a cherry pie. She was nice, but she was one of those people who couldn't stay quiet. She was always talking, and the one thing she talked about the most was Margaret. It was always the same story. After a while we stopped paying attention. But whenever the two of us started acting up, she'd threaten us with the story of the bogeyman MD who absconded with Margaret in his shiny black car. If we didn't behave, she said, he'd come back and get us too. I thought it was just a silly story until a couple of years ago."

"What happened to change your mind?"

"Florence, my grandmother, got this dementia thing. She'd forget stuff that happened last week, but she started remembering things from the past. That's when the story about Margaret became more real."

"What do you mean?"

"Before, the story was pretty general, but slowly more details came out. Like the business about the man calling her Peggy and offering her candy. It was creepy and made everything seem more real. Then one day she told us to go up to the attic and look for Margaret's crutches. That was the first time anything tangible was connected to the story. I didn't think we'd find anything but we did."

"Margaret's crutches?"

"Somebody's crutches. Plus a box with a pair of shoes and a couple of old dresses. I remember it really weirded us out."

"There's no record of her birth."

"There wouldn't be." The chair protested again as Fadim pulled forward and rested his elbows on the desk. "From what I finally pieced together, Margaret was born at home. Nothing unusual about that, is there? But she was sickly and weak from the start. The midwife said she wouldn't live more than a day and told my great-grandparents not to bother with calling a doctor or with registering the birth. Maybe the midwife was right, or maybe she didn't want a dead baby associated with her name. At any rate, she was dealing with immigrant farmers who spoke little English and didn't know any better than to listen to this woman who to them was a figure of authority. Somehow Margaret survived, and by the time my great-grandparents realized their mistake, they were afraid to do anything to try to correct it. As the story goes— or at least one version of it—when Margaret was four months old, she got polio. Again, they thought she would die, only she lived. Except now she was left crippled up pretty bad. They must have been embarrassed to have a deformed child. Worse, they probably thought they were being punished. They kept her in a back room and never sent her to school or took her to church. Whenever anyone visited, which wasn't often, she was kept out of sight. Florence once told me that she was forbidden to mention Margaret's name to any of her friends. She was supposed to pretend she didn't have a sister. And then one day, Margaret was gone."

"Gone?"

"Yeah, you know, sent off with this doctor to be cured. Only she never came back. I'm figuring that at some point she must have died."

"There's no record of her death either," Cubiak said.

"I don't know about that. I don't know anything more than what I just told you."

Fadim looked at the sheriff. "You're asking an awful lot of questions about someone who may or who may not have existed. What's this all about?"

"Curious. A little old lady tells me that someone is missing, and I figure it's my job to look into the situation. No harm done, is there?"

The CPA grunted and glanced at the clock.

"Just one more thing." Cubiak showed him the picture that Mrs. Fadim had given him. "She told me this was Margaret."

Fadim laughed. "Oh, geez. That's a picture of my daughter, actually my adopted daughter! It's one of her old school photos, you know, the kind the kids have taken every year. This one's probably from the second or third grade. It's kind of funny, but she does look like my sister Lorene at that age. Lorene was her birth mother—and yeah, the kid knows the whole story. We have pictures at home of the two of them, and if it wasn't for the clothes and different hairstyles, you'd think they were twins. Doesn't this sort of thing happen in families?"

The sheriff nodded. One of the few times he would ever see his mother genuinely amused was the day he brought home his third-grade school pictures. Laughing so hard she could barely talk, she had hurried to her bedroom, leaving her confused son standing at the kitchen table. A few minutes later she came back with a shoebox full of photos. "Wait,

wait," she said as she rummaged through the collection. Finally, she pulled out a gray-tinged snapshot of a boy with straight, heavy bangs across the middle of his forehead and set it down next to Cubiak's picture. The clothes and haircuts were different but the faces were identical. "My son. My cousin Mateusz," she said, pointing first to one image and then to the other. Two boys, separated by a generation and an ocean but linked by genes.

"It does," Cubiak said. Then he added, "You said your daughter lived in the area."

"The prodigal child returns. Linda Fadim, now known as Linda Kiel. She took her mother's name after our divorce. Nasty business. You know how that goes."

He didn't. "I've met your daughter, but she introduced herself as Cody Longe," he said.

Fadim laughed again. "Oh, that. Her nom de plume!" he said with obvious sarcasm. "Cody Longe: intrepid journalist. Something else, ain't she? These kids, you send them off to college, and they come back all revved up and ready to save the world. She was going to do her part by writing exposés about the evils of corporate America. All idealistic and such. I didn't pay much attention, just let her be, figured that one day she'd wake up and realize that her idealism wasn't going to pay the bills."

Nothing wrong with a little idealism, Cubiak thought. In fact, the world could probably use more of it. "You probably wanted her to follow in your footsteps," he said.

"Now you're talking." The accountant grinned. "It wouldn't have hurt none either. What with the way things are going in this crazy business, there's no question that having a female name on the door would attract more clients. People seem to like that now, and I would have been happy to have her. I'd have set her up right over there," he said, pointing across the room. "Plenty of space in here for another desk."

"She doesn't strike me as a numbers person."

"No? Well, she's counting them now. Do you have any idea what those folks over at IPM are paying her to write that nice book about them?"

He paused, waiting for Cubiak to respond. "No, I don't."

"Thirty thousand dollars." There was triumph in his voice. "Can't argue with that, now can you?"

Cubiak didn't bother to try.

The sheriff finally escaped after listening to a fishing story. In the jeep he texted Lisa: *Get me everything written by Linda Kiel aka Cody Longe.*

He was still holding the phone when it rang.

"Sir!" It was Lisa, sounding panicked. "Someone broke into Doctor Pardy's office."

"Is she okay?"

"Yeah, she thinks it must have happened last night, but she's there now and says she's fine, just a little upset."

"I'll bet."

A week prior, there had been a break-in at the drugstore in Sister Bay, but the alarm scared off the intruders before they breached the barrier to the pharmacy. Wisconsin wasn't immune to the opioid crisis that plagued the country. The rate of opioid use had more than tripled in fifteen years to the point where overdoses killed more people than auto accidents. Addicts desperate for a fix would rob—even kill—for the next dosage. Emma Pardy was a fit and athletic woman in her late thirties, but she'd be no match for a crazed druggie. Should he have done more to warn her?

"I'm just around the corner. Tell Doctor Pardy not to touch anything. Tell her I'm on my way."

BREAK-IN

9

Pardy paced the sidewalk outside her office. With one hand on her hip and a cell phone in the other, she walked back and forth, talking into the device and watching the cars come around the corner. When the white jeep made the turn, she ended the call and stepped to the curb.

"I touched stuff," she said as soon as the sheriff slid from the vehicle. "I know I shouldn't have done that, but I just forgot. Did I mess up everything for you?"

Cubiak slammed the door and handed her a pair of latex gloves. "I'm sure it's fine. Don't worry about anything. It's human nature, wanting to protect our turf. Put these on," he said.

For a moment they were preoccupied with the gloves.

"How'd they get in?" he asked finally.

"Through the front door."

From the parkway, the door looked untouched, but close up the sheriff saw the panel that the intruder had kicked in. The door was light blue, but several different layers of paint were visible on the edge of the dislodged piece.

"Looks like a pretty old door," he said as he crouched down for a better look. "Whoever did this reached in and undid the lock from the inside and then tried to maneuver the panel back into place."

Pardy peered over his shoulder. "Well, they did a pretty damn good job. I was on my phone when I got here, and I didn't notice that anything was wrong until I put my key in the lock and realized the door was open," she said.

"What about inside?"

"See for yourself," she said.

Under normal conditions, Pardy maintained a casual approach to office keeping, not too dissimilar from the sheriff's, which meant that the room was generally on the far side of untidy. Her books were piled on the floor as well as the bookcase. Her papers were distributed between the desk and the visitor's chair. A stack of medical journals nestled on the window ledge, next to a row of bright purple African violets. Desk drawers were rarely completely closed, and the same was true of the drawers in her three-tiered file cabinet. The scene that greeted the sheriff this day was chaotic in a different way. Papers were tossed around the room. Every drawer was open and the contents strewn about. Books were knocked off shelves and the floor piles dislodged. Under the window, clots of dirt dotted the floor where the flowerpots had been knocked off the sill.

Cubiak waded into the mess. "Is anything missing?"

Pardy picked up one of her daughter's preschool paintings from the floor and glanced around. "I don't think so. It doesn't look like it, but I can't say for sure." She hung the painting back in position. "I don't get it. There isn't anything here worth stealing."

"Drugs?"

She shook her head. "You mean opioids, don't you?"

"That and speed or antidepressants."

"I don't keep pharmaceuticals here. Nothing other than aspirin and a few antacid samples from the company reps."

"What about equipment?"

Pardy smirked. "My old stethoscope?"

"I mean your laptop or camera. If someone needed money for a quick fix, they'd grab anything they thought they could sell."

"I had my laptop with me." She checked the bottom drawer of her desk. "And the camera's still here."

Cubiak approached the window. The steel bridge was up, and a long line of cars idled on either side of the bay. A dozen people had abandoned their vehicles and stood along the rails watching the giant red-and-black boat that was gliding into the shipyards. Normally the big ships came in for repairs during the winter months, so the arrival of the vessel was an unusual sight this time of year. When the tanker cleared the bridge, he turned back to the room.

"How about medical records? Someone could be trying to hide a diagnosis or get information they can use to blackmail someone else."

"Blackmail?" Pardy was startled by the suggestion.

"It's been known to happen."

"Well, it won't happen here. All my records are online and secured."

"Could a hacker get into them?"

"From what I've read, a good hacker can get into anything, even the Pentagon files. But if that's the case, they wouldn't need to do all this." She waved a hand around the room.

And take the chance of getting caught, Cubiak thought.

"Whoever did this was looking for something they thought they'd find here. The questions are who and what."

He bent to the floor and picked up a photo.

"I'll have the room dusted for prints. It's just routine and I don't expect we'll find much. Offhand, I'd say this was the job of an amateur or someone who wanted to make it look like that."

The sheriff turned over the picture. It was the photo that usually stood on the corner of the medical examiner's desk. She kept it angled toward her chair, out of the view of her visitors. Every time the sheriff sat down, he had glimpsed an edge of the frame and the shoulder of someone in a dark blue jacket. This was his first time seeing the entire photo. It showed Pardy with her family, four smiling faces caught in a moment of sheer joy and permanently sealed behind glass. Pardy, the athletic mom, on one side and the quiet lawyer-husband with the wire-rimmed glasses and the blue jacket on the other. Caught in a bear hug between the parents were the two children, a girl with an uncanny resemblance to her dad and a boy who had his mother's eyes and mouth. It was the kind of candid shot that captured a perfect moment in the life of a happy family. The moment when it seems nothing can ever go wrong, that every hope and dream will come true. The moment every parent retreated into at the first sign of a dark shadow. There would be one—there always was—and when it descended the plan would go awry, perhaps skittering a degree or two off base or erupting entirely in flames. Cubiak hoped that Pardy would be one of the lucky ones, that her path forward would remain more or less straight, that the detours wouldn't amount to more than a few blips. Nothing that would completely rewrite her life.

"You okay?" Pardy asked as she settled the photo back on her desk.

"Yeah, just thinking." He pulled out his phone. "Take another look around while I get someone to secure the premises."

Out in the hall, he called Rowe and filled him in on the few details he had.

"You know what to do," he said when the deputy arrived.

Then he steered Pardy to the door. "Come on. I'll buy you a coffee."

Their drinks came in tall white mugs, which they carried out to the brick patio. Pardy headed to a table in the sun where they sat facing the bay half a block away. She wound a scarf around her neck against the breeze.

"Would you rather sit inside?" Cubiak said.

She shook her head. "It's nice here. I like looking at the water," she said as she circled her hands around the warm cup.

Cubiak poured a packet of sugar into his latte. Then another. He usually drank his coffee black, and on the rare occasions he ordered a dressed-up version he figured it may as well pass as dessert.

"You're awfully quiet," Pardy said as the sheriff stirred the foam into submission.

"I'm thinking." He laughed. "It's the part of the job no one sees."

She let him be and turned her attention to the trio of sparrows that had alighted on the otherwise deserted terrace. One by one the birds edged toward their table.

"Why break into your office now? What's different?" Cubiak said after a few minutes.

Pardy brushed an errant crumb toward the sparrows. "I haven't done anything out of the ordinary for at least a month. Except the autopsy on Doctor Melk. I mean, I do them, but not that often."

"And the findings?"

"Sorry, I was going to call you when all this happened. The results were well within the normal range on all counts. Melk was a fairly robust man for someone his age."

"That's what Sage said."

"He had cardiac issues but again nothing extraordinary. And a defibrillator, or ICD, but even that's not uncommon."

"Sage mentioned that as well."

Pardy took a small box from her canvas tote bag, opened it, and placed it on the table.

"Did you ever see one? Nothing to it, is there?"

"It's no bigger than a pocket watch," the sheriff said.

"That's the idea. The early models were huge and not very practical. Now they're small enough to implant under the skin. Usually, they go just below the collarbone in the left shoulder area." Pardy pressed a hand to her shoulder to illustrate what she meant. "There's a lithium battery inside that powers a tiny computerized generator, which monitors the heart's natural rhythm. The ICD can act either like a pacemaker, delivering low-power electrical signals to the heart, or like a defibrillator, sending stronger signals to shock the heart back to a normal rhythm. The electrical impulse travels through one of the wires, or leads, that are placed inside the heart." She looked at the sheriff. "That's the layman's explanation. It's actually a very sophisticated mechanism, an example of the very best that modern medicine has to offer."

Cubiak reached for the device. "Do you always walk around with one of these in your bag, in case of an emergency?"

"Hardly. I wouldn't know how to install one if I had to. This particular ICD is the one I removed from Doctor Melk."

Cubiak pulled his hand back. He had lost his squeamishness about dead bodies with his sixth autopsy, but the thought of touching the device seemed different. Intimate in a way that made him feel uncomfortable.

"You can hold it. It's okay."

"I know," the sheriff said, but he left the device on the table.

Pardy returned the ICD to the box and replaced the lid.

"Why did you take it out? Shouldn't it be left in the body?" Cubiak said.

"Legally, I had to remove it to prevent the lithium battery from exploding in case the body is cremated."

"Really? Is the defibrillator worth anything?"

"A few bucks maybe. You don't think someone was trying to steal it?"

"An addict can be pretty desperate."

"But no one knew that Doctor Melk had a cardiac device except his close colleagues. And I can't imagine that anyone at the institute is hard up for cash. I was there yesterday dressed like this and felt like Raggedy Ann amid all the suits."

Cubiak nodded. "I know what you mean. What were you doing there?"

"I was in Green Bay and thought I'd stop in to see Sage as a matter of professional courtesy, but he wasn't in. Lots of patients, though."

"So I gather." Cubiak pointed to the box. "What are you going to do with that?"

Pardy shrugged. "Hold on to it for a while, I guess. I had to call the manufacturer for instructions on how to disengage it so I wouldn't be shocked taking it out, and the rep said something about recycling the device. But I'd rather not do anything until I talk to the family or who-ever is in charge of the doctor's affairs."

At that moment, an adolescent boy in a T-shirt and baggy shorts whizzed toward them on a skateboard. "You need a helmet," Pardy called out as he slid past. The kid didn't even turn around, and they heard him laughing as he disappeared around the corner.

"Another one. He'll end up in the ER yet, but God knows you can't tell these kids anything. I'm already starting to see that with my two. 'Youth is wasted on the young.' George Bernard Shaw," she said and shook her head. She continued, "Speaking of Melk's affairs, whatever happened with Sage? You said he didn't want an autopsy performed and might try to intervene, but he didn't come to the hospital and he hasn't returned my calls."

"I've been leaving messages for him too. His secretary thinks he's distraught over Melk's death and taking some time off."

"You'd think he'd be busier than ever now." Pardy finished her coffee. "Funny thing though, that journalist called. Cody whatever."

"Cody Longe. That's her pen name. Her real name is Linda Kiel."

"That's her. The young woman who was at the conference when Melk collapsed."

"What did she want with you?"

"It was hard to tell. She was pretty evasive, just said she was following up on events of that day for her book on Melk and the institute. She asked a lot of questions about the autopsy. It sounded to me like she was trying to make a big story out of the doctor's death. I told her the findings were confidential until the inquest."

A bank of clouds had moved in and covered the sun. The temperature had dropped noticeably, and even the sparrows had deserted them for a warmer spot. They carried their cups inside, and then Cubiak walked Pardy to her car.

"I wouldn't use the office again until you get the door repaired and the lock replaced. In fact, you might consider putting in a new door— something stronger. Maybe something made out of steel."

"Do you think I'm in danger?"

"Not really, but there's no reason to take chances. While you're at it, I'd keep the defibrillator secured at the hospital."

"Why?"

Because instinct says it's the right thing to do, he thought.

"Why not?"

Pardy slipped into the driver's seat and started the engine. "Yes, sir," she said and saluted.

DISHONOR

10

It was nearly four when Cubiak finished talking with Emma Pardy. He waited for her to drive off, and then he headed north to the Green Arbor Lodge. He had called earlier and been told that Francisca and Lupita worked the day shift and would be finishing up soon. He didn't want to miss them again.

Lodge guests parked in the paved lot out front and followed the stone path to the entrance. The help came and went by a rear door that abutted a small graveled patch near the dumpsters. Cubiak left the jeep in a sliver of shade and positioned himself near the back door.

Five minutes after he arrived, the door banged open, and a dozen men and women emerged, all still in uniform. The men hurriedly lit cigarettes, and the women chatted and clutched the oversized bags that hung from their shoulders. It took the sheriff a few seconds to distinguish Francisca from the others. She recoiled when she saw him. Then she inclined her head almost imperceptibly and pulled Lupita aside. They waited until their colleagues had driven off to approach him.

"This won't take long, but I need to talk to you again," Cubiak said.

The women followed him back into the building, silently retracing their steps down the corridor. When they reached the lobby, they hesitated. A stylish, middle-aged couple in colorful resort attire waited near

79

the front desk, a small mountain of monogrammed, matching luggage piled up behind them. The man glared imperiously at the trio as if he expected them to deal with the suitcases.

"Enjoy your stay," Cubiak said, adding to the man's confusion. Then he motioned Francisca and Lupita forward.

"Come with me," he said as he led the way toward the conference center. He planned to talk to them in the Forest Room, hoping that Francisca would feel more comfortable there.

But when they neared the door, she started to cry.

"It's okay," he said again.

Cubiak opened the door and stepped in. The women followed.

As soon as she was inside, Francisca began talking in Spanish. Eyes downcast, she spoke hurriedly, and her words tumbled out in the soft, urgent patter of a confession.

Lupita interpreted. "She is sorry for taking so much of your time. She thinks that perhaps she was mistaken. That perhaps she only imagined the boy in the photo was her brother."

"Why?" Cubiak said. This is not what he expected.

Lupita started to explain when Francisca looked up. Her eyes were sad and heavy with lack of sleep. "It has been many years since I saw my brother."

"You speak English." The sheriff was unable to hide his surprise.

Francisca nodded. "Yes, I have learned."

"Why were you talking to me in Spanish before?"

"I was very upset, very excited. All the English words I knew escaped." With her hand, she mimicked a bird flying away.

She faced him without flinching. There was something honest in her gaze, and Cubiak remembered how his mother reverted to her native Polish whenever she became flustered.

"I understand. Please, sit." He pulled out two chairs for the women. Lupita took a seat, but Francisca remained standing. She looked at her friend. The older woman smiled her encouragement. Finally Francisca crossed herself and perched on the edge of the other chair.

As he had done at their first meeting, Cubiak sat facing them.

"It is possible that you were wrong about the boy in the photo being your brother. But I am interested in knowing what happened to

Miguel. I want you to tell me everything that you remember, from the beginning."

Francisca took a moment to respond. "My mother had six children. I was the oldest. I was thirteen when Miguel was born. He came in the middle of the night. There was no one to help."

"I don't understand. On Monday, you told me that he was your twin. Now you're saying you were a teenager when he was born." Was she toying with him? How many versions were there to her story? He tried to stay patient.

Francisca blushed. "My mother called him my twin because he was born on the same day, at the same time. We were like twins, she said. If he had been born when you were, he would be healthy, too. I don't know if that's true, but it comforted her to think that it would have made a difference."

She brushed a tear from her cheek and fell silent. When she tried to go on, she began to tremble. Lupita reached for her hand, and Francisca continued.

"The rest of us were healthy, all except Miguel. He was different. My mother knew as soon as she saw him. My father did not want a son who looked like that, and he was very angry. He was a very proud man who could not accept the fact of having a deformed child. He said that Miguel was an insult and blamed my mother. He said that she must have sinned to bring this upon us. He refused to acknowledge Miguel as his son. He wouldn't even let my mother have him baptized, and he forbade her from taking him out of the house. He made her hide him because he thought that the people in the village would scorn us. It was the curse of the devil, he said. We were to tell everyone that Miguel had been born dead and that we had buried him in the little garden behind our house. He even put a small cross in the ground, pretending to mark the grave."

Cubiak said nothing. Listening to her story, he remembered how as a boy of six or seven he had asked his mother about the strange brother and sister who lived several doors away on their street. The first time he saw the two he realized that they didn't look like the rest of his friends. He was even a little afraid of them. When he asked his mother if they could be his friends, she said no. He was to have nothing to do with them, as if whatever afflicted them could affect him. Not that it mattered ultimately, because he rarely saw them. They came out only in the evening, and they were never alone. One parent was always with them, guarding them, as they walked awkwardly, hand in hand, to the corner and back. They never crossed the street. What's wrong with them? he had asked his mother. She said they were mongoloids, and it was years before he learned that the word was derogatory. When he asked why they stayed inside all the time, his mother said it was because their parents were ashamed. Why? he asked. They think people will say it's their fault the children are deformed and that they are being punished for being bad people.

"My father wanted his son to die. He waited for his death, maybe he even prayed for it. But Miguel lived, and when he was two years old, my father threatened to leave. He told my mother that he could not stay in the same house with Miguel and would come back only after the boy was gone."

A small handkerchief materialized in Francisca's grip. The thin cotton square was white and edged with faded red flowers. Cubiak wondered if Lupita had slipped it to her, something for her to hold. Twisting the worn fabric between her fingers, Francisca went on with her sad tale.

"I loved my father, but I could not understand his cruelty. He was forcing my mother to choose between him and her son. To pick him over the baby that had grown inside her. How could he expect her to do that?"

She looked at the sheriff to see if he would come to her father's defense. Cubiak said nothing.

"She knew how difficult life would be for us if he left, and she begged him to stay. She said she would figure out some way to make things better. But he wouldn't listen. Not to her, not to me, not to any of us. I thought we'd convinced him to change his mind, but a week later he was gone."

Francisca made a sound like a sob and lowered her head. When she looked up again, her eyes were fierce. "My father thought Miguel had brought shame to the family, but he was the one who dishonored us. It didn't take long for the neighbors to discover that he had deserted us, and with him gone, we became objects of gossip and pity. My mother had to take a job working in the fields to earn money for food and rent. When that wasn't enough, I quit school and joined her."

The young cleaning woman held up her hands. "You see how rough and swollen these are from the work I do here? This is nothing compared to the way they looked after five or six months of harvesting coffee and cacao."

She dropped her hands into her lap. "The only good thing that came of my father's leaving was that Miguel was no longer a prisoner in our house. Before, my mother would take him out only on nights when there was no moon and the clouds covered the stars. She would talk to him in whispers, and she never went farther than our tiny yard. With my father gone, my mother had Miguel baptized and allowed him to play outside in the sun. I know there were people who made fun of him and said cruel things about my mother, but some of the neighbors were very kind. When they could, they gave my mother extra flour, and they'd give my brother a bit of candy after Mass on Sunday."

"Did your father ever come back?"

"Perhaps." Francisca shivered. "Perhaps he came many times. Who knows? I used to dream that he was home with us again, that he had slipped in through the door during the middle of the night and was at the window in the morning with his coffee, looking out to check the weather, as if he'd never gone away. But one day I actually saw him. I was in the back hanging up clothes to dry, and I saw him on the street. He stood there looking at me. 'Papá,' I said. He smiled a little as if he was uncertain what to do or say, and I started toward him. I had forgotten that Miguel was at a little table on the other side of the yard. I should have motioned for him to stay where he was, but I was so excited to see my father that I dropped the wet shirt on the grass and ran toward the gate. Miguel came up behind me, and when my father saw him, his smile disappeared. He made his face into a stranger's mask, and then he turned and walked away."

"How old was your brother when this happened?"

"He was around two. 'Who was that man?' he asked. 'No one,' I told him. 'It wasn't anybody.' And I made myself believe that I had only seen a ghost. Two years later, I came to America to work. I hated leaving my home. In some ways I felt I was deserting my family just like my father, but my mother could not support the children on what she earned, and there were no good jobs for me or my brothers and sisters, only to labor in the fields. I had to come here and work so I could send money to my mother."

Francisca wrapped her arm around her companion's shoulder. "Lupita helped me. She was my mother's friend when they were little girls, and when I was a child she was like my *tía*, my aunt. She still is. Lupita had lived here for many years, and she helped me to get here and to get a job."

"You were not at home when the men allegedly came and took your brother."

Francisca's nostrils flared at the word.

"I was here for two years when I received a letter from my mother. One of my younger brothers had written it for her. What she said in the letter is the story I told you before about the doctors coming to the village and saying that they could cure Miguel."

"You said you were there when this happened. Why did you lie?"

"I thought there was a better chance that you would believe me. I didn't lie about what happened. Everything I told you is exactly what my mother told me happened, except that my father was already gone. She was the parent who was left to make all the decisions for the family. The men who came told her they were from a charity and that it would cost her nothing. Every word is the truth. I still have the letter, if you don't believe me."

"I believe you," he said. What he believed was that someone had taken an impaired child from a poor, uneducated woman and not for any good reasons that he could imagine.

"You think that maybe what my mother did was wrong? Then you don't understand. What they offered was the answer to her prayers and not just for Miguel. She had found a way both to cure her son and to get her husband back. She told me to pray for my brother but not to worry. The paper she had to sign, the doctor signed too, and then he gave it to her to keep."

Francisca reached into the denim bag next to her chair and pulled out a small cardboard folder. "Someone in the village had a camera, and they took a picture of Miguel with my mother before he left. Here," she said, taking a snapshot from the folder. "I hadn't seen him for four years and couldn't believe how much he'd grown. But you see he looks like the boy in that photo, the one on the wall, doesn't he?"

The photograph was crinkled and worn; a crease ran across the boy's face where it had been folded into the envelope. Cubiak could barely make out the child's features.

"When I saw the picture on the wall, I was sure it was Miguel. But maybe I was wrong. Others have told me that children with the Down syndrome can look very much like each other. I don't know if it's true because I've only seen my brother."

Francisca took the photo from Cubiak. She looked at it for a long moment, and then she slipped it back into her bag.

"Have there been more letters?" Cubiak asked.

The young woman moistened her lips and stiffened as if steeling herself to go on. "My mother has written me many letters. At first they were full of joy and excitement. After the doctor left with Miguel, she waited to hear news of his progress. She told the whole village what she had done, knowing how the story would spread and hoping it would eventually reach my father. When he learns of this, he will return home and we will be a whole family again, she told me. Every night she got down on her knees and said the rosary, praying to the Blessed Mother to look out for her son and to forgive her husband. On Sundays she lit a candle in church, to thank God for the good fortune he had sent her way. She was almost bursting with happiness at the thought of how finally their luck had changed. Then one month, and two, and three passed, and she heard nothing from the doctors and nothing from my father. She tried to tell herself that she was being impatient, that these things took time. But after six months and she had not gotten any information, she began to wonder if she had made a terrible mistake. Every letter she wrote to me was the same: What have I done to Miguel? Why am I being punished again? I will burn in hell for my sins. Finally, she wrote and said she needed to talk to me. One of the neighbors had a telephone and said she could use it to receive a call from me if I would be the one to pay."

"Did you call her?"

"Of course. I had to. I wrote back and arranged a day and time when she would be at the neighbor's house. I knew the call would be expensive, and I did not want to waste time waiting for someone to go and get her. She was the one who answered, and at first I could barely speak. I didn't realize how much I missed my home until I heard her voice. I was so happy I began to cry and almost forgot why she had wanted to talk to me. It was all about Miguel. How sorry she was for what she had done. How she wanted me to find him. 'You are both in El Norte,' she said, as if that was all that mattered. I tried to explain to her that this was a very big country, that I didn't know where to start looking."

"Did she understand?"

"The line went dead. I was too upset to call back, so I wrote to her instead. Of course I would try to do this, for her sake and for Miguel too. But I had so many questions: What was the doctor's name? What city was he from? What was the name of the charity?"

All the right questions, Cubiak thought. "You'd make a good detective," he said.

Francisca shook her head. "My mother did not need a detective. She needed a magician. She didn't remember any of the details, and the paper that she'd signed was lost in a fire. All she knew was that her son was gone. 'He is in America, and you are there too,' she said. 'You must find your brother and bring him home.'"

The handkerchief in her hands was twisted into a tight rope.

"Perhaps that is why I was so excited when I saw the picture on the wall. I wanted so badly to find Miguel and I thought I had."

There was a knock. Cubiak ignored it. The door opened and a lanky, sandy-haired young man in a pressed blue shirt and creased khakis stepped in. The sight of the two cleaning women sitting and not at work seemed to confuse him.

"Excuse me, these are private meeting rooms," he said. He tried to sound important enough to warrant the title of assistant manager that was printed on his badge, but Cubiak doubted that he had yet to reach voting age.

The sheriff pointed to the badge on his belt. "And we're having a private meeting," he said.

"I see."

He didn't, but Cubiak didn't feel compelled to explain further.

"If you don't mind."

The staffer smiled obsequiously, the way he'd been instructed to when faced with difficult guests. "Of course," he said as he backed into the hall.

Cubiak got up and closed the door. How many children like Miguel were there? he wondered. Thousands. Tens of thousands perhaps. Innocents like this boy stolen from their unsuspecting parents, runaways misled into prostitution, youngsters kidnapped for forced labor and worse. Promises of miracle cures, bright futures. There were times the world seemed populated by predators. He felt helpless in face of the statistics.

"I wish there was something I could do to help, but it seems impossible. You must realize that."

"Sí. Yes."

"You should take comfort in knowing that you have done everything you can, both for your mother and for your brother."

She gave a quick ironic smile. "But I have failed."

Just as I have failed many times, the sheriff thought. Just as we all do in one way or another.

"As long as you keep telling your brother's story, there is hope."

"Do you really believe that?"

"Yes. It may not help you find Miguel, but it could save others." He paused and gave her time to take in the full import of his words. "That may be the most you can ask for."

Francisca had tears in her eyes, but she returned his look with a somber, steady gaze. "You are a very honest man, Sheriff. And I thank you for that."

A moment of understanding passed between them.

The women stood to leave.

Cubiak got to his feet as well, but he wasn't finished questioning them yet.

"The other day, I came back to talk with you, but you were gone. Why didn't you wait for me, like I asked you to?"

Francisca pulled a scarf from her bag and draped it across her shoulders. "That young woman came in and told us that you said we could leave."

"What woman?"

"She didn't tell us her name."

"What did she look like?"

"She had hair of two colors, and she wore a jacket like this," Francisca said, pointing to her denim tote bag.

On the day Leonard Melk died, Linda Kiel's hairstyle and outfit had branded her an anomaly among the well-coifed and well-heeled conference-goers. It had to have been her. She was the only woman with bicolored hair and a denim jacket. After the second scream, she must have slipped out of the Woodlawn Theater and followed him to the Forest Room. Was it journalistic instinct that sent her scurrying down the hall in search of a story, or did she have a different motive? And how much of Francisca's tale had she overheard, eavesdropping at the closed door? What the hell was she up to?

"Did she say anything or try to get you to talk?"

"No. She just shooed us out the door."

"Did she take the laptop?"

"I don't know. When we left, it was still in the room and so was she."

"If she comes around again and starts asking questions about your brother and the photo, don't say anything. But let me know, okay? In fact, if anyone asks you about Miguel, call me." He wrote his cell number on his card and gave it to her.

"Sí, señor. But why?"

"Because I want to talk to them first."

Cubiak walked the women back to Lupita's rusty Fiat. The older woman shook his hand and said good-bye in a way that implied she didn't expect to see him again. Francisca surprised him with a quick hug, but even that felt like an ending. Once inside the car, the women didn't wave. He waited until they were out of sight, and then he called Linda Kiel. The journalist owed him answers, but again he was unable to reach her, and her mailbox was still full. He tried texting, but the message was undelivered.

He could swing by her place and leave a note. Did people still do that? Cubiak wondered. He wasn't sure if he had a piece of paper to write on. Not that it would matter because he didn't know her address. His only alternative was to try to reach her through her father. After seven rings, Tom Fadim's answering machine came on. The sheriff left his number and a message asking the accountant to tell his daughter to call. "Tell her I've got an exclusive."

That'll get her attention, he thought.

PICTURES ON THE WALL

11

"Don't let your mother see this," Cubiak said as he popped the cap off the can of whipped cream. While Cate was out walking, he had made pancakes, his usual Thursday ritual, and Joey wanted his with a face. As Joey watched, his father rimmed the pancake on his plate with a giant grin. The boy made a smile to match and then dropped in two blueberries for the eyes and a strawberry for the nose.

"Perfection," Cubiak said. He leaned over and winked conspiratorially. "Remember, not a word."

"Gotcha, Dad," Joey said. He clamped his mouth shut and looked up, unaware of how deeply his response tore into his father's heart.

Cubiak had played the same game with Alexis. When he had told her mum's the word about the forbidden treat, she would say, "Right, Daddy," and then draw a finger across her mouth as if zipping it shut.

Ever since Joey had been born, Cubiak had seen flashes of his daughter in the boy. How could he not? When Joey took his first step, Cubiak saw Alexis taking hers. When he made his first snow angel on the beach, he remembered how his daughter lay on her back and gleefully slid her arms and legs back and forth on the front lawn outside their Chicago bungalow. The joy of watching his son grow up had been matched by the pain of remembering his daughter, who had died.

In four months, Joey would turn five, a birthday that Alexis never reached. What happened then, when reality outdistanced memory? Cubiak wondered.

At the moment Joey crammed the last bit of pancake into his mouth, Cate came in from the beach. When she left for her morning walk, she had been wearing her jacket, but now it was tied around her waist. She flung it over a chair and gave her son one of her all-knowing looks.

"I hope you had some fruit with your breakfast," she said, pouring coffee into a tall blue mug.

"Yep," Joey and Cubiak said together.

Cate scowled at them and then laughed. "I'm onto you two," she said.

The next few minutes were lost to the usual rush of getting the table cleared and Joey into his socks and shoes and out the door in time for his mother to drive him to the morning preschool session.

In the quiet of the empty kitchen, Cubiak checked his email. Lisa had forwarded a batch of articles that were bylined by either Linda Kiel or Cody Longe and had been published within the last eighteen months. The sheriff skimmed the titles. The young woman had been busy. As Kiel she had authored a half-dozen fluff pieces on the latest trends in fashion scarves, hairstyles, decorating accessories, and foods with names he didn't recognize. These were followed by more serious pieces that dealt with environmental issues. Two offered advice on how-to-go-green, but one delved into proposed industrial pollution guidelines for the Great Lakes. Six months ago, she started writing as Cody Longe, and the tenor of her work shifted toward investigative reporting. The titles of her most recent pieces were both sensational and dramatic: "How Modern Medicine Can Kill You" and "What Computer Nerds Don't Want You to Know."

Cubiak was about to start reading when Rowe appeared at the back door. The sheriff waved him in. "You're out early," he said.

"I got that meeting with the neighborhood watch volunteers up at Ellison Bay. Since I was going this way I figured I'd stop and drop off today's paper. Thought you'd want to see it." He handed Cubiak a copy of the *Green Bay Press Gazette* with the page 1 banner headline: "Death by the Bay."

"By Cody Longe. Did you read this already?" Cubiak said.

"Yep."

"And?"

"You're not going to like it." Rowe stepped toward the door. "I'll let myself out," he said and was gone.

The story was an eyewitness account of Leonard Melk's death at the Green Arbor Lodge. Kiel played up her role as one of the last people to talk with Melk before he collapsed. That was true enough, but she got many of the other details wrong and exaggerated much of the situation. Cubiak didn't begrudge the journalist her opinions and take on events, even if he thought they were sensationalized, but he resented her misrepresentation of facts. She had seen everything that happened that day, and he had said nothing that didn't confirm her observations, yet she referred to him as the "tight-lipped sheriff." Pardy had answered her questions as well, but in the piece Kiel portrayed her as the "uncooperative medical examiner who refused to divulge critical information." Even Sage's straightforward comment that Melk appeared to have suffered a fatal heart attack came across sounding suspicious. From start to finish, the article implied that the Door County sheriff and the medical examiner as well as the head of the IPM were covering up the truth about the doctor's death.

Interestingly, she didn't mention the second scream and what she had picked up, eavesdropping outside the Forest Room. If Kiel had heard Francisca's story, why hadn't she included it? Or was she writing a sequel about missing children and mystique by the bay?

"Damn it to hell," Cubiak said.

He tossed the newspaper aside and fished Kiel's card from his wallet. Staring out at the lake, he dialed the number and counted the rings. After nine, the message kicked in: the person he was trying to reach was not available and the mailbox was full.

He was about to lay the phone on the counter when it rang in his hand.

Probably Kiel, he thought. He wondered if she was calling to excuse herself or maybe even to apologize. But caller ID flashed an unfamiliar number on the small screen. He hesitated but finally took the call.

His greeting was met with a raspy cough. Then a woman whispered in his ear. "He's here again."

"Who is this?" Just what he needed to top off his morning, a prank call.

"It's me!" The voice was low and sluggish with age. Cubiak realized that he had heard it before.

"Mrs. Fadim, is that you?"

"Of course it's me. Who else would it be? You said to call if I needed help."

Cubiak pictured his card lying on the table next to her chair where he had left it yesterday.

"Are you hurt?"

"Don't be ridiculous. Would I be calling you if I was hurt?"

Point taken, Cubiak thought. "You said someone's there. Who is it?"

"I don't know, but I've seen him sneaking around before."

"Where is he?"

"In the barn."

The sheriff had seen the abandoned barn from the kitchen when he made tea for the frail woman. The building was a wreck. Decades of wind and rain had eaten the paint off the wood and turned the boards a sickly gray. The roof sagged and the concrete foundation was crumbling in spots.

"What's he doing in the barn?"

"How should I know? Up to no good, I imagine." Mrs. Fadim wheezed, and when she spoke again her snappishness had turned to panic. "What if he gets in the house?"

"Stay where you are. I'm sending help."

"You come," she said and hung up.

Rowe had left a half hour ago. By now he would be nearing the tip of the peninsula, too far away to double back. One of the deputies was giving a talk on summer safety at Southern Door High School; another was due in court that morning. Cubiak was the closest.

On his way to the Fadim farm, the sheriff checked in with Lisa. He had no calls to return, no meetings that morning. Reading Linda Kiel's article had ruined his good mood, and he drove fast down the empty roads. The notion that he was off on a fool's errand fueled his annoyance. If Mrs. Fadim's intruder was as genuine as much of the information in her great-granddaughter's article, then his visit was a waste of time. Maybe the tendency to blow things out of proportion ran in the family.

Sooner than he expected, he reached the long, straight stretch of pavement that ran past the farm. Everything looked the same. Cubiak groaned. He had only himself to blame; he should never have given her his number. Now he would never be done with her. He had a sudden taste for a cigarette. Instead he reached for a stick of gum. He was unwrapping it when a black car popped out on the road ahead. He was too far away to see if it had come from Mrs. Fadim's driveway or from one of the fields beyond. As the vehicle sped away, Cubiak floored the jeep, but before he reached the driveway, the car had disappeared. He swore under his breath and braked hard. Turning in, he slowed enough to avoid skidding into the shallow ditch. It seemed there was an intruder, and if Mrs. Fadim was hurt, he had to get to her quickly.

As before, the front door was not locked. Cubiak swore again, but this time out loud.

The house was quiet. He called out, but the elderly woman didn't respond. The house seemed to be caught in a time warp. The dim light, the musty aroma, the heavy stillness remained the same, like remnants of a life frozen in amber.

He stumbled as he hurried into the living room.

"It's about time you got here," Mrs. Fadim said. She had forsaken the whisper she had used on the phone and reverted to her usual bark.

Cubiak had expected the worst. Instead he found the old woman in her chair at the front window, seemingly unperturbed.

"Are you okay?" he said.

"What a silly question. Of course I'm not okay. I've been sitting here since dawn waiting for my tea. A good son makes his mother a cup of tea before he leaves for school."

"Mrs. Fadim, Florence, I'm Sheriff Cubiak. You called me—"

She cut him off with a slice of her hand. "I didn't call anyone."

"You said someone was in the barn."

She snorted. "The barn's been empty for more than forty years, ever since your father died. God rest his soul." She crossed herself and then she snugged her worn shawl around her sloped shoulders.

He tried again. "Mrs. Fadim—"

She scowled at him. "Where's my tea? Don't just stand there, you know what to do."

Cubiak took a step closer to the chair. He needed to make sure that she was unhurt.

"Go!" she said and waved him toward the kitchen. "And don't forget my biscuit. I like a biscuit with my tea."

After he put the kettle on, Cubiak studied the barn. It was a relic from another era, and from the house it looked no different from the dozens of abandoned barns that were scattered around the county. Barns like the one on the Fadim farm were the product of many hands, built in an era when dozens of neighbors rallied to help, everyone sure in the knowledge that when their time came their friends would join the workforce. Gone. All gone. Desperate for cash, the farmers had forsaken work in the field for jobs in the city; instead of talking to their neighbors over barbed-wire fences, they communicated by email. Once proud symbols of prosperity, the old barns were emptied of cattle and feed and then left to decay in lonely isolation, so many sad legacies of defeat splotched across the American landscape.

When Cubiak finished in the kitchen, he escorted Mrs. Fadim away from the window. Over her protests, he settled her in front of the television with a tall mug of sweet, hot tea and a plate of cookies.

"I hate that thing," she said, kicking a foot toward the TV.

On the screen two women who would have looked better with less décolletage and longer dresses ranted at each other in a packed courtroom while a judge pounded a gavel and told them they needed to be civil or she would find them both in contempt.

"Damn foolish nonsense," the old woman said. She dunked a cookie and smirked at the scene that was unrolling before her.

Can't argue with that, the sheriff thought as he switched channels until he came to a rerun of *Shane*.

"Better?"

Florence harrumphed and settled in.

The yard had turned to jungle. A few clumps of dried brown grass remained, but most of the lawn was blanketed by a leafy green vine. The voracious plant coiled around shrubs and spiraled up the trunks of trees where it reached into the branches, threatening death by suffocation. Was this one of the invasive species he had heard so much about? Cubiak wondered as he tromped down the gravel driveway.

At the barn, he checked the milk house first, but the panes in the window were intact and the tarnished lock on the door was covered with spiderwebs that hadn't been disturbed in years. A second door on that side was also battened down with an ancient lock.

Whoever had broken in had gotten in a different way.

Near the rear of the barn, the sheriff climbed over strands of sagging barbed wire and stepped into the pasture. Thistle and weeds were thick and knee-high and had grown up to the center double doors, where the cows used to enter. The metal door handles were lashed shut with wire that had rusted together. Cubiak searched the rest of the structure for a broken window or loose board, but the barn appeared impenetrable. He was about to give up when he discovered a third entryway, behind the silo. The door was narrow and low and led into a short passageway that connected the silo to the barn. A shiny new lock hung on the door.

Mrs. Fadim hadn't imagined an intruder.

In broad daylight, a prowler wouldn't venture past the house to get to the barn. There had to be a back way. Beyond the boulders and scrub brush on the other far side of the barn stood a thick forest. Fifty yards into the trees, the sheriff came upon an old logging road that was nearly overgrown with weeds. Twin trails of broken stalks showed where a vehicle had driven up the lane and stopped.

Cubiak walked back toward the barn. From the edge of the tree line, he could make it partway to the hidden door without being seen from the house. If the prowler had come this way, it was his bad luck (Mrs. Fadim had said *he*) to choose one of the rare times the old woman was in the kitchen facing the back window.

Or had she been lying in wait? "He's here again," she had said. She had sounded angry, as if she knew that someone was up to no good in her barn.

Given the farm's remote location, the building could be used as a warehouse for stolen property or as the site for a meth lab. It wouldn't be the first one Cubiak had discovered in the county. But there were no burn pits or other tell-tale signs. It had to be something else. To find out, he had to get inside. Shooting off the shiny new lock on the silo door was one option, but that would alert the intruder that he had been found out. His only other alternative was to undo the wires on the double doors at the cattle entrance.

Time and rust had melded the wires together. He couldn't untwist them by hand so he tried using pliers from the jeep. As he separated the strands, the pliers slipped and the wire pierced the skin between the thumb and index finger on his right hand. He sucked at the blood and worked clumsily with his left. It took him another five minutes to pry away the last bit of wire.

He pulled the handles but the doors didn't budge. They were swollen in place. He pulled and kicked at the thick wood slabs until the doors gave way and the cavernous interior opened before him. Like the disemboweled, haunted hold of a sunken ship, the deserted barn carried a cargo of memories and spectral images. History was written in the emptiness of the space. First the cows had disappeared—sold, auctioned off, or shipped to market. Then the tall iron stanchions and drinking cups had been ripped from their moorings and traded for cash, as was the conveyor system that had nudged the manure through the gutters. Every shard of metal had been stripped away and sold in a last desperate attempt to reap a few dollars from the once proud enterprise known as the family farm.

The air inside was saturated with mold and dust. Cobwebs hung like lace curtains at the long row of windows on either side, filtering the light and casting shadows on the floor where the mice scurried unseen. Water pooled in one corner where the concrete foundation had begun to crumble.

With his bleeding hand against his mouth, Cubiak walked down the center aisle. Each step left a mark on the detritus of a past that had been created by decades of hard physical work. From dust to dust. The words held not only for humanity but for the fruits of its labor.

At one point, the sheriff stopped and looked around, puzzled. The barn had appeared bigger from the outside. He kept going, and when he reached the end of the center aisle, he discovered a small door that had been cut into a wall, indicating another room on the other side. The door stuck. He put his shoulder to it and shoved several times before it gave way. The door was low. He ducked to avoid hitting his head and then, once inside, nearly tripped over a bale of hay. The space was cold and damp and even dimmer than the rest of the barn. The only light came from a slit near the ceiling where a ray of sun slipped in beneath the eaves. The narrow beam illuminated the high arched roof and fell like a miniature spotlight on the edge of the loft space beneath it. The scent of dried hay mingled with the ubiquitous musty aroma. But there was another, more familiar smell.

Coffee.

Whoever had been inside the barn hadn't been gone for long. Cubiak swore under his breath. It must have been the intruder driving the black car. If he had gone after it, he would have caught him.

As the sheriff let his eyes adjust to the dark, the surroundings revealed themselves. The floor was wood. Two dark squares on the side walls were blackout cloths that had been tacked over the windows. He considered removing the fabric and then changed his mind. If he wanted to catch the intruder, he had to cover his trail and leave things in place. Otherwise he risked scaring off the trespasser.

A sleeping bag was rolled out on the floor near the hay bale that he had almost fallen over. The bag was generic and nondescript, the kind sold in hundreds of stores and on online outlets. The bale itself served as a makeshift table. On it were a pen but no pad, a small battery-powered lantern, and a Styrofoam coffee cup from the truck stop outside of Sturgeon Bay. The cup was not yet completely cold. Someone was camping out in the barn.

The interloper wasn't a runaway kid. A runaway wouldn't have a car, unless it was stolen.

Who was the intruder and why had he chosen this barn, this farm?

How long had he been coming there?

Was he trespassing, as Mrs. Fadim implied, or had she given him permission to use the vacant building? Given her mental condition, it was possible that she had done so and then immediately forgotten. But if the mystery visitor had permission to be there, why didn't he drive up past the house? Why sneak in from the woods? Unless there was another trail through the pasture that had eluded the sheriff.

Cubiak scanned the walls with the lantern. The aged wood was pitted, and the discolored surface absorbed the light as he moved across it. There was nothing on the wall behind him or on either of the side walls. Then he held up the lamp and looked across the room.

"What the hell," he said.

Twenty feet in front of him, hundreds of pieces of paper were tacked to the barn wall in a giant collage that snaked across the wooden boards like a long, wide river. Most of the montage was white, but there were splotches of yellow as well. Superimposed on it was a trail of small dark squares and a network of red strings that varied in length and ran in every direction, like vectors that were tracing a path on a map.

The whole business was bizarre.

Throughout Door County, farmers hung brightly colored wood designs on barn exteriors as part of a statewide barn quilt project. For a moment the sheriff wondered if the installation in Mrs. Fadim's barn was part of a partner initiative, an indoor project that hadn't been made public yet. New art installed inside old barns. For all he knew, there were dozens of such projects in progress throughout the area.

It was also possible that the collage wasn't connected to an official program but was an example of a new trend. Weren't kids pulling all manner of crazy stunts and then filming them and posting short videos on the internet? The montage might even be the work of an underground art movement. There were hundreds of artists in the county. Maybe the more avant garde among them were competing to find unique ways to repurpose old buildings. Cate might know. She was tuned in to that world.

Cubiak appreciated the straightforward simplicity of representational art and was confounded by the abstract design. "Paper on Wood Wall," he would call it, if he had to come up with a title.

Still, he found himself unable to turn away. His inner voice urged him forward for a closer look.

Assuming there was logic to the collection, it probably ran from left to right. The sheriff started at the beginning. From across the room, the white papers appeared blank, but as he got closer he realized they were pages torn from old notebooks. Each one was covered with rows and columns of faded letters and numbers that had been recorded in pencil. Some of the white papers had titles scrawled in a language he didn't recognize. The yellow sheets were filled with notes carefully written in the same unfamiliar language. And pinned to this paper backdrop were the small dark squares.

Photographs.

A dozen or more.

Black-and-white pictures of young children and adolescents. They wore plain smocks and their hair was chopped short. With their un-smiling faces and sad, haunted eyes they looked like a lost tribe of primitive youth.

Who are you? What happened to all of you? Cubiak wondered as he followed the red strings from one photo to another.

Suddenly a familiar face stared back at him. It was a picture of a girl who resembled the child Mrs. Fadim had identified as her long-lost, crippled sibling. Several pieces of red string radiated out from the photo, linking the picture to sheets of white paper covered with the letters MS and thick with tabulations. There were several yellow pages as well, all filled with indecipherable notes. None of it made sense to Cubiak. Just as he started to move on, he saw the word *polio*.

The sheriff went very still.

The letters MS could be the initials of Mrs. Fadim's sister, Margaret Stutzman. If so, the collage had nothing to do with art but could be evidence linked to her disappearance. Whatever he was looking at, instinct told him it wasn't good.

He searched the rest of the room. In the corner, under a layer of loose hay, he found a long, narrow cardboard box, the kind once used to store files. The carton was soft with mold and age. Although faded, the wording stamped on the lid was legible: "Confidential: Property of Northern Hospital for the Insane. Cleona, Wisconsin."

A new sense of dread came over the sheriff. Since taking office, he had heard tales of these government-run institutions. Now defunct and relegated to a history no one wanted to remember, they had been established as regional treatment centers for the mentally ill and those considered dangerous to themselves and others. Too often they ended up as warehouses or worse for juvenile delinquents, drunks, adulterers, and free-spirited women who willfully disobeyed their husbands or fathers.

Inside the box were fifteen manila envelopes, each filled with material similar to that on the wall. Inside a folder were dozens of consent letters from parents, voluntarily giving up their sick offspring in the hopes they would be cured of their afflictions. The letters were simply worded, some barely literate. Several were signed with X's. All of them were addressed to Leonard Melk.

On the bottom of the carton Cubiak found a framed photo of a young Doctor Melk standing next to a black sedan. The sheriff remembered that Mrs. Fadim had said the man who took Margaret away had a nice car, and she had urged Margaret to get in it.

Cubiak sat back on his heels and let out a long, slow breath.

What the hell had Melk been up to? Treating private patients at a public facility violated both state law and professional protocol, but what if he had been doing far worse things to the children entrusted to his care?

Cubiak called Bathard.

"Can you come out to Southern Door?"

"Now? Why?"

"There's something here I don't understand, something I need you to see."

BLOOD SERUM

12

Cubiak lit the room with a set of floodlights that he kept in the jeep for emergencies. He wanted Bathard to get the full impact of the collage immediately.

Like the sheriff, the coroner had to stoop to get through the low doorway. When he straightened up he saw the wall and frowned. "What in the name of heaven is this?" he said.

"That's what I'm hoping you'll tell me."

Cubiak led the physician across the room to one of the yellow papers. "The writing is pretty faded, but do you think you can make anything out?"

Bathard put on his glasses and took a closer look. "It's German."

"Do you know German?"

"A little but hopefully enough." Bathard scanned the montage. "I'll start at the beginning, shall I?" It was the coroner's polite way of asking Cubiak to leave him be.

While the physician worked, the sheriff paced along the back wall. For the second time in two days he wanted a cigarette. It had been four months since he last smoked, and he thought he had exorcised the need. The morning runs, the long walks along the beach, and the yoga breathing he had learned from Cate helped him withstand the craving.

Until now. Tension weakened his defenses. But smoke in a barn? He almost laughed. Even if he had a pack in his pocket, he wouldn't dare.

Cubiak watched as the coroner moved from one scrap of paper to another.

What's taking so long? the sheriff wondered.

He hoped he wasn't wasting Bathard's time. Perhaps he had read too much into the material and had overreacted. It wouldn't be the first situation where he imagined clues where none existed. He had made mistakes as a cop and knew he wasn't immune to making them as sheriff. Another concern nagged. To whom could he turn for help if the coroner was stymied by the collage?

The barn was damp, and Cubiak wished he could make a cup of hot tea for Bathard, but he didn't dare go into Mrs. Fadim's kitchen and chance disturbing her. Instead, he got a wool blanket from the jeep and draped it over his friend's shoulders. The doctor murmured his thanks and pulled it tight as he kept reading.

When Bathard finally turned away from the collage, his expression was grim.

"Where did you get all this?" he said as he settled uneasily on a hay bale.

"I found it here, tacked to the wall."

"I realize as much. I am asking if you know the source, from whence it came."

Cubiak showed him the cardboard box.

Bathard read the inscription on the lid and recoiled as if he had been slapped. "The Northern Hospital for the Insane! That place burned down years ago, killing so many, but it is a wonder more people did not die. I remember seeing pictures in the newspaper. There was nothing left."

"Then how the hell did this box survive?"

"Someone must have removed it from the building before the fire. Why, it is not difficult to surmise," Bathard said. There was pain in his eyes. He glanced from the box to the collage and then back again. "What you have there on the wall are fragmentary records of very rudimentary and in my opinion unethical medical research. I assume there is more of the same in the carton."

Cubiak nodded.

"The photos indicate that the experiments were performed on children and teenagers," Bathard said.

The coroner's assessment confirmed the sheriff's worst fears. Cubiak nodded again.

Bathard went on. "As a physician, I am loath to admit it, but historically children, especially those in orphanages and hospitals, were often used for such purposes."

"That's hard to believe, even looking at all this."

"I know, but unfortunately, it is true. In many respects, children and infants were ideal candidates for medical research. For one, they were readily available, and for another, they were defenseless. Melk was immune from public scrutiny, given the hospital's location, but this type of travesty went on elsewhere as well. There were more than a few doctors at highly regarded institutions who used the very young as unwitting test subjects. One physician even called them 'animals of necessity' when it came to research."

Cubiak shot to his feet. "Jesus. Weren't there laws against that?"

"You would think so, but such protections did not exist until relatively recently. In fact, there were no laws governing research in general until the Nuremberg trials after World War Two."

The sheriff was incredulous. "So these kids"—he pointed to the collage—"were essentially fair game for anyone who wanted to test a new theory or treatment."

"I am afraid so."

Cubiak handed the file of letters to Bathard.

The coroner read the first one and paled. "Leonard Melk. That fucking bastard," he said.

It was the first time Cubiak had ever heard his friend curse.

The retired physician skimmed several more of the crude letters and then dropped the pile in his lap. "Melk deserves to burn in hell for this abomination. Not only did he abuse these sick and disabled children, but he misled their parents, offering hope where none existed and then using their children as guinea pigs for his theories."

"I need to know the specifics," Cubiak said.

The coroner struggled to his feet and walked across the room to the start of the collage. "Melk seemed to be have been trying to find a polio vaccine. He may have been looking for treatments for other illnesses as well, but everything on the wall concerns that particular disease. Initially his experiments involved horse serum. I know it sounds bizarre, but there was some scientific basis for thinking the serum could work as a preventative. You've heard of the English physician Edward Jenner?"

"The name's familiar but I don't really remember . . ."

"Doctor Jenner is credited with discovering the smallpox vaccine. When entire villages were being ravaged by the disease, he noticed that the young milkmaids on the local farms seemed immune, even though they worked around animals infected with cowpox, a variation of the disease. Jenner surmised that something in the animals' blood protected them. To test the idea, he scraped particles from a cowpox lesion on one of the milkmaids and injected them into a healthy eight-year-old boy. He then exposed the boy to smallpox. The boy didn't get sick and humanity had its first effective vaccine."

"And horses don't get polio?"

"That is correct. But for reasons no one understood, their blood serum didn't protect humans from the disease. In fact, there were often severe and even fatal side effects. Having encountered that problem, Melk switched tactics and tried a different approach."

Bathard pointed to the photo associated with the letters MS.

Cubiak felt light headed.

"Once again Melk hoped to emulate Jenner's success, but this time he used blood serum that he took directly from polio victims themselves. He injected the serum into healthy subjects, on the mistaken theory that he was inoculating them against the scourge of the disease. He probably thought he was being logical. Although polio affects the nervous system, it enters the body through the mouth. Once it reaches the digestive system, blood distributes it to the nervous system. After this discovery was made, the hope was that researchers could find a vaccine that would stop the virus in the blood."

"Before it reached the nervous system," Cubiak said.

"Precisely. But like so many others, Melk's approach didn't work on his initial subjects. At least he was honest enough to admit that, but it doesn't mean that he didn't try again, perhaps with more frequent or higher dosages. There might be records of additional experiments in that carton."

Cubiak struggled to keep up. "In order to know if the serum worked, Melk had to expose the inoculated subjects to the virus and then wait to see if they became ill."

"I am afraid so. And given his position at the hospital, he had an almost limitless supply of patients on which to test his theories. Polio is a highly contagious disease. An occasional outbreak at a place like the Northern Hospital for the Insane would not have been considered cause for alarm."

"Innocent people crippled at his own hand?" The horror was almost more than the sheriff could take in. "I'm sorry the man's dead. I'd like the privilege of killing him myself," he said. Maybe someone else felt the same way. For the first time, Cubiak wondered if perhaps Melk had been murdered and his death made to look like a heart attack. The doctor's experiments were decades old, but if someone had learned about his research methods, someone related to one of his victims, they might have decided to get even. Revenge had a long shelf life.

"But why?" he continued. "By the time he was doing this, wasn't a polio vaccine already available?"

"There were two. Sabine's and the one developed by Salk that eventually was most widely used."

"Then what the hell was Melk up to?"

"Vaccines cost money to develop and produce. Melk had access to the blood he needed for free. All he had to do was to match blood types. If the treatment worked, it would be cheaper and he could claim it was 'natural.' Even back then, that was a deciding factor for many people."

Bathard looked at the wall again. "He may have had another reason as well."

"What do you mean?"

"Melk claimed that he was an only child, but he had two brothers, both of whom died before he was born, and his parents took up residence in Green Bay. They moved to Wisconsin in 1918, two years after a polio epidemic killed more than six thousand people in the United States. A third of those who perished lived in New York City, and most of them were children, among them Melk's two siblings."

"How'd you find this out?"

"I told you, I still have contacts."

"Do you think Melk was trying to find a cure for the disease that killed his brothers?"

"That may have been his initial incentive. In fact, I would like to believe so. Eventually, however, I suspect that his motivations became muddled and that he merely wanted to make a name for himself."

"And his position at the hospital gave him the cover he needed."

Bathard sighed. "For his purposes, the situation was ideal. Consider the location: In a society unequipped to deal with the insane, the mentally ill were hidden as far away as possible. What better location for a mental asylum than the remote north woods? And who was there to question him? The staff was probably overworked and minimally trained. Melk was free to act with impunity."

"I don't understand how he found these kids. I can't imagine him traveling from farm to farm searching for immigrant or desperate families with crippled children."

"He didn't have to do that, Dave. It was a different time. Today farmers order goods off the internet like everyone else. Back then they either drove to town or relied on traveling salesmen to bring the wares to them. Pots, hairpins, fabric, ointments, whatever was needed. I imagine a good sales rep would get pretty close to the families on his route and would sniff out the vulnerable fairly easily."

"And the rep would pass along the information to Melk."

"For a price, yes, or even in the mistaken belief that the doctor meant to help."

"He couldn't go on after the hospital was destroyed."

"Without the cover of the institution, Melk had no viable means of conducting his experiments with blood serum. But as a doctor with a private practice, he could test any number of drugs on unwitting patients and report his findings back to the pharmaceutical companies. For a fee, of course."

Cubiak opened his phone to the photo of the boy Francisca had identified as her brother. "Unwitting patients like this boy with Down syndrome?"

Bathard looked appalled. "That's the picture you showed me the other day." He grew more dismayed as Cubiak told him the story behind the photo.

The coroner was quiet for a several moments. Finally, he spoke. "It would appear that at some point Melk moved on to more contemporary problems and found new sources for his subjects."

"Do you think Sage knew?"

Bathard made a sound like a laugh. "How could he not? Perhaps he wasn't fully aware of his mentor's history, but eventually he had to realize that something untoward was going on."

"'For the greater good,'" Cubiak said.

"Are you trying to justify what Melk did?" Bathard sounded incensed.

"No. That's the IPM motto. I think that's how Melk rationalized his research. Sacrificing a few for the good of the many."

The coroner turned away in disgust. "All those innocent victims. How many were there over the years? And who were they? You may have a lead on the one boy, but there have to be so many others."

The sheriff moved up to the wall. "As it turns out, I may be able to identify one of the polio victims."

"What do you mean?"

"I believe the girl in one of the photos is Margaret Stutzman. If I'm right, she went missing years ago. The woman who lives here may even be Margaret's sister."

"How?" Words failed the normally erudite Bathard. He looked around the bleak room as if the answer to his question were hidden in a corner just out of sight.

Cubiak told him Florence Fadim's story and showed him the picture of Melk with the car.

"That doesn't prove anything."

"But the photo of the girl does."

"If it is she."

"It's her."

"Dave . . ." Again Bathard failed to go on. His silence was recrimination enough.

Cubiak still lacked proof and he knew it. "It certainly points to something," he said in his own defense.

Outside the rising wind rattled the windows and banged a loose board.

Bathard put an arm around the sheriff's shoulder. "What are you going to tell Mrs. Fadim?"

"I don't know."

With Bathard trailing behind, Cubiak plodded across the yard. His thoughts were as tangled as the wild vine that had overgrown the native plants and clung to the soles of his shoes. What would he say to the old woman? Did he owe her kindness, or the truth as he understood it?

Just as important: Who had discovered the files and hid them in the barn? What did they intend to do with the incriminating information about the illustrious Doctor Melk?

As the sheriff struggled with the questions, he pulled out his phone. He had turned it off when he first entered the barn and forgotten to turn it back on. Perhaps there had been a development, something that would point the way for him. He glanced at the bright screen and stopped so abruptly that Bathard blundered into him.

"Something's happened," the coroner said. "What is it? What's wrong?"

TIRE TRACKS
IN THE GRASS | 13

Harlan Sage is dead. An apparent suicide." Even as Cubiak repeated the news to Bathard, it struck him as surreal. "I've been trying to reach him for two days." And thinking the worst of him for the lack of a reply. Chagrined by the realization, the sheriff kept it to himself.

"Can you check on Mrs. Fadim? Give her my apologies and tell her I was called off on an urgent matter."

"What about the intruder and the barn?" the coroner said.

"She may have forgotten all about that, but if not, say as little as possible. Make her a cup of tea. She'll appreciate it."

Sage lived at the far western edge of Door County. His address took the sheriff along a narrow road that wound through heavy woods and was lined with upscale homes set along the Green Bay shore. Every few minutes, the forest opened to another imposing structure. McMansion heaven, Cubiak thought as he flew past the expensive properties. Each house sat in a sea of tranquility that was guarded by security cameras posted along the periphery. Each could easily shelter an extra family under its roof. The houses reminded him of a scene in *Doctor Zhivago*, the one when the peasants invaded the physician's home after the czar was overthrown. Through hate-filled eyes they took in the luxury of space enjoyed by Zhivago's family, and with a greedy vengeance they staked out their claims to the finely appointed rooms. By the time the serfs were finished, it seemed as if half the village had poured in through the open doors, dragging the muddy squalor of their past lives with them.

Sage's home differed from the rest of the houses in one respect. While the others were built of wood or brick or even stucco, his was carved from blocks of white granite—a three-story house with oversized windows and a great arching black door. A miniature forest of evergreens dotted the doctor's acre and a half, but even the gentle trees did little to offset the mausoleum-like feel that the house projected, almost like a Keep Out sign.

A vehicle from the sheriff's department stood along the edge of the road, and Cubiak saw a familiar figure wrapping yellow caution tape around the house. Rowe had beaten him to the scene.

The four vehicles that lined the wide half-circle driveway faced toward him, which meant they had entered from the right. The ambulance stood nearest the door, lights flashing. Each time the warning beams clicked around, red streaks splashed across the house's shiny white exterior like rivulets of blood. The last car in the lineup, a lime green compact, belonged to Emma Pardy. The other two cars were black. According to the message Cubiak had received earlier, Sage's assistant, Noreen Klyasheff, had made the call, so one of the vehicles belonged to her. Who else was on the scene?

The sheriff drove in from the left and parked far enough away from the house and the other vehicles so the ambulance could leave unhindered. The ground was still soft from the previous day's early morning rain and speckled with footprints. At one point, a stretch of tire tracks cut into the edge of the lawn. The tracks pointed in the direction he had just come from and were evidence of an earlier visitor, perhaps someone who left in a hurry and had carelessly driven on the grass. He took his time passing the two black cars, curious about what the interiors might reveal about their owners. One was obsessively bare and antiseptic. The other held an accumulated mess of empty water bottles, snack food wrappings, and miscellaneous items of clothing, including a crumpled black jacket that had been tossed on the back seat.

Sage was even more security conscious than his neighbors. An alarm company sign was planted in a flower bed near the front door, and security cameras were mounted on all four sides under the eaves. These were in addition to the cameras posted along the road and driveway. Unless the doctor kept a store of gold bullion in the basement, the fortresslike protection struck Cubiak as excessive.

At the moment the sheriff was about to knock, an EMT opened the door. They exchanged nods as the medic put two fingers to his mouth indicating a need for a smoke.

Cubiak let him pass, resisting the urge to join him. Strike three, he thought.

The black door opened to a two-story foyer that was as colorless as the exterior of the house. Everything in sight was white. Not just the walls and ceilings but the couches and chairs in the living room that opened to one side, the grand piano that stood in front of the large window, the statues of nudes on marble pedestals, the paintings hung at eye level. Even the wooden floor planks and stairs to the second floor were made of ash that had been drained of any tint. Nothing of warmth. More like the sterility of an operating room.

Cubiak thought of the man he had met at the conference. The house seemed to reflect the owner.

"In here," Pardy called out to him from the other side of the entrance hall.

The sheriff pushed through a second door and entered Sage's library. The room was as large as the living room and lined on three sides with floor-to-ceiling bookcases that were crammed with thick, oversized books—medical tomes, surely—bound in white to match the shelves they filled. A beige brocade wing chair sat in one corner, under an arching, silver reading lamp. Its twin faced the side window and the lush stand of cedar trees outside. Sage slumped over the arm of the chair. It looked as if he had been reading one of his medical texts when he dozed off and his shoulders slipped, letting the weight of his head and upper torso gently pull him into the awkward position—except for the handgun that lay on the floor near his dangling fingers.

"A peaceful spot to die," the medical examiner said. Her bright orange jumpsuit was a welcome splash of color and the only one visible from where Cubiak stood. Then he stepped around to the front of the chair and saw a color with which he was all too familiar. It was the deep red, almost black, hue of dried blood—a substantial amount of it. The stain defiled Doctor Sage's tie and spread across the front of his crisp white shirt and light gray suit like a Rorschach test that allowed only one interpretation: death.

"How long?"

"Two days at least. Whoever did this knew what they were doing. The bullet went up under the rib cage, directly into the heart." Pardy pointed to the entrance wound. "Death was instantaneous."

"Self-inflicted?"

"It looks that way. He was shot up close. I've swabbed for gunshot residue on his hand, for what that's worth." She shrugged. They both knew it was no proof that Sage had pulled the trigger.

"He left two notes." This time she pointed to a low table on the other side of the chair. "One was addressed to me, saying he wanted to leave his brain to science. But it's too late for that by at least twenty-four hours. The other note is for you."

Cubiak picked up a white envelope with his name neatly written across the front. Not the physician's typical illegible scrawl, he thought. The message inside was brief. "I meant no harm. I did it all for the greater good."

He read it aloud to Pardy.

"Sounds like a suicide note," she said, not bothering to look up.

"Or a confession." *Father, forgive me for I have sinned.* The familiar refrain tunneled up from Cubiak's past. All those Saturday afternoons spent on his knees inside the dark confessional at the parish church, beseeching God to pardon his boyish indiscretions. The sheriff turned back to the windows. Whose forgiveness was Sage seeking, if, in fact, that was the purpose of his final missive?

"What about a rationalization?"

The question—or was it a challenge—came from Rowe, who had suddenly appeared in the doorway.

Cubiak hid his smile. He had taken a chance when he hired Rowe, hoping that the spark he had spotted in the brash young man was evidence of intelligence and not conceit. He hadn't been disappointed. In the ten years that Rowe had been with the department, he had shed much of his bravado and matured into an insightful investigator, one who had learned to see beyond the obvious and to think before acting or speaking.

"That's another possibility. Maybe the message is a combination of all three: suicide note, confession, and rationalization."

Cubiak gave his colleague time to consider the suggestion. Then he led Rowe into the hall. "Are you finished out there?" he asked, motioning toward the front door.

"Not quite."

"We'll need crowd control for when the media gets wind of this."

Rowe looked toward the porch. "I got backup coming."

"Good." He's learning, Cubiak thought. Every day, getting smarter, better.

"Did you notice the security cameras on Sage's house and the ones on the other properties along the road?"

"Could hardly miss them."

"See what you can get from them. It would be interesting to know if anyone beside Ms. Klyasheff has been out to see Doctor Sage recently."

"Right. And there are the tire tracks on the lawn as well."

Cubiak was pleased that his subordinate had noticed them.

"I thought you might want a cast made before they're washed away or someone drives over them," Rowe said.

For the second time since arriving, Cubiak stifled a smile. "Right."

"It's on the list," the deputy said as he moved aside for the EMT who was returning from his smoke break.

"Are you the one who answered the call?" Cubiak asked the medic.

"Yes, sir,"

"Who found him?"

"Some lady. She's in the kitchen. Down there," the medic said, pointing to the white hallway that extended back behind the stairs.

By now Cubiak was accustomed to the muted white of the house and expected to find the same monotonous tone in the kitchen. Instead he was surprised with a blaze of color: pale orange walls, scarlet cabinets, sea green countertops, and a porcelain sink as shockingly blue as the lake under the bright summer sun. Even the floor was a patchwork of tiles dyed like Easter eggs. The overall effect was dazzling. It seemed as if Sage or his decorator had finally tired of the tedium of the rest of the house and in revolt created a kaleidoscope of clashing tints in this one room.

Inside, another surprise awaited the sheriff. There were two women at the table: Sage's assistant, Noreen Klyasheff, and the elusive journalist, Linda Kiel.

With their hands curved around vivid purple mugs, the women sat stiffly and watched him approach.

He was tempted to ask the writer if she had gotten his message, but instead he stuck to the business at hand.

"Which of you?" Cubiak started to ask.

"I did," Klyasheff said.

Her eyes were red and burdened with dread and fear. She had aged a decade since he had met her three days earlier at the conference. Shock had deepened the lines that spread weblike across her forehead and cheeks. She had chewed off her lipstick, leaving only a thin border of red that outlined her mouth like a strip of fresh blood. Only her coifed hair and smart suit hinted at her professional status.

With her wrinkled blue dress and disheveled hair, Kiel looked like the local dog walker. But her appearance didn't fool Cubiak. She was on high alert, excited to be on the scene with another dead body.

He had a litany of questions for the journalist, questions that went far beyond asking the reason for her presence at Sage's house, but he would save those for later.

"Do you mind waiting outside?" he asked her.

Kiel ignored him and glanced at the other woman, as if seeking permission. A look passed between them, and Kiel got up. She moved slowly, carrying her mug to the sink and then sliding out the back door, leaving Cubiak alone with Klyasheff.

"Are you drinking tea?" he asked.

She arched forward and looked into her cup, as if she couldn't remember and needed to check. "Yes."

"Would you like more?"

"No."

Cubiak eased into the chair that the younger woman had vacated. "I'm sorry for this. And that you had to be the one to find Doctor Sage, but it's important that you tell me everything you remember."

She stared at him with vacant eyes.

"In your own words."

She blinked. More time passed in silence but Cubiak waited. He knew this was hard for her.

"I was worried," she said finally. The statement was definitive and seemed to open a floodgate of memory.

"Doctor Sage hadn't been in the office this week since . . . well, you know. It wasn't like him to stay away so long and not call or email. Not to return my messages. He lived alone and I worried that maybe something terrible had happened. What if he'd fallen down the stairs, or had a stroke or . . ." Her voice trailed off. She shuddered. "My mother always said I had an overactive imagination, but I couldn't help it. These things do happen, you know."

"They do," Cubiak said. Not often, he thought.

"This afternoon, I decided I'd call one more time, and if there was no answer, then I'd come by. I brought some letters to be signed and figured that gave me an excuse, that I needed his signature."

"Were you ever at his house before?"

"Many times. Doctor Sage often worked from home on the weekend. If he needed me, he'd ask me to come out for an hour or two. Usually we sat in his study, at the back of the house, but sometimes he'd be working in that room . . ." She grabbed a green cloth napkin from the table and twisted it in tight, angry swirls. "I'm sorry."

"It's okay. You're doing fine." He waited and then he began again. "When you got here this afternoon, was the door locked?"

"Of course. It's always locked. I had to let myself in." She wrenched the fabric into a tight tourniquet. "I wasn't sure if I had the right to do that, but he didn't answer the bell and his car was in the garage."

"You checked that first."

She nodded.

"You know the alarm code?"

Klyasheff blushed. "Doctor Sage gave it to me a couple of months ago. He'd left some documents at the house that he needed, and he asked me to retrieve them." She studied the twisted napkin in her lap. "I don't know what I would have done if he'd changed the code!"

"What did you notice first?"

"I saw Doctor Sage!"

Having come through the front door, the sheriff knew that wasn't possible, given the location of the body relative to the entrance. "You walked in and saw him immediately?"

"No," she stammered. "You're right. I didn't, not right away. I came in and stood in the hall and listened, thinking I'd hear him, but it was so quiet, and cold, too. The AC must have been on high. I went directly to his study—he spends so much time there—and then to the kitchen. It was almost dinnertime and I thought maybe he was fixing something to eat. But he wasn't there either. I came back to the hall and glanced into the living room and finally the library. That's when I saw his arm hanging over the side of the chair. At first I thought that maybe he'd fallen asleep or, you know, something worse, like a stroke." She pinched her mouth. "I walked around to the front of the chair and saw the blood. So much blood."

"Did you touch him?"

The woman shuddered. "I couldn't. I was afraid to. I was certain he was dead. He had to be." She caught her breath. "At first I couldn't move. Then I wanted to run. I thought that whoever had shot him might still be in the house. I didn't know what to do. But when I saw the gun on the rug I realized the horrible truth of what had happened." She looked at Cubiak, her eyes full of pleading. "How could anyone do that? Why would someone do that to themselves? It was horrible. Just horrible. The poor man . . ."

Cubiak brought her a glass of water and waited until she was calm. "Anything else?"

A lace-edged handkerchief had replaced the tortured napkin in her lap and was being subjected to the same fate.

"The phone rang. It was the one on his desk in his study—where I'd come for the papers that one time. I didn't know what else to do so I went in and answered it."

"Why?"

"Out of habit, I guess. I answer his phone at the institute, so it was an automatic reflex, and it got me out of that room. Maybe I thought that if I left and then came back I would find everything would be back to normal. Maybe I worried that I'd been hallucinating or seeing things, you know, letting my imagination get the better or worse of me."

"Who called?"

"It was that writer. Linda Kiel. She said she had an appointment with Doctor Sage and was calling to confirm. She seemed surprised that I answered the phone. I don't know why but I told her what had happened, and she said she'd come right over, that I shouldn't have to deal with the situation on my own."

Pretty considerate of her, Cubiak thought. "Did she say anything else?"

"No. Oh, only that I shouldn't touch anything."

"What happened after that?"

"I hung up and called nine-one-one."

The murmur of voices drifted in from the front of the house. Cubiak couldn't make out what was being said, but he picked out Pardy's voice and figured she was talking to the EMTs.

"When you arrived, did you notice anything unusual outside the house?"

She frowned. "I don't think so. But I wasn't really paying attention. I was thinking about what I'd say to Doctor Sage. Everything seemed fine. Normal."

"Where did you wait for Ms. Kiel?"

"I went outside and sat in my car. I couldn't stand being in here."

"Did you have to wait long before she arrived?"

She squeezed her eyes shut and rubbed her forehead. "I don't know, Sheriff. I was distraught. It seemed like only five minutes or so went by before she pulled up, but it could have been much longer."

"Did she get in the car with you?"

Klyasheff's frosty response told Cubiak that she did not allow anyone to invade her private space. "There was no need. I got out as soon as I saw her car in the driveway. We hugged, as one does in those circumstances, and then she said she had to go inside the house."

"She wanted to see the body?"

"Yes. I told her it was gruesome, but she insisted."

"Did you go into the room with her?"

"No, I waited in the doorway."

"What did she do?"

"I don't know. I didn't pay attention."

Cubiak didn't believe her. Her antipathy toward Kiel had been obvious at the conference. She would have watched her every move in the library.

"Did she say anything when she came out?"

"Oddly no, just that she'd left some papers with Doctor Sage and needed to see if they were in his study. Before I could say anything, she went there and then came right back."

"Did she find what she was looking for?"

"I don't know. I didn't see any papers, but she could have shoved them in her bag. Should I have tried to stop her?"

Cubiak ignored the question. "How long have you worked for Doctor Sage?"

"Fifteen years."

"And before that?"

"Before he joined the institute staff, I was Doctor Melk's assistant. And now both of them . . ." She pressed the handkerchief to her mouth and stifled a sob.

Cubiak touched her arm. "It's okay, you're doing fine, and I'm sure that both of them would want you to help as much as possible."

The assistant sniffled and sat up in the chair. "Of course," she said, but Cubiak could see the doubt creeping into her eyes.

"The questions I'm asking are all routine."

"I understand."

"Were there problems at the clinic involving Doctor Melk? Anything you're aware of?"

She sat up as if startled by the suggestion. "Nothing. Absolutely not. He hadn't been involved in the day-to-day operations for ten years. During the past year, he rarely even came to the institute."

"What about Doctor Sage?"

She shook her head.

"Did either man have any enemies?"

"Enemies, no. Jealous colleagues, maybe, but enemies, no. Do you think someone tried to hurt them? That doesn't make any sense. Doctor Melk had a heart attack. And Doctor Sage—bless his soul—took his own life." She hesitated. "It was suicide, wasn't it?"

"It appears so."

Klyasheff sank back into the chair, as if relieved that Sage himself and not an intruder had blown the hole in the doctor's chest.

"Were the two men friends?" Cubiak said, shifting tactics.

"Friends?" She repeated the word as if she had never considered the possibility and was unsure what to make of the question. "I don't know. After all, there was a considerable age difference between them. I can't say if they ever got together socially, but I know that neither of them golfed or had any other interests that I was aware of."

"How did they get along at the institute?"

"Oh, very amiably. Their interactions were always congenial, as far as I was aware."

Cubiak noted the qualification. "What about family?"

"Doctor Melk was widowed some thirty-five years ago. He and his wife had no children. Doctor Sage never married. They both lived for their work." She said the latter with pride, as if determined to convince Cubiak that they were good men and that she'd been right to dedicate her life to them. Instead, she aroused the sheriff's suspicions.

Working that closely with the doctors, she could have been privy to their secrets. If what she had discovered tarnished them in her eyes, she might feel she had been maligned. Noreen Klyasheff was an intelligent, attractive woman. Had she forsaken marriage and family for Melk, Sage, and their precious institute? Her unyielding good posture, the upright tilt to her chin, and overall manner spoke to more than strict professionalism. Cubiak sensed a deep well of fierce pride lurking beneath her competent façade. Those who crossed her would suffer dire consequences. The more serious the insult, the more grievous the response.

Cubiak remembered something she had said earlier. "You mentioned that you sometimes went to Doctor Sage's house for an hour or two on the weekends to help with work. That sounds like an inconvenience."

"Not really. I live just outside Sturgeon Bay, about twenty minutes from his house."

"You're from here originally."

"I inherited my parents' house. I don't see what that has to do—"

"Did you ever go to Doctor Melk's house?"

"Of course. He and his wife had me out for the occasional dinner. What are you trying to get at?" She was becoming indignant.

"Nothing. These are standard questions," Cubiak said. But her answers could have a lot to do with things. She had grown up near enough to the Fadim farm to have heard the story about the missing girl. What if she had stumbled onto the old files in a back room at the institute or hidden away at Melk's house?

The sheriff couldn't picture Klyasheff breaking into Mrs. Fadim's barn, but he didn't doubt that she had the acumen to assemble the collage. At the conference, she had been near Melk minutes before he died, and she had been the first to report finding Sage's body in his home library. If there had been a way to kill both men without tipping her hand, she was smart enough to have figured it out.

Cubiak knew he was reaching. He also knew that at times it was the only option.

Noreen Klyasheff wanted to go home when they had finished, but Cubiak asked her to wait for a while on the chance he might have more questions for her. "You're still distraught and probably shouldn't drive, anyway," he told her.

He made her a fresh cup of tea—he was getting good at this, he realized—and left her on the patio under a tall heat lamp.

From there Cubiak ducked behind the garage. He needed a moment to think. Based on what Bathard had gleaned from the old hospital files,

Melk had plenty to hide. If Sage was tainted as well, then both physicians were prime targets for blackmail.

Noreen Klyasheff was the last person to see Melk alive and the first to find Sage dead. But Linda Kiel was also on the scene both times, and the files were found in her great grandmother's barn, meaning she might have either put them there or seen them. In public, the two women acted as if they despised each other, but what if that was a ruse? If they'd uncovered the truth about Melk and Sage, they might be implicated in the men's deaths and could be working together to profit from what they knew.

The sheriff called the circuit court and requested an emergency warrant for the release of Klyasheff's and Kiel's financial records. Then he texted Lisa and told her to run the necessary background checks on the pair.

"The usual. As fast as possible," he said.

Out front, the sheriff found Kiel leaning against the hood of the second black car. As he walked toward her, he pretended not to notice the tire tracks that cut across the grass. She watched him approach, at the same time appearing to draw his attention to the onslaught of boisterous chatter that she directed into the cell phone pressed to her ear. Something about the scene seemed contrived, and Cubiak wondered what she had been up to before she saw him.

"I'll meet you in the kitchen," he said when he reached the car.

"Five minutes?" She flashed an open hand at him.

"Two."

The sheriff found Rowe in the library with Pardy. "Don't do anything about the tire tracks until Linda Kiel leaves," he said.

The deputy's question was written on his face, but he swallowed his curiosity and said he would see to it after he finished his calls about the security cameras.

In the kitchen, Cubiak took the same chair he had sat in for the interview with Klyasheff and waited for the journalist. More late than on time, she strode through the door with a studied nonchalance, as if it wasn't at all unusual or upsetting to be interviewed by the sheriff in the home of a man who appeared to have put a bullet through his heart. But she wasn't fooling him; he could almost see the tension in her step.

He pointed her to the seat across the table. As soon as she was settled, he started in, not bothering to ask if she would like a cup of tea.

"Do you live nearby?"

"No."

"How did you get here so quickly when Ms. Klyasheff told you about Doctor Sage?"

"I was on my way to Green Bay. In fact, I was just a few miles from here when I called. I was surprised when she answered the phone, but then she told me what had happened."

"What did she say exactly?"

"She told me that Doctor Sage had committed suicide and that she was alone in the house with his body. She sounded hysterical. I couldn't just leave her here by herself."

"When was the last time you saw the doctor?"

Kiel pulled her chair in, stalling for time. "We met at one on Friday, last week. Then I saw him on Monday at the conference, of course." She took a breath and frowned, pretending to take a mental sprint through her calendar.

She's wondering how much to tell me, Cubiak thought.

"After that, I heard from him on Tuesday morning. He said he needed to see me and asked me to come out to the house."

"Had he done this before?"

"I'd met with him here once or twice when I was researching the book, but this was the first time he ever called and invited me to come out."

"What did he want?"

Kiel laughed. "It was kind of embarrassing, really. He said that he thought I deserved a bonus for my work on the book. I'd already been paid so it was a real surprise, something out of left field."

"Does that kind of thing happen often?"

Kiel smirked. "Maybe to other writers, but it was a first for me. Usually I end up dealing with people who have no concept what's involved in a project and think they've overpaid for the agreed-upon work."

"Did Sage write you a check?"

She shook her head. "He paid me in cash."

"That sounds odd," he said. Also, it meant that there was no paper trail, no proof that she was telling the truth. Just her word.

Kiel hurried to agree with his assessment. "It seemed strange to me, too, but hey, money is money."

"What was his mood like?"

"He was very subdued. I think we both were, having witnessed Doctor Melk's death the day before. But he seemed resolute. He thanked me for all I'd done to document the institute's history, and then he said that the work had to go on."

"He didn't seem despondent?"

"Not at all, just thoughtful, maybe a little preoccupied."

"And you didn't see him after that? Not until today?"

"I didn't see him today, at least not in the way you mean," she said.

"Why did you call Sage this afternoon?"

"He'd asked to see things at every stage of production. The first typeset pages had just come in, and I figured he'd want to take a look at them."

"You told Noreen Klyasheff there were papers here that you wanted to pick up."

Kiel looked sheepish. "I lied to her. Technically no one is supposed to see the book yet, and I didn't want her to know what I was doing."

"Did she show you the body?"

Kiel colored. "Actually, I asked to see it."

"Why?"

"I'm not sure I fully believed what she'd told me on the phone. I said that she sounded hysterical. What if Doctor Sage was badly wounded but still alive? What if he needed help?"

"Did she go in with you?"

Kiel shook her head. "She wouldn't go near the room. She said she couldn't bear to see him again, not like that. I went in alone."

"Did you touch anything?"

Kiel's eyes snapped open. She's wondering what I'm trying to get at, Cubiak thought.

"Of course not. I know better."

Cubiak let the assertion go unchallenged.

"It wasn't a pretty sight."

Kiel turned her head away, as if to emphasize the truth of the statement.

"Then you went into Sage's study, even after you realized that he was dead."

She looked at the sheriff and primly folded her hands together on the table. "I had to. I'd told Noreen I had to pick up the papers and didn't want her asking any questions."

Kiel's answer didn't sit right. "That was pretty clear-headed thinking, considering what you'd just seen in the library."

She said nothing.

"May I see the book?"

Kiel quickly reached for her canvas bag, her nonchalance an attempt to hide her relief at the change in direction. "It's not quite Hoyle but why not?" she said as she rummaged in the tote. After a moment, she handed him a thin volume with Proof Only stamped across the front cover.

Cubiak set it aside. "You knew the code?"

Kiel stiffened. She knew what he meant, he was certain of that.

"Excuse me?" she said, in a voice that feigned surprise.

"The code that allowed you to unlock the front door without setting off the alarm. Did you know it?"

"No. As far as I'm aware, no one did, unless maybe Noreen. Why would I?"

"No reason." Not unless the tire tracks across the lawn were from her car and her story about Sage calling and inviting her to the house was a lie meant to cover up the real reason for her coming to his house prior to today.

Kiel pushed her chair back and started up. "Are we done? Can I go now? I have a meeting in town."

Dressed like that? Cubiak thought. Her appearance seemed decidedly unprofessional. "I'm afraid you'll have to reschedule. I need you to come to the station and make a full statement about the events here."

She looked at him, incredulous. "Why? I didn't find the body."

"You were on the scene minutes after it was discovered. You may have seen something that Ms. Klyasheff missed. It's important."

Her tone grew strident. "But Doctor Sage committed suicide. Didn't he?"

Cubiak left the question hanging.

"Follow me," he said, pushing to his feet.

Kiel hesitated again.

The sheriff opened the back door. "Please," he said as he motioned toward the patio where Noreen Klyasheff waited.

SETTING THE TRAP

14

With the sun low in the west, Cubiak led the four-car parade from Sage's estate. They cruised into Brussels at five miles under the limit and then at slightly faster speed onto the highway that led back to Sturgeon Bay and the justice center. The sheriff kept his eyes on the road with an occasional glance at the rearview mirror just to make sure neither of the women decided to bolt. Noreen Klyasheff was directly behind the jeep in her compulsively tidy, like-new black sedan. Then came Linda Kiel in the lived-in compact, also black. Rowe took up the rear in a departmental patrol car. The sheriff had already gotten as much information as he could from talking with each of the women, but given the circumstances, he felt that formal statements were in order. There was always the chance that they would remember more details than they had first recounted. Beyond that, he wanted to keep them busy and out of his way for as long as possible.

At the station, Rowe put each woman in a separate interrogation room.

"Which one should I tackle first?" he asked Cubiak.

"Neither. I'll have one of the other deputies take their statements. You and I are heading to the Fadim farm. You go now. Bathard's already there. I'll call Mrs. Fadim and tell her to expect you as well. When I'm finished here, I'll meet you at the house."

"What am I supposed to do in the meantime?"

Cubiak grinned. "You can start by making a cup of tea for the nice old lady. Then get her to start talking and listen carefully to everything she says. She can be a little dotty at times, so she may think you're her son or nephew or someone else from her past. Don't let that put you off."

With Rowe on his way, the sheriff briefed one of the other deputies on the situation and the background on the two women.

"Start with Noreen Klyasheff. I want a detailed accounting of what she did from the time she arrived at Sage's house until Rowe got there. Make her go through the sequence of events step by step. Don't rush. Take your time with her. There's no hurry getting to the second one, and when you do, follow the same line of questioning. It's critical that you keep both of them here as long as possible without them making noise about calling their lawyers."

Lisa was gone for the day, but her reports on the two women were on Cubiak's desk.

Noreen Klyasheff was a frugal lady and a shrewd investor. She had a quarter million in the bank, and besides having clear title to the house and land she had inherited, she owned three farms in Southern Door that totaled more than seven hundred acres. She had one credit card, which she used for groceries, the occasional meal out, and her utility bills. She didn't shop for clothes often, but when she did, she bought quality. The monthly balance was paid in full. Taken together, the numbers revealed the kind of woman who lived modestly and who would stun the world at her death with a generous bequest to her church or the local animal rights foundation. As Cubiak surmised, Klyasheff's life centered on her work at IPM.

In contrast, Linda Kiel's bank balance teetered toward zero. What had she done with the thirty thousand dollars from IPM and the additional cash bonus from Sage?

The writer appeared to exist on credit. She charged everything—cat food, her morning latte, a notepad, two pens. She had fourteen different cards, issued under her name and that of her alter ego, Cody Longe. All of them were maxed out.

Lisa had flagged one of the statements from April. On it, a series of twenty charges was highlighted in yellow. Each was for an ad Kiel had placed in a local small-town Wisconsin newspaper. Cubiak had told his assistant to look for anything out of the ordinary and she had. "See attached," she had scrawled in the margin.

It was a copy of one of the advertisements.

"Missing Children: Were they taken from your town?" Pictures of children bordered the text. They were copies of the photos from the collage. At the bottom was a number to call. It was Kiel's cell number.

"What the hell?" Cubiak said.

He emailed Lisa and asked her to pull up the telephone exchanges for the locales where the ads had run.

"Once you have those, trace any calls made from Kiel's phone to numbers with those exchanges. Forward anything you get ASAP," he said. Then he pulled Kiel's credit card statements from the previous two months. In early March, she had charged two nights at a motel in Cleona, the one-time home of the Northern Hospital for the Insane.

"I'll be damned if she wasn't there," Cubiak said.

When the sheriff reached the farm, Mrs. Fadim was entertaining Bathard and Rowe with stories about the one-room schoolhouses of her youth. As usual, she occupied the chair by the window, a cup of tea in her gnarled grasp. The two men stood to one side. From the front hall, Cubiak heard her urge them to "take a seat and get a load off," but they demurred, presumably fearful that they would splinter the antique furniture into matchsticks. They both looked relieved when the sheriff stepped in from the entryway.

"Such a nice young man," she said of Rowe when she saw Cubiak.

"Indeed," the sheriff said, adding to the deputy's embarrassment. "He's here to help catch the person who's been sneaking into your barn."

The old woman skewered Cubiak with her blue eyes. "Isn't that your job?" she said, her sharp tone reinforcing the message that she did not approve of those who shirked their duties. Nor did she suffer fools or take kindly to being treated like one.

"It is, but my deputy is part of the team."

She took his response under consideration. "Well, if it helps you to find Margaret, okay." With that, she settled into her chair, picked up the mug from the side table, and thrust it at Bathard. "It's empty. Could you make me another cup of tea, please?"

Cubiak left the coroner in the kitchen and slipped into the yard with Rowe. In the fading light, dark shadows fell across the jungle growth and twisted into grotesque shapes.

"Man, this is creepy," the deputy said as he followed the sheriff through the undergrowth.

Cubiak's abbreviated tour around the barn ended at the silo door on the far side of the building.

"The lock is new. Unless there's a hole in the roof, this has to be the intruder's way in," Rowe said.

"That's why I've left it untouched. I don't want to give away our hand," Cubiak said.

From there, he walked his deputy across the pasture and into the woods to the overgrown track.

"The lane comes out about a quarter mile east of the house across from a cornfield. It's the only way in by car without going past the house, but someone on foot could walk in from any direction. This used to be pastureland," Cubiak said, flashing a narrow yellow beam at the trees that loomed around them. "But I doubt that the fences have been kept in good repair. I want you to look around for a trail or pathway and set up a twenty-four-hour stakeout. It won't be easy, given the terrain."

"Starting when?"

"Now. This evening. You can make the necessary adjustments in the morning."

"How many deputies do you want out here?"

"As many as you need. They'll be happy for the extra pay."

Rowe toed the soft earth and looked around. "Where will you be?"

At that moment, the sheriff's phone lit up with a text from Lisa. The message was succinct, but it contained the information he needed: George Wilcox, Pikesville. And a phone number.

Cubiak glanced up. Overhead the first stars were emerging. In Chicago, light pollution dimmed the night sky, but on a cloud-free evening in Door County, the stars would keep appearing, so many that he wondered if it was possible for anyone to count them all. The sheriff allowed himself a moment to consider the matter. Then he turned back to Rowe.

"Me? I'll be looking for a ghost named Margaret."

TWO SMALL TOWNS

15

Over a quick, late dinner Cubiak explained his last-minute plans to Cate.

"What do you expect to find out there?" she said.

"A trail that's still warm enough to follow."

"After all these years, do you think it's even possible?"

"I won't know until I've looked," he said.

Before he left, Cubiak read a story to Joey. Unlike Cate, who occasionally traveled solo on assignment, he rarely ventured far from home without either his son or his wife, and Joey was not happy to see him leave.

"Where are you going?" Joey asked as he stood in the doorway with his father.

"Pikesville and Cleona. Two small towns you never heard of."

Joey glanced at the overnight bag on the floor. "Are you running away from home?"

Cubiak smiled and tousled the boy's dark curly hair. "No. I'm off on official sheriff's business. I'll be back tomorrow."

"Promise?"

"Absolutely."

Joey grinned and, just as Mrs. Fadim had done hours earlier, gave him permission. "Well, in that case, okay," the boy said.

It was nearing ten when the sheriff departed. In the past, he enjoyed driving in the dark, but not so much anymore, as his night vision had become increasingly compromised. Oh, he could see all right, just not as well as when he was younger. Mostly he worried about deer and about his reaction time if one leapt out onto the highway.

He was near Shawano when the first text from Rowe came in. *All set.* An hour later, there was a second message: *Nothing.*

At midnight, the sheriff pulled up to the Wayside Inn outside Pikesville, where he had booked a room. This early in the season, there was only one other car in the motel lot. He checked in at the small, overheated office and was crossing the gravel parking lot to his room when his phone dinged with Rowe's third text: *No one. Yet.*

Klyasheff and Kiel had been released from the station several hours ago. From the information Lisa had garnered, Cubiak suspected that the journalist had organized the material on the barn wall and assumed she would make a quick trip to the farm to retrieve it. Either she had outwitted Rowe and the deputies and snuck in without their noticing, or he had been wrong about her. Unless she was playing her own game of wait and see.

The sheriff's phone dinged again at 1 a.m. No sign of anyone at the Fadim barn.

On Friday morning, Cubiak was up at six, but there was still no news about the intruder. At the local diner, he downed three cups of bitter coffee and, with a silent apology to Bathard, ate a farmer's breakfast: eggs, bacon, hash browns, and pancakes smothered in butter and maple syrup. He was finishing up when Lisa texted him the address that went with the name and phone number she had forwarded the previous evening.

In Pikesville, the sheriff passed a row of empty storefronts, a scene that was sadly emblematic of many small communities across the state and the nation. He was practically out in the country again when he reached his destination.

George Wilcox lived in a one-story frame ranch on the eastern edge of town. The house was painted a sickly olive green and sat in the middle of a weed-choked, cluttered yard, the kind that would draw tsks from the nearby neighbors, if there were any.

Cubiak made his way past a collection of old tires, metal fence posts, and wooden tubs to a front door marred with long, deep gouges. Claw marks. He knocked and a deep growl came from inside, then silence. When the door finally creaked open, a round, wrinkled face appeared and a pair of dark eyes blinked into the light from behind thick glasses.

"George Wilcox?"

The stooped figure nodded. Seeing the sheriff's ID, he reacted not with alarm but with curiosity.

"What'd I do?"

"Nothing that I know of. I just have a few questions for you. May I come in?"

"Sure. I guess," Wilcox said and stepped back to make way.

Cubiak hesitated. "You've got a dog?"

"Yep, sure do, but he's as old as me. He won't bother us none."

Crude pieces of art made from the stockpile of junk outside were scattered around the claustrophobic living room. "My hobby," Wilcox said as he pointed the sheriff to one of the two chairs in the room.

Cubiak refused the offer of coffee, and when his host settled into the other seat, he showed him a copy of the ad Linda Kiel had placed in the Pikesville newspaper.

"Oh, that. I already told that Cody Longe gal everything I knew. I'm not in some kind of trouble, am I?"

"Did she come to see you?"

"She called. Well, actually I called her and she called me back. We talked on the phone for about an hour. She had a lot of questions."

"What did she want?"

"Exactly what she asked for in the ad: information about kids who went missing years ago. She said she was a reporter and that she was writing an exposé about the hardships and abuses suffered by immigrant farmers. Not only about how they struggled to raise decent crops in their rocky soil but how they were taken advantage of. She said she'd heard rumors about doctors, or people pretending to be doctors, who convinced people that they could cure their sick or feebleminded kids and then made off with them. She wanted to know if the stories were true and said she had money to pay for information." Wilcox colored, as if embarrassed by admitting as much.

"And you knew someone that this happened to?"

"Not in my family, thank God. But I'd heard about it happening. Years back the son of the people who lived on the farm next to my uncle disappeared. I think his name was Henry."

"His folks lived near here?"

"About twenty miles from town. They were small-time dairy farmers, a whole bunch of them who'd come from the same village in Czechoslovakia. When I was a kid I spent summers on my uncle's farm and, well, you know how you hear things. Little kids, big ears. Henry was a cripple. Polio, I gather. And he was an only child. His folks needed him to help on the farm, and when this doctor said he could fix the boy up, well, they believed him. I guess they needed to because they sent him away to be healed."

"The parents never saw Henry again, did they?"

Wilcox shook his head. "Nope, not as far as I ever heard."

"Did you recognize his picture from the ad?"

"I wasn't sure, but there was something about one of the boys that made me think of him."

Wilcox peered at Cubiak. "What's this all about anyways? First this Cody Longe calls and now you show up. Something must be going on, and I'd like you to tell me what."

While the man talked, a mangy bullmastiff plodded into the room and flopped at his feet. The dog looked big enough to swallow a sheep. Cubiak didn't like big dogs.

"That's what I'm trying to find out."

Wilcox rubbed the dog's head. "The story about Henry was part of the local folklore. I didn't make it up just to get a few bucks from that reporter."

"Folklore can be based on rumor as much as reality."

"I asked my uncle about it once when I was older, and he swore by it." Wilcox moved his hand down the dog's back. "I don't know nothing more than that. I guess it could have happened just the way people said.

Henry's parents were uneducated immigrants who barely spoke the language. But why would someone do that?"

"I'm afraid there are reasons."

Cubiak's phone vibrated in his pocket. It was probably Rowe reporting in. The sheriff was tempted to check his message, but the way the dog looked at him gave him pause. He was sure the beast would pounce and tear his hand off if he reached for his cell. He ignored the phone and slid his foot farther from the dog.

Wilcox leaned forward, his hands on his knees.

"Those other kids whose pictures were in that ad, did the same thing happen to them?"

"It seems so."

Wilcox shook his head. "That's pretty hard to believe, ain't it? But then there's things going on out there that you just don't want to know about. Man's inhumanity to man and all that."

Outside and away from the slobbering dog, Cubiak read Rowe's message: *Nothing. Thick fog.*

Coming from Rowe, *thick* meant pea soup, the kind of fog that would keep most people at home. But was it bad enough to stop Linda Kiel from sneaking through the woods under its cover?

Stay put, Cubiak texted back.

There was no fog in central Wisconsin, and he retraced his path through town under a sky so blue and bright it hurt his eyes. He had forgotten his prescription sunglasses and rummaged through the glove box for the spare clip-ons as he drove. He found them just as he reached the highway and headed north.

The road had two lanes, and although each was wide enough for the approaching cars and SUVs, the logging trucks that came toward him seemed to take up more than their share of space. Each time one roared past, he felt the jeep shudder and edge toward the shoulder. After a hundred miles, a sign announced that he was entering the Oneida Reservation. Beneath the thick forest canopy, the jeep's automatic headlights flicked on. The temperature dropped immediately, but he kept the window open several inches. He liked the feel of the cool air on his face and the sound of the wind as it whistled past. The forest was a world unto itself, and for twenty minutes, the jeep was the only vehicle on the road. Then a massive pickup whizzed around him and disappeared around a bend so quickly that Cubiak wondered if he had imagined it. He drove for miles without seeing anyone. The few homes along the route were nestled into small parcels that seemed to be more threatened than sheltered by the surrounding tall pines. In the dense forest he felt as if he were alone in the world. The last surviving man. Besides the trees, there was only a river. The waterway paralleled the road and occasionally ran near enough for him to glimpse the rushing water and catch its murmur. In several spots the river flattened out into calm, wide pools, but in one stretch it passed through a jumble of massive boulders. The rocks peeked out above the surface, and the water foamed and protested as it pushed downstream. Not a good place for canoeing, Cubiak thought.

Abruptly, he came to a junction with a tin-roofed tavern on one corner, a rundown shack that housed a combination gas station and grocery store on the other, and a cluster of used cars for sale on the third. The fourth was choked with weeds. Welcome to Cleona. The sheriff spoke out loud, as if welcoming himself back to reality and the mission at hand.

There wasn't much to the town. It was half the size of Pikesville but had twice the number of vacant storefronts. A small craft store anchored one end of Main Street and a used furniture store the other. The parade of yellowed For Rent signs between the two establishments was interrupted by a tavern that declared itself to be a genuine saloon. Two swinging half doors at the entrance reinforced the claim. The three cars parked on the street were in front of the bar.

Outside Cleona, Cubiak entered a forlorn landscape. There were no homes, no cultivated fields, no fences—only a narrow, potholed road that was crumbling along the edges where the weakened asphalt gave way to the forest that flanked it on both sides. The dense proximity of the trees was threatening and claustrophobic. Cubiak was seized by an immediate sense of dread that deepened the farther he ventured from town.

He had difficulty finding the hospital site. Blackberry brambles had overgrown the entrance, and he nearly missed the fissure that allowed him to drive through. Some twenty feet in, he came to two stone pillars. According to old photos, an iron arch had once risen up from the columns, but it was gone, sold for scrap.

Cubiak stopped and took a second look. Something wasn't right. The pillars had been recently tuck-pointed, and the grounds, or what he could see of them from that vantage, appeared reasonably well kept. The weeds along the circumference were whacked knee-high and the small patch of lawn inside the circle driveway was freshly mowed, as if in anticipation of his arrival. Rather than make him feel welcome, however, the prospect added to his unease.

Halfway up the drive, he got out of the jeep and continued on foot.

When it opened its doors in the mid-1800s, the Northern Hospital for the Insane was the largest building in the state, far bigger and grander even than the old capitol in Madison. The regal, red brick edifice had been located five miles from town, close enough to give the residents who worked there an easy commute to work, especially during the harsh winter months, but far enough away to allay any fears that escaped patients would reach them before the authorities caught and redeposited them behind locked doors. By the time Melk arrived, the hospital was ninety years old and had lost much of its luster. Eventually, patients were reallocated to newer treatment centers, until fifteen years later, when the aging facility burned. Its population had dwindled by half.

Now, the magnificent building was gone. All that remained were the concrete steps and a layer of rubble that formed an ugly scar along the surface of the earth. He climbed the wide steps, stood where he imagined the massive double doors had been, and peered into a great maw littered with shards of glass that had exploded from the window frames and the misshapen remains of metal desks and beds that had melted in the heat. Beer cans and trash lay scattered amid the ruins. At one time the hospital had been a beacon of light, a depository of the best that the medical profession could offer to the mentally and emotionally tormented. All vanished.

The destruction was complete. Cubiak shuddered to think of the fire and the innocent victims—many of them children—trapped behind locked doors and barred windows. Surely their desperate screams would have penetrated the thick masonry walls and soared above the treetops to reach the townspeople. But even if they had known, what could the local residents have done? What kind of volunteer fire department would a town like Cleona have had back then? How many buckets and how many hands would have been needed to douse the flames? And from whence the water?

The site was eerily quiet. In the stillness, it seemed as if nature itself had bowed its head in sorrow those many long years ago and was still offering up prayers for the dead.

There's nothing left here, Cubiak thought. Yet he lingered.

Compelled by a need to honor those who had suffered and died, he walked alongside the serrated ridge of broken brick, careful to stay on the grass so his footfalls would not disturb the silence. He had covered a quarter of the perimeter before he realized that the building was in the shape of a cross, with one long center section and two wings. He had read that the large center section had been reserved for adolescents and adults. The far wing was for the children; the nearest was the medical wing overseen by Leonard Melk.

During Kiel's visit to Cleona, she had stayed at the Deep Woods Motel, dined at the Dew Drop Inn, and bought two bottles of wine at a grocery store one town over. By then she was writing the book about the IPM and she would have known that Melk had worked at the hospital. The doctor hadn't wanted to delve into the past, but apparently his reluctance hadn't hindered her. It might even have piqued her curiosity or sparked her instinct to dig deeper. She would have made the drive out from town. She would have seen what the sheriff saw, walked the terrain, and absorbed the depressing essence of the place. But none of that explained how she got hold of the files. If Melk had kept them, he wouldn't have given them to her. Cleona didn't appear to have a historical society or even a library where the box of records might have been shoved into a corner and forgotten. On his way back, he would take another look around town to be certain, but he couldn't imagine that anything, much less a cardboard box filled with paper, had been salvaged from the flames.

Sadder but none the wiser for his journey, Cubiak circled back to the jeep. As he put the vehicle into gear, he looked up at the rearview mirror and glimpsed something moving across his line of vision. There one minute and gone the next. He thought of ghosts, but ghosts were white and whatever he had seen was black, like a raven's wing. He turned off the engine and slipped back outside. When he turned, he saw a small figure ambling toward him. Male or female, he couldn't determine, but definitely human and alive. The figure's head and shoulders were pitched forward as if to speed its progress. Cubiak started forward, and as the distance between the two dwindled, the figure transformed into a frail old man struggling beneath the weight of a great ebony coat.

When the two were twenty feet apart, the man stopped. He pushed back the cap that had slid down his forehead and studied the sheriff.

"I thought you'd be one of them, but you ain't. Not dressed like that," he said, taking in Cubiak's yellow sweatshirt and jeans.

"One of who?"

"The doctors, of course."

Cubiak knew the name of only one doctor associated with the site and took a chance on it. "You mean like Leonard Melk?"

The man chortled. "Melk? He'd be dead by now, I reckon, but his son wouldn't, if he had one." He moved his mouth and spat at the ground. "The son would be a doctor, too, wouldn't he, seeing as his daughter is."

Cubiak almost smiled at the thought of Linda Kiel pretending to be a physician. He said her name out loud, adding: "Doctor Leonard Melk's daughter."

The man jeered. "No, she's too young. I mean the son's daughter. Doctoring must run in the family."

Cubiak didn't tell the man that Melk had no children. "I didn't expect to find anyone here," the sheriff said.

"Oh, I'm always here. Got no place else to go."

"Who are you?"

"Who am I?" The man's voice was charged with indignation. "You tell me who you are and what you're doing here and then maybe I'll tell you who I am."

Should he lie? Cubiak wondered. He could pass himself off as another of Melk's sons, an uncle to Linda Kiel. Or he could claim that he was a historian from a local college, maybe even a realtor, curious about the resale value of the land.

He decided to tell the truth, that he was the sheriff of Door County where Leonard Melk had recently died. Hearing the news, the old man closed his eyes and crossed himself. Then he looked up, and Cubiak went on with the rest: there'd been no offspring; there was no Doctor Linda Kiel, but a young woman by that name who was writing a book about Leonard Melk, which explained her interest in the site.

"So it was okay that I gave her that box of his things?"

"Yes." It was a very good thing, Cubiak thought.

The old man grew wistful. "I knew someone would come eventually."

"And you were right," Cubiak said. He waited a moment. "I've kept my end of the deal. Now you have to tell me who you are and why you're here."

As they talked, the two men had edged toward each other one step at a time. Finally they were close enough for Cubiak to see the deep furrows that fanned the corners of the man's milky eyes and webbed across his spider-veined face.

"Name's Paul Osgood. I grew up here. Oh, not in there," he said quickly, nodding toward the ruins of the mental hospital. "Back there." He pointed a finger over his shoulder to the woods, where the faint outline of a log cottage was barely visible among the trees. "My father was the caretaker here. After the place burned he didn't know what else to do, so he stayed on; there was nowhere else to go and he had the house. At first, they let him live there in exchange for shooing off the sightseers. After a while, I guess they forgot he was here. I was just a kid then and my mother was dead, so there was no one to complain about having to live with all the ghosts."

"Why are you still here?"

Osgood's shoulders twitched inside the big coat. "Nowhere's else to go either. I came back from the war with my own ghosts. Guess I figured that if I'd stay here, they could all keep one another company. Anyways, somebody had to look after my father. When he passed, I waited for one of them officials to come by and tell me to git, but no one did, so I stayed. I get my social security money and pick up a few dollars doing odd jobs around town, but mostly I look after things here, keep the grounds tidy. That and wait for someone to pick up Melk's stuff. But I guess that part of the job is done, ain't it?"

He looked to Cubiak for affirmation, and the sheriff inclined his head a bit.

"It's a wonder the files weren't destroyed in the fire," Cubiak said.

"Not really."

The sheriff didn't push. He knew the rest of the story would come out sooner or later.

Osgood looked hot and tired. The steps had shaded over, and Cubiak suggested they sit there out of the sun. He got two bottles of water from the jeep and gave one to his host. The water was lukewarm, but Osgood drank his without complaint.

"I don't usually go for this stuff, but I got to admit it tastes pretty good today," he said.

"How old were you when it happened?" Cubiak asked.

They both knew what he meant. "Eight, going on nine. It must have broken out in the middle of the night, probably in the basement on a pile of old rags or newspaper. Must have been simmering for hours because just before dawn, it blew up through the building. The whole place seemed to be on fire at once. There was nothing anyone could do. The staff and doctor on call unlocked the front and the side doors but no one could get past the flames to go in. The fire was too hot. And not everyone got out either."

"The papers reported thirty-four deaths," Cubiak said.

Osgood hung his head. "That's right, and it was a damn shame. Patients and staff died, even the young girls who cleaned the medical wing."

"The cleaning crew lived on site?" That didn't sound right to the sheriff.

"Not exactly a crew, five or six crippled girls that Doctor Melk took in because their families had no use for them. He felt sorry for the poor kids and let them do simple chores in exchange for room and board. It was all unofficial, of course."

Cubiak seethed and pressed his clenched fists into the pitted concrete.

"They died, too," Osgood said. "Once the roof went, the fire just shot up into the sky." He stared at his worn boots. "I had nightmares about it for years."

Even the birds had gone quiet and for several minutes the two men sat in a mournful silence. When he finally had his anger in check, Cubiak remembered that he still had to ask about the files.

"You were going to tell me how it was that the box didn't burn," he said as casually as he could manage.

"Oh, that." Osgood tried to inject a grain of levity into the conversation. "Providence, I guess. Earlier that week, I heard Doctor Melk tell my father that the state authorities were coming to do an inspection. He said these guys were sticklers for neatness and he was worried because he hadn't kept up with the paperwork and his office was a mess. He said he needed to temporarily clear out some of the files and had tossed some stuff in a box. You know, by way of tidying up so he'd get good marks from the powers that be. My dad, being the nice guy that he was, offered to take the box and tuck it away in our attic."

Osgood tugged at his chin. "Two days later, the hospital burned to the ground and then Melk left along with everybody else. For a while, there were plenty of authorities coming back and forth, but we never saw Melk again. In all the to-do, my father forgot about the box and when he remembered, well, he figured that since these were official records and all, it was his responsibility to keep them. 'Some day someone will come asking for that box,' he said. I never questioned his reasoning and after he died and I kind of took over, I figured the responsibility fell to me." Osgood pivoted and looked over the collar of his coat to where the hospital had once stood. For a while he seemed lost in memory and then he pivoted back toward the sheriff.

"It took long enough but I guess the old codger was finally right," he said as he squinted into the afternoon sunlight.

INSTITUTE FOR

PROGRESSIVE MEDICINE

16

With a heavy heart, Cubiak sped away from Cleona. Although he was grateful for every mile that put more distance between him and the Northern Hospital for the Insane, he came away burdened by the knowledge he had gained. The crippled girls had burned to death, most likely Mrs. Fadim's sister, Margaret, among them. And Leonard Melk was to blame. As far as the sheriff was concerned, the doctor might as well have lit the match that started the inferno.

Cubiak drove blindly, oblivious to highway signs and roadside attractions, and only vaguely aware that if he kept the sun to his right, he would eventually get back. He covered the distance to Green Bay listening to the screams that had haunted Paul Osgood through his childhood. At the sight of the towering smokestacks on the northern edge of the city, he snapped into a sudden awareness that Melk had once followed a similar route. How much time had passed before he hung out his shingle and started to lay the groundwork for his IPM?

Emma Pardy said she had been to the institute. As long as he was in the area, Cubiak decided to take a look himself. He swung into the southbound lanes and then onto the bypass that carried him over the Fox River and past the maximum-security prison for men. Built in the late 1800s as a reformatory, it stood a comfortable distance from town, like the mental hospital in Cleona, but by now a familiar sprawl of shopping malls and housing developments surrounded it, making the watchtower and strings of barbed wire just another marker on the daily commute to work or school.

At the split, he followed the signs for Milwaukee. Melk's Institute for Progressive Medicine was in the rolling countryside about fifteen miles southeast of Green Bay. Around a gentle curve, a sign for the facility appeared in a grove of pine trees. Next Right, it read.

Cubiak exited the highway onto a two-lane blacktop. After several miles he glimpsed the upper floor of a large white building at the top of a heavily wooded rise.

The sheriff was more than thirty miles outside his jurisdiction. He had no legal authority in the area, but there was nothing to prevent him from visiting the facility. He could be a curious onlooker. Or maybe he was a potential patient with a persistent crick in his back that had confounded his family doctor. It was a free country.

A second right-hand turn put him on a stretch of smooth pavement that wound up a slope. Suddenly the road leveled off, and Cubiak arrived at two stone pillars that marked the entrance to IPM. Déjà vu, he thought as he drove onto the grounds. Trees, grass, and flower gardens filled the parklike campus, and wooden benches stood at intervals along paved walking paths that crisscrossed the terrain.

The building he had seen from the road towered over this island of serenity. Three stories high and constructed of pure white stone, the home of Melk's IPM managed to be simultaneously imposing and welcoming, a symbol of strength and hope in a world besieged by despair. A wide staircase led to the first level, where five Corinthian columns supported the overhanging roof. The columns as well as the cathedral-style doors combined to present a façade that was designed to intimidate as well as to instill confidence. "We know what we're doing here."

Not too shabby for the son of a truck driver and a store clerk, Cubiak thought as he followed the arrows to the parking lot. There were few empty spaces. Most of the vehicles were local, but others bore plates from the surrounding states of Illinois, Iowa, and Minnesota. Some were from as far away as Ohio and Montana. There was even a red van from Florida. Business was good. Or health was bad. He wasn't sure which.

Before he got out of the jeep, Cubiak took off his badge and secured it with his gun in the vehicle. Without them he felt oddly vulnerable, and for a moment, he wondered if it was a sense of helplessness that drew others to this mecca of hope. What power had that despair bestowed on the late Doctor Melk and his colleagues? How isolating were the innocent white walls of the institute?

The afternoon was pleasantly warm, but only a few people were out. Cubiak walked by a middle-aged couple who sat on a bench holding hands as they stared aimlessly into the surrounding greenery. Nearby a young woman pushed a stroller down the path to the rose garden. The toddler in the elaborate carriage slept with a thumb in his mouth. Another child, probably five or six, ran ahead, kicking at the small stones. The sheriff hoped they had accompanied an ailing relative and that one of the children wasn't here as a patient.

He followed two young women up the stairs. They wore stylish wigs and outfits of sunny yellow and bright pink, colors of optimism, and chatted eagerly about the new therapy they would be receiving that day. Maybe miracles were being performed behind the massive wood doors, but Cubiak was doubtful.

The sheriff didn't worry that anyone would recognize him. The only IPM physician he had met at the conference was dead. Noreen Klyasheff would be ensconced in an office in the inner sanctum. To anyone he encountered, he was Mister Average Citizen, visiting the institute to gather information for a desperately sick relative—correct that—for a dying relative, should someone ask.

The interior was nothing like any hospital or clinic that Cubiak had ever seen. IPM visitors entered a grand hall lined with rows of comfortable chairs that were arranged like pews in a church. The room was done in shades of white that taken together evoked either the simple purity of heaven or the antiseptic wonder of a medical Eden. Cubiak found it cold and impersonal and at odds with the hope that emanated from the faces of the people who waited to be summoned forth. Into what? he wondered. When Melk established the IPM, had he forsaken his fierce ambition and crude methodology, or had he found a way to incorporate them into the philosophy and practices of the institute?

In an alcove, Cubiak came upon a display rack filled with brochures and testimonials and updates on new treatments for a range of dreaded diseases. He gathered up a handful of materials and hurried toward the exit.

Inside the only sounds were the hushed voices of the patients and the piped-in white noise of a gentle surf. Outside he was greeted by the deafening roar of mowers and blowers. The grounds crew was hard at work. Relieved to be back in the real world, Cubiak smiled as he walked past the workers, but the eight men in blue paid no attention to him.

THE FARMER NEXT DOOR

Ten miles east of Green Bay, Cubiak hit fog. Pickups and trucks roared past, their drivers seemingly oblivious to the conditions. The sheriff had never worked traffic, but he had heard enough stories of bodies peeled off windshields and steering wheels to know when to slow down. For half an hour, he drove through alternating patches of heavy mist and shadowy light, but by the time he reached Door County, the battle was over, with fog the victor. He thought of Rowe trapped in a cloud in the middle of the woods, unable to see past a few tree trunks but listening for footsteps and hoping the intruder wasn't sneaking up behind him.

Anything? the sheriff texted.

A fog horn moaned in response. Then this from the deputy. *Zip.*

On my way.

Cubiak stared into the void and thought of Florence Fadim at her window. What did she discern in the fog on a day like this? Did the old mirages hold sway, or did new hallucinations take their place? Half a mile from the farm, he almost drove past the turnoff and caught himself in time. The thick fog blurred distances, and he was startled by how quickly the driveway came up. The house wasn't visible, just the gravel road to it. He kept going toward the abandoned logging lane that led into the woods. It was unlikely that the intruder had avoided the surveillance team, but if someone had gotten through and was in the barn, he wanted to try to surprise them.

But it was Cubiak who got the surprise.

A pickup truck blocked the way to the old narrow road. Nearby, a bulky man in patched overalls and green plaid shirt was hammering together several pieces of lumber into what looked like a makeshift barricade.

"You intend to plant that here?" Cubiak said.

The man started and slapped the hammer into his palm like a weapon. "What's it to you?" His scowl melted at the sight of Cubiak's badge. "Name's Stanley Smolinsky, and my apologizes, Sheriff, but this here is private property, and I'm trying to keep it that way," he said.

Cubiak recognized the name. Smolinsky was the man who was renting the fallow farm fields from Tom Fadim.

"That's awfully neighborly of you."

Smolinsky seemed puzzled, but then he laughed.

"What do you mean neighborly? I ain't doing this for nobody else. It's my land."

"Isn't this the back road that runs into the Fadim farm?"

"It's the back road all right, but this ain't the Fadim farm anymore. Hasn't been for a few years."

"Aren't you the one who's renting the fields?"

"I used to be. Then Tom said he wanted to sell and I bought. Oh, not everything at once. Just bit by bit. This here pastureland was one of the last parcels that I got from him."

"How much of the Fadim land do you own?"

"Every square foot except for the farmstead, and that's only about two acres or so with the house and the old barn and such. But I got right of first refusal on that once the old lady's gone," Smolinsky said, a note of pride in his voice.

Why hadn't Tom Fadim told him all this? Cubiak wondered.

"Did Tom say why he was selling?"

"Well, for one thing, he ain't been farming for years. Even at that, I'm sure he hated to part with the land. Each time he offered up another parcel, he made it clear that he was only doing it because he needed the money for Florence's care. People around here tend to take their time making decisions about selling land, especially when it's been in the family for generations, but with Tom, there was always an emergency of one kind or another and a rush to get the deal done."

Smolinsky stopped talking long enough to drive a nail into a board.

"He has power of attorney, you know, so it's all on the up-and-up. He told me Florence would rather die than sell, so he had to use his better judgment in terms of her medical situation. Tom asked me to not say anything to anyone, so I didn't. I guess he didn't want her to hear about it from one of the local gossips."

The farmer eyed the sheriff. "Just so we're clear, it's true that I wanted the land. But I was willing to wait as long as needed. I wasn't trying to pull the wool over the old lady's eyes, if that's what you're thinking."

But had Tom Fadim? Or had he told his grandmother about the transactions, assuming that the information would get lost in the miasma of her confused mind?

"None of that explains what you're doing here," Cubiak said, indicating the wood barrier that was under construction.

"This? Like I said, I'm trying to keep private property private. This damn road hadn't been used in years and was so overgrown I didn't think anyone even knew it was here. Then a couple months ago that started to change. I keep a pretty close eye on things and could tell by how the grass and weeds were beaten down that someone was coming and going pretty often."

"You ever see anyone using the road?"

"Nope. But I ain't got all day to sit and watch neither. Anyways, if you ask me, I think whoever's going in and out is doing it at night. You think maybe there's something illegal going on in the woods, or they got some kind of rendezvous in there?"

Cubiak shook his head. "Nothing like that, I'm sure. But do me a favor and hold off on putting up this barrier for another week or so."

Smolinsky had pulled a long, thick nail from his pocket and stood considering it. "Is that an order?"

"More like a neighborly request."

"I got my rights, you know."

"I'm aware of that, but I've got my reasons."

The farmer laughed. "Put that way, anything you want, Sheriff."

"I wouldn't be wandering about the woods either, if I were you."

"Now that sounds like an order."

"Let's just say it's more a suggestion, but a strong one."

Cubiak helped Smolinsky load the half-completed gate and materials into his pickup.

"I don't suppose you'll tell me what this is all about," the farmer said as he hoisted himself into the cab of the truck.

The sheriff reached through the open door and shook his hand. "There might not be anything at all going on, but if there is you'll find out soon enough."

"Okay," Smolinsky said and slammed the door. The motor was running when he rolled down the window and turned his grizzled face toward the sheriff.

"How's old Florence doing anyway?"

"Mrs. Fadim? She's good."

"Now that's nice to hear. She's a feisty one, I'll give her that. I always liked the old gal. Hope things work out for her."

With that he drove off.

Cubiak watched the dust settle and the taillights fade in the distance. Had Tom Fadim lied about the disposition of the farm? Or had he simply failed to tell the truth? If he had lied, it could mean he had something to hide. If he had fudged the facts, it could be that he was too proud to admit that he had been forced to sell the land out from under his grandmother and the rest of the family.

It might not even be any of the sheriff's business, but then again it wouldn't hurt to know.

He requested another warrant and texted Lisa with instructions to check out Tom Fadim's financial situation.

Cubiak pulled the jeep far enough up the logging path that it couldn't be seen from the road and entered the woods on foot. The fog was thinning. In spots it hung like gauze from the branches and parted reluctantly as he made his way through the maze of trees. The forest was silent, closed in on itself. It belonged to no one, least of all to him.

He wondered if the forest animals were watching him. Deer, perhaps, or squirrels. He wondered if years back the cows that pastured here had ever been attacked by wolves. He remembered the poster on the department bulletin board that warned about ticks and wondered if the little bloodsuckers were active this time of day. As a precaution, he stopped and tucked his pant legs into his socks. He wondered if the intruder was trailing him through the mist.

Finally the sheriff reached Rowe. The deputy was camped out behind a copse of stunted firs along the fringe of the forest. Burrs stuck to his sleeves in odd clusters of three and four, and a large silver thermos leaned against the base of a rotting stump.

At the sight of his boss plodding through the brush, Rowe clambered to his feet. He arched his back and shoulders. He was fidgety and tanked on coffee.

"Nothing going on here, sir. Do you really think someone's going to show up?" he said. The words were polite but the tone conveyed both his boredom and doubt.

"They will. They have to. It's a matter of time," Cubiak said.

From where they stood they could make out the back of the barn through the trees. The sheriff gazed at the silo door and the house beyond.

"Give it a couple of hours and then leave. In fact, make a show of giving up. Pull the crew together and all go out at the same time."

"We're done? What about the surveillance?" Despite his earlier reluctance, Rowe sounded disappointed.

"I want the intruder to think we've given up."

"You've got something in mind, don't you? A different plan?" The deputy sounded hopeful.

Cubiak rubbed his jaw. He needed a shave. "There's always a different plan."

Keeping his promise, Cubiak stopped at home to see Joey. From there he went to the office, where Lisa's report was waiting.

Tom Fadim was in a financial bind. The CPA with the shoddy office was trapped in a sinkhole of debt that grew deeper by the day. Pretty soon he would be breathing through a straw, Cubiak thought. And then, he would disappear into the muck, sucked in under the heavy weight of money owed.

After what Stanley Smolinsky had told him, the sheriff had given Fadim the benefit of the doubt. But it was clear that he had lied to his neighbor when he sold the land. The money for the farm parcels wasn't used to pay for Florence's medical bills or to buy her better care. She was stuck in that chair in front of the grimy window, dependent on the kindness of strangers for a cup of tea and a biscuit, because her grandson had robbed her. Tom Fadim had gambled away his income as well as the assets from his business and his home, and then he had started selling off pieces of the only remaining thing of worth in his control: the family farm. If there was anything decent that could be said on his behalf, it was that he hadn't put the farmstead itself on the market. At least not yet. But how much longer could he hold on before he sold the house out from under his grandmother and she was left with nowhere to go and no choice but to rely on a system that was increasingly hostile to those like her? How long before this woman who had worked hard her entire life was forced to hold out her hand and beg for crumbs from anyone kind enough to notice her?

"Bastard," Cubiak said. He tossed the printouts onto his desk and turned toward the window. In the pasture across the road, the Holsteins were lined up along the back fence like a row of dominoes. As he watched, the first cow began to move, and then one by one the others followed suit until the entire herd plodded behind the leader, sure that it would bring them no harm. Mrs. Fadim had the same kind of unquestioning faith in her grandson Tom, the sheriff thought. She had put him in charge, confident that he would keep her safe.

She had entrusted the farm and all her material goods to his care. And why not? He was an accountant. He knew the ins and outs of finance. He was supposed to be a fiscal conservative, a financial expert who understood that a nest egg had to be protected and nurtured. The whole point of having even a modest amount of money was to keep it and not squander it fecklessly.

Tom Fadim was a fraud, a reckless bean counter who had failed his most important client. Worse than that, he had cheated her.

The preliminary report that Lisa had pulled together was chilling. Fadim owed nearly a quarter-million dollars to ten different credit card companies, his house was in receivership, and his small office building had been refinanced three times.

"I'm going into town," Cubiak said, pulling on his jacket as he passed his assistant's desk.

"Are you coming back later?"

"Maybe."

The manager at the Bank of Sturgeon Bay confirmed the details about Fadim's financial woes.

"Tom's been a customer here for years, sad to see this happen to him," the manager said. He toyed with a pen, avoiding direct eye contact with the sheriff. Finally, he looked up. "I had to reject his most recent loan application. One of several, I might add."

"You think he's a bad risk?"

"More than that."

"You're saying that he's defaulted on past loans?"

"Tom and I grew up together. We were friends through high school. We played on the same basketball team, dated some of the same girls. Let's just say I went out on a limb for him, and he left me hanging."

Cubiak heard the same sad story at the two other local banks.

What the bank officials couldn't attest to was the reason for Tom Fadim's sorry state of affairs. He came from a good family, and for years he had run a solid business. There were rumors that after his divorce he started gambling—betting on sports games, trying his hand at poker, and eventually gravitating to the casino outside Green Bay, where he quickly became a regular, one of those unfortunate men who routinely bet large and lost big. The bankers knew about the land that had been sold; they also knew about the rumors of money borrowed from disreputable sources, the kind that charged usurious interest rates and resorted to threats when payments didn't materialize. They all shook their heads over their childhood friend's downfall.

At the historic downtown diner, Cubiak joined a table of the regulars. When he sat down, the eight men looked up from their half-eaten burgers and plates of liver and onions and fried perch and greeted him warmly. Then he mentioned Tom Fadim's name, and they lowered their gaze. After a moment, the man at the head of the table spoke for all of them. "Tom's messed up bad. He's put the touch on me more than once, the other guys too. We go back a long way, and I tried to keep the faith with him, but after a while I knew I could kiss the money good-bye. It's too bad but him and me aren't friends no more."

When the spokesman finished, his companions bobbed their heads in agreement.

In her lucid moments, Florence must have known something of her grandson's problems; her reference to staying away from the table had nothing to do with gluttony as Cubiak had first surmised. She had been referring to the blackjack table where he incurred most of his losses. But how much of the time was she lucid, and how many lies had Tom told her? the sheriff wondered.

From the restaurant, Cubiak headed up the peninsula. It was a beautiful evening but all he could think of was Florence Fadim sitting at her window. The elderly woman believed she owned both the farmstead and the surrounding fields, some three hundred acres in all. The family farm had once been a prosperous concern, but now it was little more than a memory that fell like a shadow across the vacant buildings, the overgrown pasture, and the lush, sprawling fields. She took pride in the heritage of the land that had come down through generations of her late husband's hardworking ancestors and been entrusted to her. She believed that Stanley Smolinsky rented the fields. She didn't know that Tom had sold the property to the neighboring farmer. She didn't realize that because of her grandson's misdeeds, she was fast running out of options.

How low would a man go to save his own skin? Cubiak wondered as he drove north.

On a hunch, he called Justin St. James, a former reporter for the *Door County Herald*. Several years ago Cubiak had given the fledgling journalist an exclusive about a local philanthropist whose misdeed left three innocent boys dead. The story catapulted St. James to the big time and the two had stayed in touch. Without mentioning specific details, Cubiak filled him in on what Melk and Sage had been up to and asked if he thought there was enough material for a book.

"Are you kidding? Publishers love stories about medical scandals. The more appalling the better. With documentation, the author can write his own ticket," he said.

Maybe that was Kiel's game plan. She would write an exposé about the nefarious physicians. And maybe her partner in crime wasn't the financially solvent executive assistant Noreen Klyasheff but her own father, a man desperate for money.

THE INTRUDERS

18

At a few minutes past eight that evening, Cubiak picked up Bathard. The elderly doctor had jettisoned his cane and looked jaunty as he made his way to the jeep. As requested, he wore a black raincoat. He also carried his black medical bag.

"I may as well try to check Florence's vitals as long as we're out there," he said by way of explanation. "If she'll let me," he added, as Cubiak opened the passenger door.

If Bathard was surprised to see Rowe in the rear, he didn't let on.

"Michael," he said, nodding to his fellow passenger. "I see you are comporting yourself admirably these days. You are in good health, I hope."

"Yes, sir," Rowe said and grinned. This was the physician who had stuck a needle into his backside more times than he cared to remember when he was growing up. "Just fine, Doc, thanks."

Their easy chatter made Cubiak nostalgic for his former partner Malcolm and the Chicago friends he had left behind when he moved to Door County. He had lived on the peninsula for more than a decade, but there were few people he could talk to with that kind of familiarity. A large percentage of the locals were from families that had been in Door County for generations, and to them he was still a newcomer.

Cate shared in the old-timers' legacy by virtue of the many summers she had spent here as a child, the niece of the well-loved sheriff Dutch Schumacher and her claim to The Wood, the estate her wealthy grandfather had built in the previous century. Some of her heritage would pass naturally to Joey, and for that Cubiak was grateful.

Bathard cleared his throat, a signal that he was waiting for the sheriff to explain what the evening held in store.

They were headed to the Fadim farm. That much, he had told them both earlier. He had even called it by that name, which he knew was false.

"You've both seen the collage on the barn wall. There's a good possibility that whoever is responsible for it will want to retrieve the material and do it soon. I'm counting on the intruder to return this evening. Chances are they've got the farmstead under watch, and if so, they will see me and Bathard arrive and enter the house together."

"What about me?" Rowe said.

"I'll drop you off a quarter mile down the road. From there, you'll walk toward the farm. Stay away from the road and circle up through the woods behind the barn. I want you in the trees but someplace where you can get to the barn fast."

"I got a good idea where that'd be," the deputy said.

"Once you're in position, text me."

Cubiak touched Bathard's arm. "That's when you come in."

"Meaning what? Am I to participate in a covert operation?" He was teasing but there was a hint of excitement in his voice.

"Something like that. After I hear from Mike, you'll leave the house wearing my hat and jacket and drive off in the jeep. We're about the same height and weight, so anyone watching will think that I've left and that you're still in the house with Mrs. Fadim."

"Which means they won't come in."

"Exactly. Once you're gone, I'll turn off her phone, so there's no chance that she'll get or make any calls while this is going on. She's not always lucid, but we can't take a chance that she knows more than she's let on. I don't want her inadvertently spoiling things."

"Then what?" Rowe said.

"While Bathard is heading out the front door and driving away, I'll sneak into the barn."

"To wait for the intruder."

"That's it. If I'm right, the trespasser will think the coast is clear and take a chance on getting in under cover of night. Meanwhile you'll be in the woods, ready to come in if I need you."

Bathard turned toward the sheriff. "Where am I supposed to go with the jeep? You don't want me to drive all the way back to town, do you?"

"Stanley Smolinsky owns the farm just to the east. You can pull in there and park behind the house. I talked to him earlier and he's expecting you."

Mrs. Fadim was dozing in her chair when Cubiak and Bathard walked into the living room.

"What a pleasant surprise. You're just in time for tea," she said.

She had a tenuous hold on time, and with the curtains closed, she apparently thought that they had stopped by for a late afternoon visit.

Cubiak took his cue and retired to the kitchen. By now he knew the ritual. Her favorite teapot with the matching cups, the platter of cookies, even the tray she preferred. He set everything out, and as he waited for the water to boil, he disabled the wall phone.

From the other room, he heard Bathard talking to the elderly woman. The doctor sounded cheerful going through his list of questions. How long had it been since he had taken a blood pressure reading? Or checked a patient's pulse? Cubiak wondered.

When the sheriff reappeared with the refreshments, Bathard was holding his finger out in front of Mrs. Fadim's face and asking her to follow the movement with her eyes.

"Excellent," he said, and she beamed.

They were finishing the tea when the sheriff felt the phone vibrate in his pocket. It was a text from Rowe. *All set.*

After Cubiak carried the tray back to the kitchen, he and Bathard spent another ten minutes saying good-bye to Mrs. Fadim. She clutched their hands and begged them to stay.

"Just a bit longer, gentlemen. Surely you can spare me a little more time," she said.

Against Cubiak's better judgment, they lingered. Knowing the full extent of her circumstances, he found it hard to leave her. The dreadful reality that Tom Fadim had fashioned would collapse on her soon enough. If dallying for a few extra moments would lighten her load even briefly, then he would take the chance.

Finally, in a gallant gesture, Bathard lifted Florence's veined hand to his lips and bowed. It was a finale enough for her. Delighted, she waved the two men out of the room.

In the hall they stood out of her line of sight and prepared. Cubiak handed his jacket to Bathard. As the coroner put it on, the sheriff slipped into the doctor's dark coat.

Under cover of night they left. Bathard walked to the jeep, while Cubiak ducked low and slipped along the front of the house. By the time the coroner pulled away, the sheriff was hidden in the thicket of trees along the side. The pine scent teared his eyes, and the soft needles whisked his face and hands. He imagined droplets of resin dotting Bathard's coat like sequins. Nothing to be done about that now. From the rear porch he paused to look across the yard at the barn. There was no cover in the open space between the house and the dim hulk, but during the times he had spent in Mrs. Fadim's kitchen waiting for the kettle to boil, he had studied the yard and knew its obstacles well. Guided by instinct and memory, he made his way to the rear of the barn without incident. Once there, he let his hands play lightly over the rough surface until he reached the double doors. In quick order, he loosened the wire and slipped inside.

The dank aroma of the interior was familiar, but the cold surprised him. There was more dust than he remembered, and he swallowed a cough as he tried to get his bearings. He didn't dare use a light. The last time he was in the barn, the middle aisle was clear. Rowe and the surveillance team hadn't seen anyone enter the building, but there was no guarantee that the intruder hadn't snuck in and booby-trapped the path. As he moved forward, he held out one arm and swung it back and forth as he slowly crept through the dark interior. Finally, his fingers grazed against the rough wood of the far wall.

The soft thump of his hand against the wood was no louder than the skitter of a mouse, but had it been enough to alert someone hiding in the dark to his presence? He held his breath and listened. Outside, a soft wind had come up, but the silence inside the barn seemed deep and eternal. He waited several seconds. Then he exhaled and felt for the cut-out door. When he found it, he pushed it open and stepped through. At the last moment he remembered to duck but he still grazed the top of his head against the rough frame.

The room was void of light. Even allowing for his eyes to adjust, he couldn't see anything. It was cold like the rest of the barn, and the smell of coffee had dissipated. Only the familiar faint scent of hay remained.

Relying on luck and memory, Cubiak stole to the corner where the bales had been haphazardly piled. Careful not to dislodge them, he slipped behind the artificial hedge and lowered himself to the wooden floor. There wasn't enough room to stretch out his legs, so he sat with his back to the wall, his feet flat, and his knees bent. He had silenced his phone before he left the house, but once settled, he dared a quick check of the time. It was 9:17. He snugged the black raincoat around his chest and waited.

The sheriff was certain that Linda Kiel had created the collage. She had had three months to study the files from the Northern Hospital for the Insane and to figure out, even superficially, what Melk had been doing. She had to retrieve the material from the barn because she needed it for the book he was convinced she planned to write. Not one that sings the praises of Melk and the IPM but one that portrays the physician as a monster and broadcasts his unscrupulous and heartless methods to the world. How many people in addition to George Wilcox had she reached through her ads? She had her family's story to tell about Margaret. Perhaps all she needed was another five or six to round out the tale. She had plenty of graphic material to supplement the details: Melk's charts and research notes and the old photos, the letters and the faded black-and-white images of the children whose parents had been promised cures and instead been left with nothing but guilt, shame, and anger. Even a hack would be able to cobble together a decent book out of all that incendiary material, but Cubiak had read enough of Kiel's work to know she was capable of better. On one deft stop in Cleona, the struggling journalist had stumbled onto fodder for a best seller and the path to literary stardom.

Cubiak flexed his fingers. His hands were numb and his feet had lost feeling as well. He tipped forward and shifted to his knees, careful not to dislodge the top layer of bales. Using the wall for support, he stood. As quietly as he could, he moved his arms and marched in place until his extremities tingled in protest. He had to stay limber. What good was he if he couldn't move when Kiel arrived?

Hours passed. He struggled to stay awake and alert. He had deliberately not brought any coffee because he knew the aroma would give him away. Cate had got him drinking tea, but Earl Grey, his favorite, wouldn't have worked either. She had a shelf full of teas. If he had been thinking ahead, he would have asked her to recommend one that would go undetected and brewed enough to fill a travel mug. Hot tea would do double duty; it would keep him focused and warm.

A rumble of thunder rattled the windows, and a sudden gust of wind whistled around the corner of the barn. Within minutes, rain and hail pelted the walls with the fury of a giant hurtling rocks against the building. Cubiak wondered how Rowe was doing and if the shift in weather would lure Kiel to the farm or keep her away.

The sheriff hadn't done this kind of surveillance in years and was beginning to regret the plan. He and Rowe couldn't stay in place indefinitely. Cubiak was about to check the time again when a solitary click penetrated the noise of the storm. He listened hard. The sound could have been made by a loose wire slapping against the building, but given the wind, it would keep repeating. And it did not. The sound could also have been made by a lock snapping open. Cubiak shifted into a kneeling position. Moments passed and he heard a different noise. It was close and familiar. It was the scrape of wood against wood as the cut-out door was pushed open.

A bright white light flashed around the room and hit the wall several inches above the sheriff's head. Then it swung around, bouncing from floor to rooftop and then from one side to the other. Finally, the light landed on the collage and stopped.

Hurried footsteps moved through the dark. Too many footsteps, Cubiak thought. He stayed low, still not willing to show himself. Something wasn't right.

A hushed conversation broke the silence. Cubiak strained to identify the voices, but he was too far away.

One thing was clear: two people had entered the room. The sheriff assumed one was Linda Kiel, but who was the other?

Cubiak peered over the top of the bales and watched the intruders. The two were a matched set: both of them average height, slender, and dressed in black, like midnight raiders. They wore gloves and had pulled their hoods up over their heads, hiding their hair and keeping their features in shadow.

The duo stood with their backs toward him, murmuring and gesticulating at the collage as they conferred. Their headlamps followed their gestures, moving in a wild profusion that created an odd strobe-light effect.

When they finished their secretive exchange, they moved to opposite ends of the display and settled into the task at hand. Using short metal files, they pried the tacks from the rough boards and dismantled the collage piece by piece, pulling off the bits of string and lifting the sheets of paper from the wall. At first, they worked slowly, but as they grew accustomed to the routine, their pace quickened. Although they were careful not to tear any of the photos and documents, they paid little attention to them and dropped them in loose piles on the floor.

They cleared away the two end sections in about ten minutes and moved in toward the middle. The sheriff had to act soon. Having expected Linda Kiel to come on her own, he hadn't anticipated having to deal with two people.

The low, crude door was the only way out of the room. That meant Cubiak needed to get between the intruders and the exit before they spotted him. To nab both of the interlopers, he had to wait until they reached the center of the collage and were standing alongside each other. Otherwise, he would be able to grab only one while the other did an end run and sprinted away out of his reach.

The hard, uneven floor pressed uncomfortably against Cubiak's knees, and the tight hiding spot clamped his arms against his torso. The storm had died down, and he wasn't sure if he could move into position without alerting the two to his presence.

Just as they reached the middle of the montage and stood nearly shoulder to shoulder, the squall started up again. Rain slammed the roof and south wall with a staccato fury. The noise was loud enough to mask any subtle sounds Cubiak would make. Gingerly, he pushed up from the floor and rubbed his sore knees and tingling arms. As he did so, he watched the two for any sign that they were aware of his movements, but they remained oblivious.

The sheriff was eager to grab the trespassers, but he forced himself to wait. The fragile documents littered the floor. A scuffle would damage the material irreparably. The two had come to retrieve the documents; there had to be a next step.

Finally, the wall was bare.

The mystery intruders high-fived each other. Then they quickly gathered the documents and stuffed them into two large brown envelopes.

When they were finished, Cubiak stepped out from behind the barricade and advanced toward them.

"Party's over," he said, as he grabbed the unsuspecting intruders by an arm.

The two were surprisingly strong and tried to yank free but he kept his grip tight.

Startled, they both yelled at the same time. "What the fuck!" and "Shit, who are you?"

They spoke in the voices of young men. Cubiak spun them around and looked at their stunned faces. Teenage punks.

"I'm the sheriff and you're trespassing."

The one on the right sniggered. "The fuck we are, we got permission to be here."

"From who?"

"The owner."

The other teen kicked at his partner. "Shut up."

"And who would that be?" Cubiak said, ignoring the interruption.

The boys grew sullen. One was pimply faced; the other sported a scraggly soul patch under a thin lower lip.

"Okay, then, let's try another question. Who sent you here?" the sheriff said.

"We ain't doing nothing wrong." The one with the patch snarled the response.

"Besides trespassing? How about breaking and entering and burglary? I gather that the material you were removing from the wall doesn't belong to either of you," Cubiak said and glanced toward the brown envelopes they were holding.

They looked away.

He nudged the boys against the wall and frisked them with one hand. They were trembling. "Sit down."

They slid to the floor.

"You can make this easier on yourself and tell me the whole story now. Or you can spend a night in jail and wait until the morning to talk."

The teens exchanged furtive glances.

"I'll give you a few minutes to decide how you want to proceed."

He walked backward to the door. "It's the only way out," he reminded them and turned so that both his badge and his gun were caught in the glare of their headlamps. Wouldn't hurt to scare them a little, he thought.

While the two whispered back and forth, he texted Rowe: *Come now.* Then to Bathard: *Bring jeep.*

The soul patch kid spoke first. "What do you want to know?"

"Let's start with who you are. You got any ID on you?"

"Yeah, but we need to reach into our pockets, and we don't want to get shot."

Cubiak almost laughed. These two had been watching too many TV cop shows. "Fine. One at a time. Then toss your credentials to me," he said.

They were from De Pere, both of them barely seventeen.

"Who sent you?"

"We don't know."

166

"What do you mean, you don't know? Someone hired you for a job or called in a favor. You're not out here for your health. Who was it?"

"We're getting paid, but we don't know by who," the second boy said.

"It was on Craigslist. Somebody needed someone to come out to the farm and get this shit off the wall. We got fifty dollars on PayPal upfront and another fifty when we're done."

"There was a name on the account?"

"A company name, something LLC. It sounded legit."

The stupidity of it infuriated Cubiak. "You came all the way out here in the middle of the night not knowing what the hell you were getting into?"

"I guess, something like that," the second boy said.

"There could have been a lunatic killer waiting for you. Didn't that ever occur to you?"

The boys' bravado melted away.

"We needed the money." They spoke in unison, nearly choking on the words.

"Yeah, well, next time ask yourselves what's more valuable, your lives or a few bucks."

The intruders stared at the floor.

Cubiak shook his head. "Try thinking first," he said. When he went on, his tone softened, and he became more conciliatory.

"So what comes next?"

The boy with the patch took over again. "We're supposed to put the envelopes in a black garbage bag and leave it in the trash barrel at the tourist center outside Sturgeon Bay."

"When?"

"Anytime between three and four."

"In the morning?"

"Yeah."

"Good. That gives us plenty of time to get ready."

The rain had stopped, and the house was dark by the time Rowe and Bathard reached the barn. Cubiak gave them a quick rundown on what had happened and told them his plan for the rest of the night. There wasn't time to drive Bathard home, so the sheriff called Cate and asked if the coroner could sleep over.

"Of course. I'll get the guest room ready," she said before he was half-finished explaining the situation.

"I owe you," he said.

"Nonsense. Joey will be thrilled."

It was true, the retired doctor was the closest to a grandfather that the boy had. He would be delighted to see him at the breakfast table.

"I feel bad keeping you up so late. Are you okay?" Cubiak said to Bathard as they sped toward Jacksonport.

By the time the sheriff had left his friend and the jeep with Cate and was back on the road in his wife's car, the Big Dipper was high in the northern sky. He raced to catch up with Rowe and the teens. The three had headed out together from the Fadim farm, following the plan that Cubiak had hatched in the barn. They were driving toward the justice center outside Sturgeon Bay in the rusty VW the kids had driven from De Pere. The boys sat up front, and Rowe squeezed into the back, holding a black garbage bag stuffed with old newspapers from Mrs. Fadim's back porch. The material that the intruders had removed from the wall was safely tucked into a red canvas bag on the floor behind the driver's seat in Cate's car. The sheriff was taking no chances on being recognized.

At twenty minutes past three, Cubiak pulled into the parking lot behind his office. The others were waiting.

"What were your exact instructions about tonight?" he asked the boys.

"We already told you."

"I want to hear it again."

"Like we said, we were told to get to the farm after midnight and take the stuff off the barn wall. When we were done we were supposed to put everything into a black plastic bag and head toward town and dump it in the trash barrel at the tourist center."

"Then what?"

"That's it. After that, we were supposed to head back to De Pere."

"How were you supposed to be paid for finishing the job?"

"The directions said that the rest of the money would be in a plastic bucket by the sign for the turnoff to the airport."

Trusting souls, Cubiak thought. "What if it wasn't there? What would you do then?"

The boys exchanged anxious glances.

"Go ahead, show him," the one with the patch of chin hair said.

The second boy pulled a folded piece of white paper from the front pocket of his jeans. "I kept this. It looked important and I figured we'd hold onto it. You know, like for insurance."

Like so many of the pages in the collage, the sheet was covered with numbers arranged in neat columns, probably another record of test results. The faded initials L.M. were barely visible in the bottom left corner. Cubiak regarded the boys. Out of all the documents on the wall, they had had the dumb luck to hold back one of the most incriminating pieces.

"I'll keep this," he said. "Otherwise you stick to the plan exactly."

"You're letting us go?" the first kid asked. His eyes opened wide with surprise.

"Not quite. Deputy Rowe will be waiting for you at the airport road."

"You mean that you're arresting us? We didn't . . ."

Cubiak cut him off. "For now, you're not under arrest. Let's just say I'm playing it safe. We don't have a lot of time now, and I'll probably need to talk to you again, so the closer you are the better." He didn't want to tell them that he was making sure they weren't followed on their way to De Pere and that he didn't want them to meet with an accident on the drive back home.

The bearded boy looked at Rowe. "Why doesn't he just come with us?"

"Because if there's a chase, he wouldn't catch anything in that car of yours."

"Oh." The teen sounded insulted.

"When you get to the tourist center, I'll be waiting at the gas station across the highway. There's always a row of cars parked along the west edge of the lot, and I'll blend right in."

Cubiak turned to Rowe. "Mike, you go on ahead now, using back roads only."

"Got it."

After the deputy left, the sheriff regarded the two adolescents again.

"Don't even think about skipping out after you've made the drop. Right now I could arrest you for trespassing. But try to get away and I'll charge you both as accomplices in what may well be a murder case."

The color drained from the teens' faces. The sheriff gave them a moment to come to terms with what he had said before he spoke again.

"Well, what's it going to be?"

Without hesitating, they blurted out their answer together.

"We follow orders."

"We do as you say."

"You got that right."

Cubiak checked his watch. "It's three fifty-four. I'm leaving now. You wait another twenty minutes and then follow."

"Yes, sir," they said in unison.

The sheriff held out his hand. Uncertain how to respond, the boys hesitated. Finally, they realized it was gesture of goodwill. First one and then the other shook Cubiak's hand.

THE PICKUP

19

At four o'clock on Saturday morning, Sturgeon Bay was deserted. The die-hard fishermen were already at the harbors prepping their boats, and anyone working the third shift at the hospital or shipyards was on the job. Everyone else was either home in bed or half-asleep in front of a television or computer screen. Despite the empty roads, the sheriff followed a roundabout route to the gas station. When he was half a block away, he turned off the headlights and bumped across the uneven terrain to the station's paved surface, where he wedged Cate's orange hybrid into the row of parked cars and cut the engine. The station was in dark shadow. Across the road, a solitary streetlight lit the entrance to the tourist center. The building was set back, with a small lot in front. There were two barrels on each side, one for trash and one for recyclables.

Fifteen minutes after Cubiak settled into place, the roar of a car engine rattled the predawn silence. The sheriff recognized the sound. It was the boys' old auto, in need of a new muffler. The teens pulled into the center, and with the engine running, one of them jumped out and tossed the black garbage bag into the trash barrel. He wore his hood up, and from where Cubiak sat, it was impossible to know which boy was behind the wheel and which was in charge of the bag. Don't stop. Don't look this way, the sheriff thought.

As if he had heard the directive, the hooded figure dove back into the car, and the driver peeled away. Within moments, the taillights disappeared into the darkness, dragging the roar behind until the obnoxious noise faded away. Silence again. Five minutes later, Rowe sent a two-word text: *They're here.*

Cate's compact car did not accommodate Cubiak's six-foot frame well. He had pushed the driver's seat back as far as possible and still felt cramped. To keep limber, he rubbed his knees and tried flexing his arms toward the steering column. He wished for a cup of coffee and settled for a sip of warm, stale water from the bottle his wife kept in the console. He opened the window and then closed it against the mosquitoes that buzzed his face and neck. He trained his eyes on the tourist center and waited.

He had been fooled earlier that night when the two boys showed up at the barn to retrieve the material on the wall. This time he was confident that Linda Kiel would come to claim her prize. Would she drive, or sneak in by foot from behind the center? For all he knew, she might ride up on a bicycle or even on horseback.

One hour went by. No one. Nothing.

Cubiak jolted awake. Damn. He'd dozed off. Judging by his watch, twenty minutes had passed since he had last looked across the road. Had he missed Kiel? He scrubbed his face and rocked his head from side to side. His neck was stiff. His left shoulder had knotted tight.

He had two options: he could either maintain the vigil and hope he hadn't slept through the pickup, or he could check the trash barrel for the bag and risk being seen and ruining the setup. Rock and hard place.

He decided to stay put for another hour. By then it would be light and unlikely that Kiel would show. Still, he felt uneasy. Had he botched the job or was there a reason for the delay? Perhaps it was part of her plan. Or something had gone wrong on her end.

At 5:38, a dusty red car pulled up near the tourist center. Cubiak sat up, ready to spring from his seat. The car stopped and a woman got out from the driver's side. She wore jeans, a red sweatshirt, and a yellow cap that was pulled down to her ears. She was too short to be Kiel, but something about her was vaguely familiar. He waited for her to approach the trash barrel. Instead, she walked to the center, unlocked the door, and went inside.

That's it, Cubiak thought. One of the employees had come in early, probably needed to catch up on paperwork. He was about to leave when the woman stepped back onto the small porch. She carried a broom and made a few perfunctory swipes across the floor. Her attention was focused on the pickup truck that approached from the direction of town. As soon as it passed, she propped the broom against the building and stepped down into the driveway.

Head up and eyes on the highway, she hurried toward the trash barrel. Cubiak opened the car door and slipped out. She pulled the bag from the metal can and carried it to the car. As soon as she turned her back, he bolted across the road. By the time he reached her, the trunk was open and she was about to toss the bag in.

"I'll take that," the sheriff said.

The woman uttered a cry of dismay and turned around.

It was Francisca Delgado.

You!" Cubiak said, unable to suppress his surprise. "What are you doing here?"

"I clean," she said and glanced back at the building.

"No, I mean what are you doing with this?" He pointed to the bag. "You need to tell me. Everything!" he said, nearly shouting.

Francisca pressed her mouth shut. She was trembling.

"I can't help you unless you talk to me." He tried to keep his voice calm and steady. "Do you understand?"

She shivered. "Yes," she said quietly.

Another car approached from town. They were too conspicuous standing behind the car with the trunk open. "What time does everyone show up for work?"

"I don't know—I think ten. I am not here when they come."

"Can we go inside?" he asked.

She hesitated and then closed the trunk and led him up the porch steps and into the center. Except for a corner office, the interior was one large room. A counter divided the space in half. Three desks were crowded together on one side, and on the other side two white plastic molded chairs stood along a wall, amid racks of colorful brochures and tourist literature.

Cubiak shifted the chairs so they faced each other. He waited for Francisca to sit and then he followed suit.

The sheriff knew he shouldn't have been surprised to find her working at the center. Many Door County residents put in long hours and took on more than one job during the summer season. The old adage about making hay while the sun shines didn't apply just to farmers. Francisca was young enough to handle a heavy workload for several months of the year. People like her—like his mother, who had cleaned office buildings in the Loop for decades—were invisible to their employers. They sometimes saw and heard more than their bosses realized.

"You work here part time?" he asked.

"Sí. Yes. For two years. It is an easy job."

"You work other places, too, besides the Green Arbor Lodge?"

"Yes."

He took a stab in the dark. "Perhaps at the Institute for Progressive Medicine?"

Francisca shook her head. "Not there. It is too big. They have a regular crew. No part-time help."

"Where are these other places? Tell me."

She looked puzzled. Why did this matter? "I clean here and for people at their homes. Some, one day a week. Some, every two weeks. Usually on Saturdays and one place on Sunday. One very big house, I help my friend at the beginning of summer and again at the end. We 'open' and 'close,'" she said, with a singsong lilt.

"Do you clean for any of the doctors who work at the institute? At their homes, not at their offices?"

"I clean for three of them." She mentioned their names; the first two meant nothing to Cubiak, but the third stopped him. Harlan Sage.

"How long have you been working for Doctor Sage?"

"Three years, maybe a little longer."

"You have the code to his house."

She frowned. "Of course. Usually he isn't home when I come, and I must get inside."

"When was the last time you were there?"

A touch of pink tinged her cheeks. "Yesterday." She balled her hands into fists. "I did not clean after—" She hesitated. "You understand?"

"Yes."

"It is more than a person like me can do. There are people trained to do that."

"I know. But why were you there yesterday?"

"The real estate agent called and asked me to come in. She said she wanted the house 'polished' before she put it on the market."

That's awfully quick, Cubiak thought. Too quick.

"Do you remember the name of the woman who called you?"

Francisca shook her head. "No. I forgot to ask. I didn't want to go in there. I was nervous."

"Was she at the house when you got there?"

"No." Francisca avoided his glance.

"Was anyone else there?"

The question hung in the air.

Francisca hugged herself and slowly rocked back and forth.

"Someone was there. You need to tell me who."

"The journalist. I don't know her name."

"The young woman you saw at the lodge, the one who told you and Lupita to leave?"

"Yes. It was her. She opened the door for me. I didn't understand what she was doing in the doctor's house, but she didn't seem surprised to see me."

Because she was the woman who pretended to be the realtor, Cubiak realized. She was the one who lured Francisca to Sage's house under false pretenses.

"Tell me what happened."

Francisca sat up and looked at him. Her eyes were moist. She took a deep breath and then exhaled slowly.

"At first nothing. She let me in and said she'd come for some papers, that she had permission from the institute. When I asked where the real estate lady was, she said she didn't know but that the woman would be back soon and not to worry. Then she went into Doctor Sage's office, and I went to the kitchen to start cleaning. Someone had made coffee and left the cups in the sink, so there was a little bit of work to do there. I wiped the stove and counters and swept the floor. I dusted all the downstairs rooms and then started to vacuum. It seemed useless because everything was so clean. I was vacuuming the rug in the front hall when she came out of the office. She pulled the plug and told me to come with her, that she had something to show me."

Francisca twisted her hands and Cubiak remembered how she had knotted the handkerchief the first time he had talked with her.

"I was scared. I wasn't sure she was supposed to be there, and I started to think that maybe I shouldn't be there either. She took me by the elbow and led me to the office. There weren't any papers anywhere, nothing but a photo on the desk. It was the same picture that I saw on the wall at the conference, but bigger. Not bigger like this"—she held out her hands—"but bigger because it showed the man standing behind my brother. He was very young, very tall, and he was smiling. He didn't look like someone who would hurt anyone."

"Did you recognize him?"

"No. I never saw him before. I asked her if she knew who he was, and she said it was Leonard Melk. I didn't know who that was. She said Doctor Melk had stolen my brother because he needed him for his research. She said he'd taken many other children, and adults, too. Some who had Down syndrome and some who had different diseases. Why did he do these terrible things? I asked her. She said that he was trying to find cures for many bad diseases. When I told her the doctor who took Miguel promised my parents that he knew how to cure Down syndrome and that he would bring him back when he was healthy again, she laughed. It was a lie, she said. It was the same lie he told many other people."

Francisca looked past Cubiak at the rows of colorful brochures advertising wine tastings and kayak tours, boat rides, and gourmet restaurants. The wall was filled with literature that promised fun days and romantic nights in Door County. "A good doctor does not lie to people. He does not steal their children. This man was a monster," she said.

Cubiak remembered what Bathard had said about the Hippocratic oath and those who abused it.

"Did you ask her if she knew what had happened to Miguel?"

"Yes, of course. I had to, even though I was frightened by what she might say. For a long time, I had believed that my brother was dead"— she shuddered and inhaled sharply—"and I had come to accept this as God's will, but I had to know, didn't I?"

Cubiak nodded.

"She told me that Miguel had not been cured. She told me that people like Miguel had knots in their brains. She said that the doctor gave him different medicines and then took pictures of his brain to see if any of the drugs made the tangles go away."

A small, sad smile flitted across Francisca's face. "I am not an educated woman, Sheriff, but I am not stupid either. I know that if someone discovered a cure for the Down syndrome, it would be very big news. There would be many stories in the newspapers and on the television. So I did not expect to hear that my little brother had been freed from his affliction. But I did not think that someone would do experiments on him. I asked her if Miguel was hurt, and she said no. She said he was alive, that he still had the disease, but that he was okay."

Francisca's face was wet with tears. "When I asked her if she knew where he was, she said she did. She said he was not very far away, and that if I brought the black bag to her, she would take me to see him."

"Are you supposed to meet her and give her the bag?"

"No. No. She told me I should bring the bag to Doctor Sage's house and leave it on the closet floor in his office."

"When?"

"Today, after two o'clock but before three. She said it wouldn't be a problem if anyone else showed up because we both had reasons to be there."

And you both know the alarm code, Cubiak thought.

"Did she tell you to wait there for her?"

Francisca shook her head. "She said I should leave and call her when I was back on the highway."

"And your brother? When will she take you to see him?"

"She didn't say a date, but she promised that she would keep her word. She said I had to trust her."

"Do you?"

Francisca looked down at the floor and then back up at him. "Yes, of course. I have no choice." Her words were full of hope, but her eyes were clouded with doubt.

Cubiak left Francisca at the tourist center with her broom and dusters. He also left her with the decoy black garbage bag. He didn't tell her that the bag with the genuine material was in his car across the road and the one in the trunk of her car was crammed with old newspapers. For his plan to work, she had to believe she was transporting the documents that would lead her to her brother.

From Cate's car, he called Rowe with the latest developments.

"Sounds like a game of cat and mouse. Which are we?" the deputy asked.

Cubiak laughed and told Rowe to put the boys' old car in the airport lot—somewhere discreet, if possible—and then drive them back to the station.

"You want me to book them?"

"I want you to make them comfortable and assure them they are not under arrest. This is for their protection. Don't ask, because I can't explain. It's just a feeling I've got."

"Right." Rowe had learned to rely on the sheriff's instincts.

"Then get over here to the center. Drive your own car and keep tabs on Francisca. Make sure she gets to Sage's place safely and that when she leaves she gets back home without incident." He didn't elaborate.

"How long should I hang around there?"

"Until you hear from me."

"Where are you going to be?"

"At Sage's house. I'm heading there now."

The sheriff was exhausted and hungry. He had been awake all night and hadn't eaten since Friday lunch. He bought a muffin and coffee at the bakery on the edge of town and headed to Brussels. He didn't trust Linda Kiel. He didn't know if she was working alone or had an accomplice, and he figured the best way to outsmart her was to be on the scene hours before Francisca arrived with the fake goods.

A mile from the house, he turned down a narrow lane that he had spotted his last time out that way. Twenty yards in, he abandoned the car in a thicket of bushes and started hiking to the house.

Francisca had told him that there were alarm pads on both the front and the rear doors. Using the code she had given him, Cubiak came through the back entrance and into the kitchen. He needed more coffee but was too tired to brew any and knew the aroma would linger and give him away.

He set his phone alarm to ring in one hour. Careful to make sure he couldn't be seen from the front hall, he stretched out on the living room sofa. The sleep that came was restless, disturbed by the images of children standing in long rows beside tiny beds. They were barefoot and wore ragged hospital gowns, their eyes wide with fear and their faces distorted in silent screams.

At ten, he jolted awake. If Kiel kept to the plan, she wouldn't show up for another four hours. But Cubiak suspected that she had her own timetable. He went upstairs to the guest bedroom and angled a chair toward the window so he could sit and have a sideways view of the entrance.

He didn't have to wait long before the journalist's black car turned in to the driveway. Cubiak shoved aside his fatigue and went on full alert. He leaned toward the window as far as he dared, but the sun's reflection on the windshield made it impossible to see inside. The car slowed but didn't stop. Instead it continued past the house. There was no question that Kiel was behind the wheel. She stopped out back, hiding the car where Francisca wouldn't see it. The door slammed, and a few moments later the alarm chimed, signaling the all clear for her to enter. Then it chimed again, indicating that she had reset the alarm, just as he had done earlier.

Cubiak pictured her walking through the kitchen on her way to the rest of the house and was doubly grateful that he hadn't bothered with coffee or even had a drink of water. He had come to appreciate Kiel's attention to details. She would notice a hair out of place on a poodle.

For a slight young woman, she had a heavy step, and he had no trouble following her progress as she moved from one room to another. She walked fast, like someone taking a cursory glance around the premises. Then he heard the sound of drawers being opened and closed, papers being tossed on the floor. She was in Sage's office. What was she looking for? he wondered.

Moments passed.

"Ah!" Followed by a sharp laugh. The sound of victory. Then silence descended on the house, and the two waited.

Kiel stayed on the first floor, perhaps sitting in the dead doctor's chair. Cubiak remained upstairs and wondered what would happen next.

A few minutes before two, Kiel's phone rang, playing a silly girlish tune. Apparently she hadn't expected the call.

"What?" Her voice was loud and harsh. "Don't be so fucking greedy. You'll get the rest when I get my advance."

By then the afternoon sun had reached the guest bedroom window and raised the temperature beyond the point of discomfort.

At 2:20, Kiel's phone jangled again. This time her response was sugary.

"Oh, good," she said. "Aren't you sweet to help me?" And then she added, "Of course, I will. I promised, didn't I?"

Ten minutes later, Francisca's car pulled in to the driveway. She stopped in front of the house and entered as she normally did. Cubiak strained to listen. He knew she was going straight to the office, but she walked so softly he had difficulty following her progress.

Then he heard the telltale squeak of the door to Sage's office.

"Buenos días," Kiel said, her voice heavy with sarcasm.

Cubiak jumped to his feet.

Francisca yelped in surprise, and the office door slammed shut.

As the sheriff raced down the stairs, he heard Kiel yelling inside.

"What is this shit? Where's my stuff?"

"I don't know!" It was a wail of truth.

Cubiak pounded on the door.

"Where is my brother?"

"Fuck your brother," Kiel said.

"Where is Miguel?"

Cubiak kicked the lock free and lunged into the office.

The trash bag had been ripped open and the newspapers strewn across the floor. Kiel had pinned Francisca to the wall. The journalist slapped her and raised her arm to take another swing when the sheriff grabbed her wrist and pulled her away.

Kiel swore and struggled to get free.

Francisca crumpled to the floor, sobbing.

The sheriff shoved the journalist into Sage's chair.

"I have your stuff," he said.

Kiel turned red with rage.

As he helped Francisca to her feet, a car pulled up outside.

Cubiak wasn't expecting anyone else and feared that Kiel's accomplice had arrived. He put a hand on her shoulder to keep her from bolting out of the chair. Then he kicked the battered door shut and stepped in front of Francisca to shield her from danger.

Footsteps came down the hall, and Rowe burst into the room with his gun drawn.

"We don't need that," Cubiak said.

The deputy holstered his weapon and took in the scene. The newspapers on the floor. Kiel in the chair. The frightened woman who peeked out from behind the sheriff.

"Thank goodness you're safe," he said, addressing Francisca. Then to Cubiak, he said, "Sorry, sir. She went home first, and I lost her when the bridge went up. She was already on the other side."

"It's okay," the sheriff said.

Three bridges connected the Door County peninsula to the mainland. More than once he had ordered them raised to keep a suspect from escaping. In a situation like today's he couldn't put them out of commission for hours without wreaking havoc with traffic. Rowe had had no choice but to take his chances tailing Francisca.

"I'm bringing Kiel in for questioning."

The journalist glared at him. "You've got nothing on me," she said.

Cubiak ignored her and told Rowe to follow with Francisca.

"We'll need a statement from you. Don't worry, you're not in any trouble," he said, motioning her out of the room.

Francisca looked at the sheriff with eyes rimmed red and full of fear. When she spoke, her voice was a whisper.

"My brother."

Cubiak rested a hand on her shoulder. Miguel's fate was not his concern, but he couldn't ignore Francisca's torment. He was sure that the missing girl Margaret had perished in the fire at the Northern Hospital for the Insane, but he had no idea what had happened to Francisca's brother. Kiel said Miguel was alive, but how would she know?

"I'll do everything I can to find him," he said. Or to learn what happened to him, he thought.

A STORY IN TWO PARTS

20

Late Saturday afternoon, a demure Linda Kiel faced Cubiak across the interview table. On the ride to the justice center, she had taken control of her rage, and now she sat with her hands folded primly on the shiny surface. After they arrived, she had asked for permission to use the restroom, and a few minutes later she emerged with her face scrubbed, her hair fluffed, and her blouse neatly tucked into her jeans. She had said yes to the offer of coffee although the cup remained untouched. She had rejected the suggestion that she needed legal counsel. An empty chair rested along the back wall should she change her mind and decide to call a lawyer.

Cubiak had read the journalist her rights. The recorder was running. Kiel spoke up immediately.

"I've done nothing wrong and want it on record that I have agreed to questioning of my own free will. I have nothing to hide." The statement was a polite echo of her earlier outburst.

She looked at Cubiak as if expecting him to contradict her. When he remained silent, she went on.

"I acknowledge using my great-grandmother's barn without her permission, but that hardly constitutes trespassing since I am included in her will as an heir to any and all of her property, including the barn and the land surrounding it."

Cubiak didn't react. He wondered what she would say when she learned that her father had sold her inheritance out from under her.

"I also acknowledge using an unconventional method of recovering the material from said barn, but there was nothing illegal about my actions. The material is mine. It was freely given to me by a Paul Osgood in the town of Cleona. I have every right to use it in any manner I wish."

"Perhaps you do," Cubiak said.

Her eyes flashed. "Then why am I here?"

"Two people are dead, and I'm trying to sort out the details."

She bristled. "I had nothing to do with any of that. You have no right to accuse me."

"I haven't accused you of anything. But tell me, what made you go all the way up to Cleona earlier this year, in March to be exact, where Leonard Melk, one of the deceased, had worked as a young physician? Wasn't the book you were writing about him nearly finished by then?"

She smiled. "It was. But I didn't go all the way up there, as you say, with the intention of poking into the doctor's past. He'd told me about his position at the mental hospital in Cleona. In fact, it's listed on his vitae. I had nothing to learn by going there," she said.

"Then why did you go if you weren't still researching the book?"

She laughed. "Oh, that. It was pure coincidence. I drove up there with my boyfriend, for his cousin's wedding. The party went on all hours on Saturday, and on Sunday he was too hungover to get out of bed. I didn't know any of the other guests and didn't have anything to do while he slept it off, so I drove out to the old hospital and looked around. I'd heard about the fire and didn't expect to find much of anything, but I thought I could absorb some local color, maybe a hint of how things used to be. I was about to leave when Osgood walked out of the woods and nearly scared me half to death."

"You didn't find his story odd, about Melk giving his father the records to hide from the authorities?"

Kiel didn't take the bait.

"Is that what he told you? The version I got had more to do with tidying up a messy office, so he could pass inspection," she said.

"You believed that?"

She shrugged. "Why not? To be honest, I didn't give a damn why Melk did what he did. I wanted to see the files. When I interviewed him for the book, he said he couldn't trust his memory when it came to discussing his early days as a doctor, and I hoped to glean an anecdote or two to fill out the first couple of chapters."

"And did you?"

"Yes. In fact, I did."

"Why put the material up on the barn wall?"

"The files were a mess. It really did look like he'd just thrown everything into a box, like he said. I needed to get it organized and started working on it at my place. But I didn't have enough room to spread out. I was trying to figure out where to go with it when I remembered the barn. When we were kids, Nana always let me and my cousins play there. She even gave us chalk so we could draw pictures on the walls. It seemed like the perfect space to use."

"Certainly a good hiding place," he said.

Kiel stiffened. "What are you insinuating?"

"Just stating the obvious." Cubiak took a sip from his coffee. "Tell me about Margaret."

"My father told me that you'd talked to him about her. So you know the story." The journalist was back under control.

"I want to hear your version."

She sighed and in a casual, off-hand fashion recited the details of Mrs. Fadim's sad family saga. Almost as if the past events had nothing to do with her, the writer repeated her great-grandmother's story about the crippled sister who disappeared and the doctor in the expensive car who took the girl away, promising a cure.

"How did you feel about Margaret?"

Kiel twitched. "To be honest, by the time I was in high school I was pretty fed up with the whole business. Growing up, I'd heard the story ad nauseam, and frankly I was tired of the shadow it cast over my existence. I wanted my own life, but Florence kept harping at all of us about how it was our responsibility to find her 'before it was too late.' Hell, it had been too late for years. Once the old lady's mind started to go, the situation got even worse. She hounded us endlessly. It got to the point where I wasn't even sure how much of the story was true or if it was true at all. I assume you've met my great-granny. She's hardly a woman with a firm grip on reality."

"Margaret looked a lot like you."

Kiel's gaze narrowed. "Really?"

"Your father mentioned it. He suggested that around the age of six—the age Margaret was when she disappeared—you, your birth mother, Lorene, and Margaret all bore a remarkable resemblance to each other."

"So?"

"So when you found her photo in the box and the medical records with the initials MS, you didn't speculate that maybe the subject was your missing great-aunt and that perhaps your great-grandmother's story was true?"

"Of course, I did. If I could prove that the letters MS stood for Margaret Stutzman, I'd have found my big story, something that would get me recognized by the national media."

"What happened?"

"Nothing. The more I considered the possibility, the more I realized it was wishful thinking, a flight of fancy on my part. There were dozens of initials on those papers. The letters MS could have stood for anyone. Maybe they weren't even actual initials. As for the photo, who knows for certain if it was a picture of Margaret? Lots of kids resemble each other. I came to the sad conclusion that I couldn't prove a thing." She paused. "I'm a journalist, Sheriff. Creative nonfiction doesn't interest me. I write stories that are based on fact."

"Like the glorified history of Leonard Melk and the IPM?"

Kiel blushed. "The book is a work-for-hire. It's different. I wasn't even going to use my name on it."

"You took the assignment for the money?"

She snorted. "Of course, I did. I'm not a trust fundie. I have bills to pay just like most everyone else." She glared at Cubiak. "The plumber doesn't work for free. Do you?"

"Why didn't you retrieve the material yourself? Why send the boys?"

She laughed again. "I see, the plot thickens. Sorry to disappoint you, but I had a deadline to meet, simple as that."

186

"And the midnight drop at the tourist center? Getting Francisca to pick up the bag for you? What was that all about?"

"I told you I had a deadline. Although as far as Francisca's concerned, I did have the ulterior motive of maybe mining her story about her brother . . . if I could locate him."

"You told her you knew where he was."

"I told her I *might* know how to find him. It's not my fault that she misunderstood."

"And who'd take the word of an immigrant cleaning woman over that of a Door County native?" Cubiak said.

Kiel gave a smug smile and reached for her coffee.

The sheriff grabbed the drink before she could. "Let me get you a fresh cup. Cream, no sugar, right?"

She grunted.

Cubiak took his time. He wanted her to sit and to wonder just how much he knew and how much of her story he believed. When he finally returned, she was at the one-way window trying to peer out.

He set two coffees down and waited for her to retake her chair.

"I thought we'd be finished by now," she said as the sheriff sat and nudged one of the cups toward her.

"Unless you have something to add, we're done with your version of events." He waited for her to speak up, but she remained silent. "Nothing? Okay. You see, I have a different scenario of how things went."

"Oh? Do tell." Kiel pretended to be bored, but he sensed an undercurrent of concern in her response.

"I think this is a two-part story. There's pre-Cleona and the discovery of Melk's medical records from the mental hospital. That's the period when you were busy writing the IPM history as presented by Melk and his colleagues. At the time you had two concerns: finish the assignment and get paid, nothing more. Then you drove up north for the wedding and accidentally stumbled on evidence of Melk's early research. Let's call it post-Cleona. From that point on, everything changed: your attitude toward Melk and your objectives both as a journalist and as a young woman personally affected by his devious actions. Follow me?"

Kiel didn't respond.

"You've pretty much stuck to the facts about the pre-Cleona segment, but after that your version veers away from the truth. Once Osgood gave you the box of files, it didn't take you long to figure out what you had. You knew that Melk hadn't stashed all that material in a file box because he wanted to tidy up his office for the state inspectors; he was hiding records of his radical research methods. The files documented the medical tests he'd conducted on scores of unsuspecting and often underage subjects without legitimate consent. And he was doing all that at a state-funded facility. Given the lack of oversight back then, his research may not have been illegal, but it certainly constituted questionable, unethical, and perhaps immoral behavior. If word got out, it was enough to get him fired, ruin his reputation, and perhaps even threaten his medical license. But you probably figured that out on the ride back to Sturgeon Bay."

Cubiak rested his elbows on the table and leaned in. "You must have gotten quite a headache trying to reconcile that Doctor Melk with the image of the good doctor that you were fabricating in the book."

Kiel remained resolute in her silence.

"Faced with the challenge of sorting through the mass of material, you moved to the barn with it. Piece by piece you put things together: the diseases, the tests, the subjects. Did you suspect you'd come across evidence that Margaret was one of the kids involved in the nefarious experiments, or did that come as a surprise?" Cubiak went on, not waiting for a response. "Because eventually you figured out that the initials MS represented your great-aunt. You may have doubted it at first, but finding her photo confirmed your suspicions." He raised a hand to forestall any objections.

"You're right that there were other initials, other photos—mostly of young children, all taken decades ago. You guessed that they'd all lived in Wisconsin, so you reprinted the photos in ads that you placed in dozens of local newspapers around the state, asking anyone who recognized the children to contact you."

Still Kiel didn't react.

"To shore up the exposé you intended to write, you needed corroboration, other stories of young polio victims, kids stolen away from their families with the promise of a cure. Don't bother denying it, because I've already talked to one person who responded to your ad, and I have the names of others as well."

The color faded from Kiel's face.

"Somehow your father got wind of what you were up to. Either you let it slip or he discovered the collage on the barn wall, maybe while he was checking for intruders at your great-grandmother's request. You had no choice but to tell him about the exposé you intended to write, about the notoriety you'd gain, and the big advance you assumed would come your way. Your father's a practical man. He figured Melk would sue you for libel and then where would you be? The doctor had no living relatives; he was the only obstacle. How convenient for you that he died when he did."

Kiel didn't flinch. She would be a good poker partner, the sheriff thought.

"I've done my homework, Linda. Two years ago you wrote an in-depth piece on defibrillators for a lay science publication. You knew that Melk had one, an older model that had been implanted nearly a decade ago and was up for replacement. If he'd gone in for the procedure, it's possible he might be alive today. For the piece, you interviewed several experts on the ways that an ICD, especially an older model, could be hacked. You had all the information you needed for your plan to work.

"Last Monday Melk was set to give his farewell speech at the conference. You knew him well enough to realize the strain he was already under when you went up to him, ostensibly to show him the cover of the new book. That's another lie, isn't it? I'm guessing you showed him Margaret's photo and a copy of the results of the tests he'd done using the blood he'd drawn from her. You told him that you knew about his experiments on children and were going to write a book about it. Taken together, the anxiety he felt at stepping down combined with your threat of revealing his nefarious past might have caused enough stress to trigger a heart attack. But then you moved closer to adjust his tie and to embrace him. To anyone who saw, it was a sweet gesture. In reality it was a death hug because you had preprogrammed your phone to send a malicious message to the defibrillator that momentarily reverse-engineered the device."

"Oh, come on, Sheriff. That's ridiculous."

"Is it? Then why break into Doctor Pardy's office looking for the device? Were you worried that she'd have it analyzed and discover the disruption?"

"You can't blame me for that. I wasn't even in town when her office was broken into."

"How do you know you weren't here? I haven't mentioned a date."

Kiel froze.

"You hit Melk with a triple whammy. You knew a younger and more robust person might survive such a hit, but you figured it would be too much for an old man like Leonard Melk. It appears that your assumption was correct because moments after you walked away from him, Melk collapsed. When Noreen Klyasheff got to him, he uttered a single word before he died. She thought he'd said *snow*. But maybe it was *no*—and maybe it was meant for you. 'No, don't ruin my name, don't destroy my reputation.'"

Kiel smiled at Cubiak, as if she had found his account entertaining. "It's an interesting theory, but I know as well as you that you can't prove any of this. In fact, all you're doing is providing more fodder for my exposé, the chapter on how I was held and unreasonably questioned by the county sheriff."

Cubiak raised an eyebrow, but otherwise he ignored the comment.

"Under normal circumstances, the situation wouldn't have been more than a tragic event. An elderly doctor suffers a fatal heart attack minutes before he was slated to give his farewell address to the conference. Like you said, anyone who was there would have attributed the attack to the stress of the moment or simply to his age. Sage would have taken over as head of the institute and that would have been the end of it.

"Unfortunately for you, I was at the lodge meeting a friend for lunch. If Noreen Klyasheff hadn't screamed, perhaps I wouldn't have known until later, if ever, what had happened." He paused. "Just as you wouldn't have known about Miguel, if Francisca hadn't screamed when she saw the photo on the wall."

A slight shift in Kiel's posture told the sheriff he was on target.

"The files from the Northern Hospital for the Insane only go as far as the early 1950s. You had no reason to suspect that Melk continued his unethical practices after the facility burned. After all, he never went back for the material. And once he'd established the Institute for Progressive Medicine, he had his reputation to protect. It would be reasonable to assume that his past was behind him, wouldn't it?"

Kiel didn't respond to the question.

"Journalists are curious by nature. They have to be to get their stories. So there we were, in case your memory has gotten foggy: Melk is lying on the floor dead, and another scream comes from down the hall. I leave to investigate, and you find an excuse to follow. What was it you told Rowe, that you needed to use the ladies' room? Under the circumstances, he couldn't refuse to let you leave, and there was no one he could ask to escort you. You were on your honor to return, which you did, but not before lingering long enough outside the Forest Room to hear the gist of Francisca's revelation. You'd been at the conference all morning, moving from one presentation to another. You'd probably seen the photo before, but it meant nothing. It was simply the picture of a young subject in a vitally important research project. The identity of the man standing behind the boy wasn't important. But Francisca's story changed all that. I'm guessing you'd seen the uncropped photo during one of your sessions with Doctor Sage, which means that both of you knew that Melk was the doctor standing behind Miguel."

Cubiak studied his notebook. The page was blank, but Kiel wouldn't know that. She would think he was checking his facts. He waited a moment and then went on.

"Melk's early modus operandi was clear: he sought out uneducated, immigrant families, people who didn't speak English and didn't know how or were too scared to contact the authorities. By the time the Northern Hospital for the Insane, the base of his operations, was destroyed, his target population had largely dwindled, and he needed a new source for his victims. After hearing what Francisca said, you realized what he'd been doing. You didn't have to connect the dots; from what you gleaned listening in at the door, the situation was obvious. Melk had found a ready supply of test subjects just across the border. Like your great-aunt Margaret, the kids he used for his research into Down syndrome and Alzheimer's were stolen in plain sight from their homes and brought to the U.S. by any means possible. For a while, I was stumped trying to understand how he managed to do that. The kids didn't have passports; but, in fact, that was better for him because there was no paper trail to worry about. But without proper documents, he couldn't fly them into the country. He had to find a different way. You figured it out, didn't you?"

Kiel sat motionless.

"No? Well, let me tell you." The sheriff glanced at the notebook again. "I talked to an old friend who works in border patrol. He said that years back it wouldn't have been that difficult to smuggle kids into one of the Canadian ports on the west coast. Assuming that's what Melk did, he'd transported them across the country from there and then had them brought by boat either to the Upper Peninsula or Green Bay or even directly to Door County—the way the rumrunners brought booze into the country during Prohibition. Things are different now with Homeland Security on the job, but for decades there were hundreds of miles of unsecured water all around here."

Cubiak stood and stretched and then sat down again. "You probably couldn't wait to tell Doctor Sage what you'd overheard that morning. When you did so, did he pretend to be shocked by the revelation, or had he suspected all along that his mentor was an unscrupulous opportunist and that he was tainted by association? Either way, once the story about Melk was public, Sage knew that he would be reviled and that his work would be viewed with disdain and suspicion. How much did he offer you to keep quiet, or did you put a price on your silence?"

The young journalist refused to be rattled. "You should be a novelist, Sheriff. You've got a terrific imagination."

Cubiak gave her an amused smile before he turned serious again. "More to the point, how much did your father have to do with your blackmailing scheme?"

Kiel stiffened. "Keep my father out of this," she said.

"By your own admission, you went to see Sage on Tuesday morning. That afternoon, he withdrew fifty thousand dollars from his brokerage account at the Bank of Sturgeon Bay. Over the next twenty-four hours, he liquated another seventy-five thousand in assets. Interestingly, the total adds up to the amount of money your father owed the casino. Let me put the question to you again: how much did your father have to do with the blackmailing scheme—and with Doctor Sage's murder?"

Kiel was on her feet, shouting at the sheriff.

"Sage committed suicide." She stabbed a finger at Cubiak to emphasize her point. "How dare you accuse me or my father of having anything to do with his death? The man shot himself in the heart!"

"Sit down."

Kiel shuddered. The muscles in her shoulders twitched. She brushed a strand of hair off her face and stared at him, wild-eyed.

"We won't continue until you take your seat."

While she fumed, Cubiak reopened the notebook and pretended to read. He could hear her fast breathing.

Then she mumbled under her breath.

"What?"

"Nothing," she said and dropped back into the chair.

The sheriff gave her a few moments to cool off before he looked up. "Why would Sage kill himself?" he said finally.

"Isn't it obvious? He was ruined. You said as much yourself. His work was tainted. He'd been duped by Melk for years. He knew no one would believe that he wasn't complicit with his mentor. More than half his early research subjects were underage Mexican kids, and the rest were from Central America, where Melk had probably gotten hold of his subjects the same way he did Francisca's brother," Kiel said.

Cubiak switched the scenario. "Melk started his Alzheimer's research while Sage was still in medical school. By the time he finished his residency and joined the institute, the tests had been underway for nearly a decade and it was another fifteen years before Sage took over as head researcher. According to Francisca, Melk tricked her family into signing a letter of consent for Miguel. He probably did the same with other families, but Sage wouldn't have known any of this. If he checked the paperwork at all, he'd find a folder of documents that looked legitimate. There's no question that if the story came out he'd have a lot of explaining to do, but he was a smart man. He'd find a way to escape any culpability."

"Sage begged me to help him. He feared that his career was on the line. He said that I had nothing to lose and everything to gain by doing as he asked."

"You don't deny being paid off to keep quiet about what you knew?"

Kiel shook her head. "He made me agree not to say anything, and he gave me plenty of money to make sure I didn't. *Gave!* I never asked for any of it."

"You took it?"

She hung her head. "Yes, I accepted the money, but I passed it along to my father. I knew he was in trouble because of gambling. It's an addiction, a disease. I had to help him."

Kiel watched as the sheriff wrote in his notebook. Trembling and near tears, she slumped back into her chair.

"I had no choice. He needed the money."

"He put you up to it, didn't he?"

"Who?"

"Your father."

"No. I already told you, the money was Sage's idea."

"I don't believe you. Your father was desperate. His creditors were hounding him, and he'd run out of options."

"That's not true. He could have taken out a loan if he wanted. He had the farm to use as collateral."

She didn't know. For the first time, Cubiak felt sorry for her.

"The farm was gone. Your father started selling it off years ago."

Kiel started. "You're lying, trying to get me riled. My father would never do that, at least not while Florence was alive."

Cubiak opened a folder and laid out copies of the bills of sale. There were six altogether. One for each parcel of land that the neighbor had purchased from Tom Fadim.

Kiel blanched. "That fucker . . ."

Did she mean Smolinsky or her father? Cubiak wondered.

Kiel snatched the papers. "Where did you get these? How do I know if they're authentic?"

She didn't give up easily, he had to give her that much. "They've all been notarized. If you wanted to, you could check county records and find out who's been paying the real estate taxes on the land."

Kiel pushed the documents back across the table.

"The two of you made quite the tag team. Your father needed you to blackmail Sage, and you needed your dad to help stage the phony suicide."

She refused to take the bait. "You're fishing, Sheriff. You've got no proof. Sage left a note. And I'm sure if you'd check, you'd find gun residue on his hand."

Cubiak placed another document on the table. "Here's Sage's note. All it says is that he is sorry for what's happened. That's a pretty vague statement. It could apply to almost anything. Also, suicide notes are usually handwritten, not typed. And notice the odd size of the paper and the rough edging here."

She leaned forward and watched him run a finger along the top of the sheet.

"It almost looks as if the top part of the page had been torn off, carefully, perhaps using a ruler," he said.

"Still no proof." Kiel settled back and assumed the same arrogant stance she had had at the start of the interview.

Cubiak went on. "Men don't generally keep stationery in the house, and if they do, you'd expect to find a box of it. But this was the only piece like it on the premises. And it doesn't look like personal stationery, does it? I think it's more likely the kind of stationery used by the institute." The sheriff laid a second sheet alongside the purported suicide note. "I got curious and asked Noreen Klyasheff for a copy of IPM stationery. It's a perfect match. That's not just my opinion. I had the two analyzed by an expert. It would appear that there are plenty of arguments against calling this a suicide note. More than likely it was Sage's letter of resignation, which you got hold of and used for your own purposes."

Kiel was unyielding. "What about the gun residue? Or did you not bother to check for any?"

"Oh, we looked, of course, and we found it. Just as you knew we would."

She started to say something and then caught herself.

"If I had to guess, I'd say that you put the gun in Sage's hand after you or your father shot him, trying to make it look as if the doctor had pulled the trigger. Why not? It's easy enough to do, and things like that happen pretty regularly on TV cop shows. The truth is that when a gun is fired, the residue spreads everywhere, so finding traces of it on Sage's hand isn't as significant as you'd like to think."

Kiel went on the offensive. "Why would I kill Sage if I was blackmailing him? Isn't there some quaint expression about cutting off your nose, et cetera?"

"Sage was well off, but he didn't have limitless assets. Once you got what you could from him, he ceased being an asset and became a potential threat. You had to kill him, too, for much the same reason you had to get rid of Melk—to make sure there was no one left who could sue you for damages after your book came out."

The journalist laughed. "You overestimate the power of the written word, Sheriff."

"Do I? Medical exposés are always big news. You figured you were sitting on the kind of sensational story that would get you on the major TV talk shows and catapult you to the top of the *New York Times* bestseller list. An explosive story like that is worth a lot of money. It also comes with the kind of name recognition that can command big advances on future book deals." He paused and then went on. "People kill for less."

"But even you said Sage was in the clear, that he'd find a way of distancing himself from Melk's activities, all of which had been going on for nearly a decade before Sage joined the institute."

"He probably wouldn't be held accountable in a court of law, but the court of public opinion is different. Alzheimer's is a hot topic. You wouldn't want to write a book that was stuck in the past. For you, probably for any writer, the temptation would be to link early research efforts to the work being done now. Sage was your answer because he bridged the two eras. A wordsmith with your skills would have no trouble casting a long shadow. If Sage was alive, he would probably sue for libel, but like Melk, he had no family. With him and his predecessor out of the way, you could write what you wanted without worrying about the consequences."

Cubiak tented his hands and tilted forward. "In the piece you wrote for the *Gazette* after Melk's death, you played fast and loose with the facts. You sensationalized where it suited your purpose and omitted details that lessened the drama. You also misquoted me. Given that sample of your handiwork, I can image the kind of salacious exposé you'd write. It used to be called 'yellow journalism.' I don't know what the term is now, but I suspect that you wouldn't hesitate to ruin Sage's reputation to embellish your own."

Kiel glared at the sheriff. "I don't apologize for what I write. Melk was a monster, and the world deserves to know it. He built his reputation and his institute on the pain and suffering of the innocent. I don't have to sensationalize what he did; the facts speak for themselves.

"As for Sage, I'm not going to shed any tears for him. He had his eye on the golden prize as much as Melk did and was willing to look the other way when it suited his purposes. Shouldn't he have thought it odd that so many subjects were at hand, that they spoke little if any English and had no families that came to visit? Melk kept them prisoners of his work just as surely as he locked up Margaret and those other children in that wing at the mental hospital. And Sage never wondered, never questioned any of it? Don't kid yourself, Sheriff. He knew more than he let on, he had to. But he looked the other way because it was in his best interest to do so," Kiel said, as if daring Cubiak to contradict her.

"But I didn't kill him. In fact, I think the assertion is ludicrous."

She stood and stepped back from the table. "Look at me, Sheriff. I'm five two and never weighed more than a hundred and twenty in my life. Do you think any jury is going to believe that I could subdue a man as tall and strong as Harlan Sage? Do you think you or the prosecutor could convince anyone that I could hold him down while pointing a gun to his chest?"

Don't be absurd.

She didn't say it, but the look on her face conveyed the message. Kiel had played her ace card. She sat back, assured that she had won.

Cubiak threw his hand up in a gesture of defeat and allowed her a moment to enjoy her victory.

She was still gloating when there was a knock on the door and Rowe entered.

"It's all here?" Cubiak said.

"Just as you suspected," Rowe said as he set a blue folder on the table.

Kiel stared at the file.

When they were alone again, Cubiak continued. "You were having an affair with Harlan Sage. The evening Sage died you went to console him about Melk's death—or maybe to celebrate. You did what a woman like you would do perched on his lap. When you finished, he relaxed and closed his eyes, unaware that at that moment you were reaching for your gun. He never had a chance."

Kiel sneered. "Prove it. Prove any of it." She tried to be resolute in her defiance but couldn't hide her nervousness.

"There are witnesses to your midnight assignations with Doctor Sage," Cubiak said.

Her right eye twitched.

"The doctor's neighbors tend to be security conscious. More than one has installed cameras to track who comes and goes. Most of the cameras point at their own driveways and front entrances but a few focus on the road, and footage from them reveals that your car repeatedly made its way to Sage's turnoff."

"I had to interview him for the book."

"Of course, and there were one or two afternoon visits, but the majority of your assignations occurred around midnight or later, and generally on those visits you didn't leave until the next morning."

Kiel started to object but Cubiak cut her off.

"The most interesting segment caught you and Sage leaving the house together. You're wearing something like a cocktail dress, if that term still holds, and you're walking together toward his car."

Cubiak slipped a photo from the folder and turned it toward Kiel.

"We were able to enhance the film enough to see him kiss you and slip his hand into a rather compromising position." The sheriff paused. "Any chance you remember where you were going that evening?"

Kiel slumped in her chair.

"I'm not saying another word until I talk to an attorney."

SHIFTING THE BLAME

21

A night in jail had done nothing to improve Tom Fadim's mood or soften his surly manner. He hadn't shaved and he sported a five o'clock shadow that might have appeared stylish on a male fashion model but had the opposite effect on him.

A nervous young man in a cheap suit sat alongside the suspect: the lawyer.

Cubiak clicked on the recorder and identified those in the room.

"Coffee?" he said, indicating the cup he had brought in for himself.

"Keep your swill," Fadim said.

The lawyer had started to say yes but changed his mind.

"Whatever," Cubiak said. He opened a green folder and took his time reviewing the contents. He knew everything that was typed up inside but wanted to keep the suspect on edge. Finally, he reached for his coffee and looked at Fadim.

"Please, state your relationship to Linda Kiel, aka Cody Longe," he said.

The prisoner made a face. "Linda Kiel, or, as she liked to call her fancy self, Cody Longe, is my adopted daughter."

"And by birth?"

"By birth, she's my niece. My sister, Lorene, was her mother."

"What happened to Lorene?"

"You must already know all this. What the hell are you asking me for?"

"I need to hear it from you."

Cubiak talked over the lawyer, who had leaned toward his client and instructed him to answer the question.

"Lorene was killed in a car accident when Linda was eleven months old. She was a single mom, no father in the picture, so my wife and I took her in."

"And you adopted her?"

"Eventually we did."

"How old was she then?"

"Eight, nine? Something like that."

"You waited nearly a decade to adopt her?"

Fadim squirmed. "Yeah. There were other relatives, and we figured maybe one of them would step up to the plate, but no one did."

"Do you and your wife have any children of your own?"

"No. And it's ex-wife."

The sheriff pretended to make a notation in the file, knowing this would worry Fadim.

"And Florence Fadim? What is your relationship to her?"

"The old lady is my paternal grandmother."

"What about your parents?"

"My father died years before. My mother was in the car with Lorene, coming home from Christmas shopping. They were both killed. The other driver was DUI. Walked away with a bruise on his shoulder." Fadim pointed to a spot at the end of his left clavicle as if he carried a similar mark under his shirt.

"Sorry," Cubiak said. For a moment, he felt sympathetic toward Fadim. Each of them was a man whose life had been changed by a drunk driver.

The sheriff closed the folder. "You know that your daughter was writing a book about the Institute for Progressive Medicine."

Fadim slipped back into form. "Sure I do. I told you about it the first time we talked."

"When did she tell you about the documents from the Northern Hospital for the Insane?"

"You don't have to answer that," the lawyer said.

Fadim waved him quiet. "She didn't tell me anything."

"But you've seen them?"

"Yeah, by accident. The old lady went on about someone breaking into the barn. When I went to look, I saw all that junk on the wall. I didn't pay that much attention to it. What I saw didn't make any sense to me. I figured Linda probably had something to do with it, so I asked her."

"How did she react?"

"At first she was pissed that I'd seen it. Then she told me what she'd learned about Margaret and all those other kids. I couldn't believe it and made her prove it to me. What the fuck, I thought. I wanted to go to the institute and wring Melk's neck."

"Or sue?"

Again Fadim swatted away the lawyer's hand. "Sure, why not? I figured he owed us something. For what he did. For the grief and pain he caused my grandmother—all of us, everyone in the family."

"You needed the money, didn't you?"

Fadim exchanged a look with his attorney and clammed up.

"Why didn't you wring his neck, as you said?"

Fadim snorted. "By the time I got the courage to do anything, he was already dead."

"Linda took care of him, didn't she?"

For the second time, the suspect heeded the cautionary look from his attorney.

"I won't answer that. You can't make me."

"What about Doctor Sage?"

"What about him?"

"Did you know that Linda was having an affair with him?"

"My daughter is an adult. What she does with her life is her own business."

"You're denying that you knew anything about the relationship between the two of them?"

"She had to talk to him for the book. I know that. Anything else, like I said, it's her business."

"Did your daughter tell you about the photo of the boy on the wall and the cleaning woman who thought it was her missing brother?"

"She may have said something."

"Did she tell you about the connection between Down syndrome and Alzheimer's, and the illicit research that Melk had started and that Sage had continued?"

Fadim shrugged.

"Is that a yes or a no?"

"It's a maybe. I don't understand all that medical stuff, Sheriff. I never was any good at science in school. Now, Linda's smart. She'd know what it meant."

A subtle way to try to shift the focus and blame to his own child, Cubiak thought. "She said it was your idea to blackmail Sage."

The lawyer put his hand on Fadim's arm, but the suspect tossed it off.

"That's a lie on two counts. I never said anything about anything, and we never blackmailed Sage."

"Where'd you get the money to pay off your debt at the casino?"

"My client has no comment," the lawyer said, chiming in before Fadim could answer.

"Where were you the night Doctor Sage was murdered?"

Fadim started to reply, but the lawyer interceded again. "No comment."

Cubiak opened the file and slid a piece of paper out. "For the record, I am showing the suspect a copy of Doctor Sage's purported suicide note. Have you ever seen this?"

"No comment." The attorney had taken over and Fadim let him.

The sheriff repeated what he had told Linda Kiel about the stationery and the torn edge along the top of the page. He ran through his theory about the seduction and the shooting and the journalist's need for an accomplice to pull off the stunt.

Cubiak slid another sheet of paper from the file. "We did a cast of the tire tracks found in the lawn at Sage's house on the day his body was discovered. They match those on your SUV. Tell me, Mr. Fadim, how do you explain that?"

"Are you accusing my client of a crime?" the lawyer said.

Unable to keep his silence, Fadim slid toward the front of his chair and rested his forearms on the table. "I just got new tires. There's probably a dozen vehicles around here with the same kind. And what about the residue? There had to be traces of gunpowder on Sage's hand," he said.

Cubiak smiled. "Ah, that old theory. You'll hear all about that in court and how numerous experts have come to disclaim it as evidence."

Fadim went white.

The sheriff stood. "Thomas Fadim Junior, I am arresting you on first-degree murder charges in the death of Doctor Harlan Sage."

A SAD VISIT

22

"Are you ready?" Cubiak stood on Bathard's back porch and pulled up his collar against the cool evening air.

"As much as I'll ever be." The retired coroner zipped his jacket and rested his hand on the doorknob. "Are you sure you don't want to come in for a minute?" he said.

The offer was tempting. "No, I think we need to go and get this over with. Don't you?" The sheriff sensed that Bathard had wanted him to delay the errand. Now he was doing the same to the doctor.

Instead of answering, Bathard stepped out into the yard. He held his black leather bag in one hand and a small white shopping bag in the other. "Seems like the only time I use this anymore," he said, indicating the medical bag. Then he lifted the other and smiled. "Cupcakes." But the smile was fleeting. "It won't be my first time delivering sad news and not yours either. We both know what to do."

"Doesn't make it any easier," Cubiak said quietly as he trailed behind. His comment was nearly lost in the crunch of gravel beneath their feet as they walked to the jeep. But he knew from the slight dip to his friend's head that Bathard had heard.

They were silent on the ride to the Fadim farm. A week ago Cubiak had rarely driven along that stretch of road, but in the past seven days,

205

he had been there so often that the jeep seemed to anticipate the turns before he did.

"I'm sorry I got you into this," the sheriff said as they approached the familiar driveway.

"Please." Bathard raised his hand in protest. "There's no need to apologize. Florence Fadim is an elderly woman in poor health. You don't know how she'll react. What would you do out here by yourself if she had a stroke or a cardiac event as the result of shock? You would have to call for an ambulance, which would take twenty minutes to get here. How would you feel then?"

The physician didn't expect a response and didn't wait for one. "I appreciate your concern for my well-being, but it's a moot point. Just as you had an obligation to ask me to accompany you, I have an obligation to be here."

As usual, the front door was open and Mrs. Fadim was in her chair at the living room window. She must have seen the headlights because she didn't turn when they came in.

"My day for visitors," she said, still without looking at them. "First the church ladies and now the both of you. Everyone with the best of intentions, is that it?"

Neither man spoke, and for a moment Cubiak wished he could pretend that he had stopped by just to make her a cup of tea and to listen to her prattle on about old times.

It took the sheriff a moment to realize that something was different. Mrs. Fadim's musky perfume had been replaced with the fresh scent of lavender. Her unkempt hair was combed and coifed, and even her clothes were different. Instead of the usual blue checked housecoat, she wore a faded pink-flowered dress that cascaded over her knees and fell nearly to her ankles. The red sweater that was draped around her thin shoulders replaced her threadbare brown shawl.

"You look quite dapper this evening," he said.

The old lady snorted. "You're not here to pay me compliments."

Cubiak leaned against the cold radiator.

"I have news for you," he said finally.

She patted the arms of the chair and then dropped her hands into her lap. "I knew you would, eventually. There will be tea, though? And a biscuit?"

Bathard took his cue and stepped forward.

"Tonight there will be something special. I brought an assortment of my favorite mini cupcakes. Hopefully one or two will appeal to you as well." He opened the paper bag and let her peek inside. When she had finished her inspection, he gave it to Cubiak and reached for the medical bag. "While the sheriff tends to his barista chores, I'm going to give you the briefest checkup. With your permission, of course."

From the kitchen, Cubiak heard the soft murmur of conversation in the living room. What were they talking about? he wondered. Were all three of them stalling? Could Mrs. Fadim actually expect good news from him? She knew he had come about Margaret. Decades had passed since the girl had disappeared. How could the old woman expect a positive outcome? Why hadn't he sat down and immediately told her the blunt truth?

He dropped the tea bags in the pot and filled it with boiling water. While it steeped, he arranged the pastries on a plate. Odd how food seemed a natural accompaniment to bad news. He remembered the dozens of casseroles and cakes that his colleagues and neighbors had left on his kitchen counter and crammed into the refrigerator after Lauren and Alexis were killed. The same had happened to Bathard after Cornelia's death and again after Sonja's funeral. All of it well intentioned but tasting like straw and the emptiness that it was meant to soften and mask, to somehow make palatable. The food didn't matter, but the gesture did. Of course he knew that. How like Bathard to remember to bring an offering, and how like himself to forget. With a pang of guilt, Cubiak stirred extra sugar into the tea. It was the best he could do.

When he entered with the tray, Bathard was helping Mrs. Fadim from her place by the window. He escorted her to the chair near the sofa and then joined Cubiak on the divan. The three of them sat, knees nearly touching. For a few minutes the sheriff kept busy pouring the tea and handing over the cups. When he held out the treats, Mrs. Fadim fussed over which to choose. She decided on one with pink icing, then looked at it for a moment and set it atop a napkin on the small table at her side. Her hand trembled. She knows, Cubiak thought.

He waited for her to try the tea. Somehow it seemed important that she approve.

"Extra sweet," she said. She tried to sound pleased, but there was sadness in her voice and her gaze was downcast.

Another moment passed and she looked at Cubiak, as if letting him know that he could proceed.

"I have news about Margaret," he said as he laid his hand over her wrist.

Mrs. Fadim stiffened, and the sheriff felt the jolt of surprise and fear that ran through her arm.

"You found the man who took her." The words came out both as a statement and a question.

"Yes."

Her pale eyes locked on his. "Was he a doctor?"

"Yes."

She nodded as if the answer were reassuring.

"Did he cure her? Did he straighten her legs so she could run?"

"No, I'm sorry, but he did not."

"He did try to cure her though, didn't he? He at least did that, didn't he?"

Cubiak hesitated. How much of the truth did the elderly woman need to hear? How much would she understand? Could he be honest without being cruel?

"I don't know if he tried to cure Margaret, but the truth is that there really was nothing he could do to help her. There was nothing anyone could do to make her condition better."

"Then why . . . ?" She found it impossible to go on.

Bathard leaned toward her. "Margaret disappeared many years ago. It was a time when there were many serious diseases for which there were no cures. Scientists and doctors around the country—indeed, around the world—were searching for drugs and treatments that would alleviate the suffering."

"I don't understand," Mrs. Fadim said. She looked around the room wild-eyed and fearful. "So why did he take her if he couldn't help her? What did he do to her?"

The retired coroner clasped his hands together. "From what the sheriff has ascertained, there are indications that the doctor was one of those who was looking for ways to cure the disease that afflicted Margaret."

"Polio," she said.

It was the first time Cubiak had heard her utter the word.

"Yes, polio, a terrible scourge. The doctor believed that her blood could protect other children from it, like a vaccine."

Mrs. Fadim gasped. Her hand flew to her mouth. "Oh, my God, no. No! He took her blood." She grabbed the sides of the chair with her clawlike hands and tried to push up.

"Mrs. Fadim, Florence, please." Bathard and Cubiak were on their feet. Speaking over each other, they took hold of her arms and slowly lowered her back down.

She breathed deeply until she was calm.

"Did she suffer? Did he hurt her?"

"No, he would not do anything to hurt her. He would have wanted her to be as strong as possible," Bathard said.

"She didn't go hungry?"

"No."

"There was never enough food for everyone back then. Not even on the farm."

Mrs. Fadim lapsed into silence.

"May I?" Bathard said as he reached for her wrist. "I would like to check your pulse."

When he finished, he rested her hand on the arm of the chair. "You're fine," he said. Then he lifted the cup of tea to her mouth. "Try and take a sip," he said.

She was quiet a long time, and Cubiak hoped that she had slipped away to a different time and place. But when she spoke, it was to Bathard and still about Margaret.

"He used her as a guinea pig, didn't he?"

The physician grimaced and didn't try to hide the shame he felt. "I am very sorry but, yes, it appears that he did. And not just Margaret, but others as well."

Mrs. Fadim took this in. "He was a beast in our midst, preying on the innocent."

She turned to Cubiak as if remembering that he was there. "You've arrested him, haven't you? You've got him in jail and you're bringing Margaret home."

"I couldn't arrest him because he was dead by the time I learned what he had done."

The sheriff held his breath, worried that she would ask how the doctor had died. What would he tell her? That part of the story was one he hoped she would never have to face.

"And Margaret? Where is Margaret?" she said.

"I'm afraid there was an accident. A fire," he said.

Mrs. Fadim frowned and narrowed her eyes as if she were struggling to understand. "I dreamed of a fire," she said quietly. "The animals were trapped inside the barn. They all died." Tears welled in her eyes. "Margaret is dead, isn't she?"

"Yes."

"And her body?"

"I don't know. I don't know that anyone does."

"Poor Margaret. Cheated in life and death both." Mrs. Fadim lifted her knobby fingers to her forehead and slowly crossed herself. Then she grabbed their wrists. "Pray with me, please, for Margaret," she said, pulling at them with surprising strength.

Cubiak and Bathard bowed their heads. It had been years since the sheriff had prayed in the usual way, and he was uncertain what to expect.

"Our Father," Mrs. Fadim began.

The doctor joined in. "Who art in heaven."

Cubiak was the third in their small trinity. "Hallowed be thy name."

As they continued Mrs. Fadim tightened her grip.

"Thy kingdom come. Thy will be done . . ."

When the prayer ended, they fell into a companionable silence that went on for several comfortable minutes. The solemn mood was shattered by the roar of an approaching car on the road. A problem with the muffler magnified the sound of the engine, and the radio blasted, leaving the incomprehensible words to a familiar tune to trail behind on the windless night.

They listened as if mesmerized by the intrusion. When the noise finally faded, Mrs. Fadim took a sip of tea and picked up the cupcake from the side table. She took a single, small bite and put it back down again. She turned to Cubiak. Her eyes were rheumy and her features gaunt.

"She never had a chance, did she? I've been fooling myself for a long time. I know that now. Life is hard and people can be so cruel. Sometimes it's difficult to imagine the amount of meanness in the world. I suppose we all get a taste of it, but some seem to get more than others."

She dipped her head and then raised it again. "How horrible for you, Sheriff."

"Me? I don't understand," he said.

"Don't you? People like me can hide in our little houses and live in our imaginations, our fantasies, but not you. You have to go out there and confront the evil. You're the one who has to face all the monsters."

Unexpectedly, Mrs. Fadim asked that they turn on the TV. They watched a sitcom until nearly nine when her other grandson, Jason, arrived from Janesville.

He was the opposite of his brother, Tom, in both appearance and demeanor. Husky and soft spoken, he seemed a kindly man, if one who was overburdened by life. When he bent to kiss her cheek, Florence swatted at him.

"Well, it's about time you got here, Tommy," she said. Then she pointed to the television. "Turn that thing off."

Cubiak clicked the remote and the room went quiet.

Mrs. Fadim fidgeted in her chair. She frowned and grabbed the sheriff's arm. "Have you found her? Have you found Margaret?" she said.

Cubiak patted her hand. "Not yet, but don't worry, I'm still looking," he said.

A DAY OF MIRACLES

23

The case left Cubiak unsettled and unable to sleep. He had no sympathy for anyone involved except the many innocent victims and their families, and he was helpless to do anything on their behalf.

Both Leonard Melk and Harlan Sage had been murdered, but the sheriff couldn't feel sorry for either one. Not after what they had done. Nor did he have any pity for Linda Kiel and Tom Fadim, the two he had arrested. The daughter-father duo hadn't acted out of a desire for revenge or justice; their motivations were unmitigated greed and self-interest. Fadim killed for the money he needed to pay off his gambling debts; Kiel killed in pursuit of literary fame. On her laptop, Rowe had found a list of the publishers she intended to approach and a draft of her query letter, which described her book as "the explosive true story of how a renowned physician used innocent children as guinea pigs in a search for miracle cures."

When sleep finally came for Cubiak, it was troubled. He woke in the dark of early morning. The numbers on the bedside clock read 3:34, an ungodly hour to be up. Cubiak closed his eyes and willed sleep to return, but when he looked again, barely an hour had passed. It was pointless to stay in bed any longer. He slid his feet out from the covers, pausing long enough to let Cate roll over to her other side. She wasn't an early riser, and he didn't want to disturb her to the point of waking. His luck held. She snuffled and went still again.

He groped in the dark for the pants and shirt he had tossed on the chair the night before and carried them down the short hall to Joey's room. The boy was sprawled nearly lengthwise across the mattress, one arm flung over his pillow and the other wrapped around his stuffed goose. Kipper lay on the floor beside him. Cubiak pulled the covers over Joey's feet and then bent and rubbed the dog behind the ears. When the boy was a toddler, the dog had curled next to him on the bed, but age made it impossible for him to jump and he settled for the rug.

"Good dog," Cubiak said. For years, Kipper had been Cate's companion and self-appointed bodyguard, and he had paid the price for his devotion with serious injuries. His loyalty never lagged, and after Joey was born, he transferred his allegiance to the boy.

In the kitchen, Cubiak made coffee. While it brewed, he dressed and watched the sky transition from night to day. When the coffee was ready, he poured a cup and carried the mug outside, letting the steam rise into his face. A scrim of fog lay over the lake. Once the sun was fully up it would be gone.

It hadn't taken long for Linda Kiel and Tom Fadim to turn on each other. Kiel claimed her father had orchestrated the murders of the two physicians from the Institute for Progressive Medicine. She said her father had been an abusive spouse and she was afraid that he would harm her if she didn't follow his directives. Tom Fadim accepted blame as the blackmailer in the two-pronged scheme but insisted his daughter was the killer. Cubiak had his own theory. He believed that Kiel had acted alone to murder Melk but that the pair had worked together to kill Sage. That was what he had told the county prosecutor who filed murder charges against the two and how he planned to testify in court.

Until then, the sheriff and his staff had plenty to do following up on the responses to the newspaper ads that Kiel had sprinkled around the state. Each story they uncovered would add another sad chapter to

Melk's legacy of deceit and abuse. Thankfully, some families would eventually learn the unfortunate fate of their long-lost relatives, but the chance of identifying and tracing the children brought from other countries was almost nil.

The only person the sheriff might hope to help was Francisca, but even that seemed an impossibility. Even though the trail had gone cold, he had promised her that he would do everything he could to find Miguel. The harsh reality was that her brother was probably lost forever. Still, he couldn't dispel the nagging suspicion that Miguel was alive and that the answer to his whereabouts had been within his grasp, only he had failed to see it.

The sun was well over the horizon when the patio door slid open and Cubiak heard the soft click of Kipper's nails on wood. He turned and saw Joey in his rumpled pajamas, the dog at his side. Bleary eyed and barefoot, the boy clutched an oversized picture book to his thin chest.

"What are you doing up so early?" Cubiak said.

Joey blinked against the morning light. "I couldn't sleep."

"I didn't wake you up, did I?"

The child shook his head and crossed the dewy wood to his father's side. "Can I have some coffee?"

"No, but you can take a whiff." He held the mug to the boy's chin.

Joey sniffed and made a face.

"Why couldn't you sleep?"

The boy shrugged.

"You got up early to read?" Cubiak said, indicating the book.

Joey held it out toward him. "I was trying to find Robert the Robot. He's supposed to be on every page but I can't find him."

"I thought you'd done that already, many times."

"I did in the first part of the book, but it gets harder on every page and now I'm stuck."

"Why is it so difficult?"

Joey looked at his father as if the answer were obvious. "Because there's lots more people in each picture, and he's dressed in different stuff on every page. Sometimes he's even wearing a hat, or a big scarf. He just looks different."

"Maybe I can help."

"Okay."

While Joey settled at the table, Cubiak went in for more coffee and a glass of chocolate milk.

When he got back, he lifted his son's cold feet to his lap and bent over the book. Joey flipped back to the beginning and pointed to the first photo. "See, he's here in this picture and then here in this one. And here, here, and here," he said, moving his finger from one page to another. "Then it gets hard. In the next picture he's wearing a green jacket instead of a striped sweater. And in the next one he's got on a cowboy hat. That one fooled me for a long time," Joey said and scrunched up his mouth.

"But you found him."

"Yeah, but first I had to figure out the clue. It's different in every picture but once you know what it is then you know what to look for. See? In the last picture it was gloves."

"But almost everyone is wearing gloves."

"I know! But his are yellow."

"Ah, and no one else has yellow gloves?"

"Right, only Robert the Robot. Gosh, Dad, now do you get it?"

Cubiak smiled. "I think so."

Joey moved on. "This is the one I can't figure out. There are lots of people in hats and gloves and lots of people with scarves. And there are pairs that match for all of those things. So the clue has to be something else."

"What else is there?"

The boy frowned and studied the picture. "Glasses! Lots of people are wearing glasses. But they're all the same color, so that can't be the clue."

"Unless there's something different about his glasses."

Joey leaned in closer, furrowing his brow in concentration. Suddenly his face brightened. "I got it! There he is! Robert the Robot's glasses have an X in the middle, right between his eyes." The boy planted a finger on the figure in the upper right-hand corner. "That's Robert the Robot. He was there all the time. He's always there. You just have to pay attention and keep looking until you find him."

Cubiak laughed and shut the book with a thwack.

"Joey, you're a genius!"

The child glanced from his father to the closed book. His face was a mixture of alarm and delight. "I am? How come?"

Cubiak tousled his son's hair. "I promised a lady that I would help her find her brother, but I wasn't sure where to look for him. You just gave me an idea."

"I did?" The boy grinned. "Do you think my idea will work?"

"I don't know, but it's worth a try."

The two went back into the house, where Cubiak called Francisca and invited her to go with him to Green Bay.

"I need your help with something," he said.

"You have found Miguel?"

"Not yet, but I think I know one place where we can look. At least it's a start."

Half an hour later the sheriff pulled up in front of her house. She was pacing on the small front porch and ran to the curb, flushed with excitement. Without a word, she climbed in the jeep and fumbled with the seat belt. Finally, it clicked and he drove off.

On the drive, Francisca alternately clasped her hands together and then flexed them nervously and stared out the windshield. At one point, he saw her counting on her fingers and wondered if she was praying, perhaps saying the rosary. At times she glanced out the side window, as if tracking their progress by the occasional glimpses of the bay that came into view. If she guessed where they were headed, she didn't say. She had put her faith in him, and with every mile they covered, Cubiak felt the weight of that trust grow heavier.

It wasn't until he turned in by the large IPM sign that Francisca spoke. "This place?" she said, her voice full of alarm. "My brother is here? He is sick?" She crossed her arms across her stomach and hunched forward.

"I don't know for certain, but I think he's here and I hope he's okay."

Francisca bit her lip and slumped into the seat as if trying to put distance between herself and the institute grounds.

IPM hadn't opened for the day, and the lot was empty. Cubiak parked where he could see everyone who drove in.

"We wait," he said.

He uncapped the thermos of coffee that he had brought from home and offered her the first cup.

"No, gracias. I cannot. I am too . . ." She waggled her hand and slid down farther.

"How long has it been since you've seen your brother?" he said, cradling the cup in his hand.

"Not since he was four, but he has a scar on his arm. I will know the mark."

"Sometimes a scar will heal and get so faint it nearly disappears. You must be prepared for that possibility."

"I know. I must be ready to be disappointed, but I must also never lose hope. When I find him, I will recognize him, and in my heart, I will be satisfied." She pivoted toward the side window. "But it is not enough, is it?" she said, as if she were talking to herself. "The world will not believe that because I say a man is my brother, that it is true. I must have proof so others will believe too."

"There are ways of finding proof." Cubiak lowered the window and tossed the dregs of the coffee on the ground. "Do you know what DNA is?"

Francisca turned toward him.

"I've heard of it on the news. It's something inside us. I know we all have it, but I don't know how it works."

"Most people don't. Today if you see someone that you think is your brother, we can do a test to see if his DNA matches yours. If it does, it will mean that you have found Miguel."

She inhaled sharply. "I know it probably will not happen, but it would be so wonderful if it did. If he is not here, then I must continue to search for him." She paused and tried to smile. "It helps to believe in miracles, Sheriff. A man like you probably does not, but I do. It is a miracle that I am sitting here with you today, that there is even a small possibility of finding Miguel, and here so close to where I live." She stopped again. "I must not be too greedy. Perhaps that is my only miracle for today. But God willing, it is not. Perhaps today is a day of many miracles."

Francisca fell silent again. She's praying, Cubiak thought. He was relieved that she hadn't asked how he felt about miracles. There was a time not that many years ago when he would have scoffed at the notion. Miracles were for the gullible and the weak, not for the rational and the strong. Still, he had come to realize that some things defied explanation. How to account for his life with Cate and Joey, the second chance he had been given for love and happiness? He had done nothing to deserve that opportunity. Was it a gift or a miracle?

Cubiak was about to pour more coffee when a dark blue van rattled into the lot. A line of rust ran along the bottom edge of the vehicle, and the left front fender was crumpled. There were no windows in the back and no insignia on the sides. Even from where he sat, Cubiak could see that both rear tires needed air.

The van drove through the lot and circled around toward the back of the building. As soon as it was out of sight, the sheriff opened his door.

"Let's go," he said.

Francisca pulled her jacket tight against the morning chill and rushed to keep up with Cubiak. As they proceeded through the lot, they heard the drone of voices on a call-in talk show. They rounded the corner of the building just as the van's radio went silent and the driver's door opened. A slim, tall man decked out in cowboy boots and jeans and a chambray shirt slipped out. As he came around the rear of the van, he scratched the back of his head with one hand and studied the clipboard that he carried in the other hand. The driver paused, still focused on the clipboard.

"The boss," Francisca said.

The supervisor kicked the bumper, and she jumped.

For a moment, nothing happened.

"Come on, I ain't got all day," he said.

The side door jerked open and a short, stocky man slowly emerged. Slipping out sideways, he put one foot on the ground and then the other. His work pants and shirt were the same dark color as the van. A matching cap was pulled low over his face. As soon as he was out the door, another man started to back out of the van. One by one, eight men emerged. They were all about the same height and build, and all moved with a clumsy but practiced intensity. The last one out pulled the door shut and joined the line with the others. So similar in appearance and demeanor were they that they could have been statues poured from the same mold.

Cubiak touched Francisca's arm and signaled that it was time for them to move forward.

The driver faced the van and didn't see them approach, but the men in the line noticed. As the two neared, the workers grew more agitated and began whispering to one another.

"Shut up."

The man with the clipboard scowled at the ragtag group, and the men fell silent. He spoke sharply in Spanish, and slowly they dropped their gaze to the ground.

But in the few moments when they had been looking up, Cubiak had seen enough of their features to know that the men were Hispanic and all had Down syndrome. Even if Miguel was not among them, the sheriff sensed that he was on the right trail.

Ten yards from the van, he stepped ahead of Francisca and put his hand out, motioning her to stop. Then he moved ahead several more feet.

"Morning," he said loudly.

The man with the clipboard twitched and wheeled around. Annoyance showed on his face.

"Who the fuck are you? What are you doing here?"

"Helping a friend."

Cubiak moved closer and pulled back his jacket so the man could see the badge on his belt.

The supervisor snorted. "They're all legal. What the hell is this all about?"

"Like I said, I'm helping a friend. I don't even have jurisdiction here, but my friend"—he turned and indicated Francisca—"is looking for her brother who's been missing for years. I have reason to believe he's somehow connected to the institute. He may even be one of the men on your crew."

"You're going to have to take that up with my boss," the man said and started to turn away.

Cubiak grabbed his arm.

"This will just take a minute."

The man pulled away.

"My brother's name is Miguel." Francisca stepped forward and stood alongside the sheriff, her head held high. There was no trace of fear in her voice.

"There ain't nobody by that name here."

"Names get changed," Cubiak said.

Francisca moved closer to the man with the clipboard. "Miguel has an old scar on the inside of his left arm below the elbow. It is like the number seven." She made the mark in the air. "Do you mind asking your workers to roll up their sleeves so I can look?"

"Now why the hell should I do that?"

"It will only take a few minutes," she said, ignoring the question.

The supervisor glanced from Francisca to the sheriff, and then he shrugged. "Whatever. As long as we get our work done, no skin off my teeth."

As the three were talking, the workers had broken out of their line and clustered together in a loose circle. Heads bowed, they murmured to each other. A few glanced at the trio and then looked away quickly. They seemed both curious and fearful.

"Line up," the super said. Then he added something in Spanish.

The men remained huddled together.

The boss laughed. "They like their routines. Anything different they can't understand. It scares 'em." He talked more to the ground than to either Cubiak or Francisca. "They don't know a whole lot. They're just a bunch of—" Whatever he was going to say next, he swallowed and instead looked at his watch.

"I ain't got all day." He turned to Francisca. "You tell 'em what you want them to do. Maybe they'll listen to you."

Speaking softly in Spanish, Francisca approached the men. Her tone was lilting and nonthreatening, and as she talked she rolled up the left sleeve of her jacket to show what she wanted them to do.

"*¿Porqué?*" said one of the men.

Cubiak didn't understand what she said in response, but the man immediately began to bare his left arm. The others followed his lead. And as if by habit or unspoken consent, they reassembled in a straight line.

By now several cars had pulled into the lot. We must be a strange sight, Cubiak thought. He watched the people exit their vehicles and look their way at the row of men with their bare arms extended. Were they worried that the workers were being checked for needle marks or gang tattoos?

Oblivious to the onlookers, Francisca went up to the first man. Whether or not he understood what she wanted, he looked at her with an eagerness that betrayed his willingness to please. He wanted to be the one for whom she was searching, no matter what that meant.

Francisca took his outstretched arm and ran her fingers up to his elbow. She said something to him and leaned over for a close-up look. A moment passed and she shook her head and began to slowly unroll his shirtsleeve.

"Gracias," she said before she moved on.

She repeated the routine with the second man. No, again. And then the third and the fourth.

With only four men remaining, Francisca turned toward Cubiak. Her shoulders drooped, and she seemed ready to cry. Why did you bring me here? she seemed to be asking. Cubiak didn't know what to say or do. He had promised to help but wondered if he had acted prematurely, prompted by little more than Linda Kiel's comment that Miguel wasn't very far away and his own hunch. In the past, he had relied on his instincts to point the way in his investigations. Maybe he was losing his touch?

Then he remembered what Francisca had said earlier.

"Perhaps today is a day of many miracles," he said.

She gave him a small smile and wiped at her eyes. Slowly she turned back to the waiting men.

No, to the fifth man. No, to the sixth.

The seventh man looked younger than the others. As Francisca approached, he bounced excitedly on the balls of his feet. When she stopped, he stuck out his arm and cheerfully pointed toward his elbow.

"*Aquí*," he said with an innocent grin.

Francisca's hand flew to her mouth. She tottered as if she might faint. Then she grabbed hold of the young man's wrists.

"Miguel?" she said.

He looked at her without comprehension.

"*¿Cómo te llamas?*"

"Carlos."

"*Hola*, Carlos," she said. "Sheriff, please," she called to Cubiak.

A thin scar was clearly visible on the man's left arm. The raised bump was about two inches across. It was no longer the vivid red that Francisca's mother had described in her letter, but the shape was just as she had said: a clear and distinct representation of the number seven.

Carlos said something in Spanish.

"He wants to know if he is the person I am looking for," Francisca told Cubiak.

"You must ask him to come with us. Tell him that you must check further."

It took a bit of convincing on Francisca's part before the man she had ID'd as her brother allowed her to swab the inside of his cheek for the DNA test. Cubiak sent one specimen from each of them to the state lab for processing but cautioned her that it could take up to three months to get the results. On her own, Francisca submitted additional samples to a company that advertised on television and promised results in as little as six weeks.

One Saturday afternoon in midsummer, Joey sat at the kitchen table reading one of his books when the doorbell rang.

He peeked out at the man and woman who stood outside on the deck. He had never seen either of them before. They seemed old to him but not as old as his parents. They held hands, which meant they liked each other, but she looked as if she were about to cry. Joey wondered if something was wrong. He wasn't allowed to answer the door to anyone he didn't recognize. His mother was setting up a show at a gallery, so he went to the back room, his father's office, where his dad was working on the computer.

"There's someone here," he said.

What happened next mystified the boy.

Cubiak opened the door and the woman thrust a sheet of paper at him.

"*Carlos es Miguel*. He is my brother," she said.

Then she flung her arms around Cubiak's neck and started to sob.

All the while, the man she had called Carlos and Miguel was smiling.

"Son, take your book to the living room," Cubiak said.

Joey picked up the book, but he went only as far as the doorway. Standing where he couldn't be seen, he watched the three adults sit down at the table.

The woman and his father took turns talking while the other man listened. He looked puzzled but happy.

After a while, the woman used the word *miracle* and kissed the sheriff's hand. A few minutes later, she and her companion stood. She had started crying again, and she was still crying when they walked out the door.

When they were gone, Joey came into the kitchen.

"Who are those people?"

"The woman is Francisca. She's a friend, and the man is her brother Miguel. She was looking for him for many years, and I helped her find him, thanks to you."

"Me?"

"Yes, you. Finding Miguel was like trying to find the robot in your book. I had to figure out the clue."

"What was it?"

"I finally realized that I had a pretty good idea about where he worked. All I had to do was go there and wait for him to show up."

The boy nodded and then he fixed an accusatory look on his father. "I don't think Francisca wanted to find her brother."

"Why do you say that?"

"Because she was crying."

Cubiak sat down and pulled his son onto his lap. "Do you remember when I told you that there are things that might not make sense to you now but will when you're older?"

"Like why you and mom drink coffee?"

The sheriff smiled. "That's one of them, and this is another. My friend Francisca didn't come here because there was something wrong. In fact, everything had turned out the way she wanted it to, and she came to thank me for helping her."

"She wasn't crying because she was unhappy?"

"No, son, she was crying for joy."

Joey frowned. "I don't understand grown-ups," he said.

Cubiak hugged the boy. "That's okay. Some things about life are confusing. Sometimes things happen that none of us ever fully understand."

"Like magic?"

"Like magic," Cubiak said. He hesitated a moment, and then he thought to himself. Or even like miracles.

ACKNOWLEDGMENTS

While reading fiction, I often wonder about the genesis of a story: did the plot originate with a news article, a comment overheard on the train, or an incident from the author's life? Unlike the other volumes in the Dave Cubiak series, which have no basis in reality, *Death by the Bay* was inspired by a real event.

In the early part of the past century, my maternal grandparents were immigrant farmers in central Wisconsin. In their community of Eastern European newcomers, most families were large. One couple had only one child, a daughter who was severely disabled. Desperate to help her, the parents sent her away with a "doctor" who promised a cure. The girl was never seen again, and the anguished parents were left to grieve and endure the pain of their tragic error for the rest of their lives.

I was horrified when my mother told me this story and even more appalled to learn that one of her younger sisters, my aunt Rose, narrowly escaped the same fate. As an infant, Rose was afflicted with polio, which compromised her speech and physical mobility. One day the same "doctor" appeared at my grandparents' door with a similar offer to heal Rose. My grandmother grabbed a broom and chased the man out of the kitchen and through the farmyard all the way to the road.

The tragedy of the stolen girl haunted me for decades. What had happened to that poor child? How could anyone be so heartless? Prior to turning to fiction, I had been a nonfiction writer, and for years I thought about trying to research the story and expose the villain, who by then was probably dead. But too much time had passed and, of course, there were no records or viable means of verifying the details. My only recourse was to fictionalize the event, which I did in this book.

For historical data on the use of children as medical research subjects, I relied on information from a number of sources. *Children as Research Subjects: Science, Ethics & Law*, edited by Michael A. Grodin and Leonard H. Glantz, was especially insightful, as were articles from the *New England Journal of Medicine*, the National Institutes of Health, and the Associated Press. The article from *Scientific American* cited in chapter 6, about the link between Down syndrome and Alzheimer's, was published in the July 1, 2014, edition of the magazine. All errors are my own.

Comments, corrections, and questions from my loyal readers helped shape the narrative. My thanks to my daughters, Julia and Carla Padvoiskis; my former boss and mentor Norm Rowland, and the women in my writers critique group—Ellen Pinkham, Esther Spodek, and Jeanne Mellet—for their diligence. A second round of applause to Julia for the original map she created for the book.

Thanks as well to Director Dennis Lloyd and the outstanding staff at the University of Wisconsin Press, who make all the pieces fall into place; to copyeditor Diana Cook, for her careful review of my work; and to graphic designer Sara DeHaan for the spectacular cover.

Finally, I owe a debt of gratitude to former executive editor Raphael Kadushin, who retired from the University of Wisconsin Press last fall. Raphy was the acquisitions editor who took a chance on the first Dave Cubiak mystery and opened the door to all those that followed. Without him, I wouldn't be here now. Former communications director Sheila Leary and former marketing director Andrea Christofferson also were part of the original team that worked diligently to ensure the success of the series. To all three of you: happy reading, happy travels, and endless thanks.